MW00413780

A COUNTRY KISS

She sighed and let herself lean against Gerry as they strolled among the swaying, whispering trees toward the banks of a silvery gill, one of the narrow, undulating streams that fed the Lesley. When he stopped in the unneeded shade of a twisted, gnarled old oak, she looked up at him questioningly. Her heart was at peace and she was ready to accept whatever her life should bring, now.

"Jenny," he said, hesitantly. He released her arm and turned her to face him. She leaned back against the trunk of the tree and looked up into his honest blue gaze.

"Yes, Gerry?"

He reached up and touched her hair, stroking it back from her cheeks, and she felt a shiver rush through her at the gentleness of his touch. His fingers trailed down her cheek and cupped her chin. His sturdy, powerful body moved closer until she could feel his heat infusing her with warmth. She gazed up into his eyes still, reading there tenderness and affection and something else, something deeper and more elemental, more to do with the night secrets that were whispered between man and woman, lover to lover.

"Jenny," he whispered.

Pinned, trapped against the gnarled trunk of the tree, the first touch of his lips was almost frightening, the intensity startling, the raw twist of restrained passion that surged from him through his lips a bewildering shock. Her eyes closed, she was a prisoner of the delicious sensations that raced up her spine and down to her fingers. . . .

Books by Donna Simpson

Published by Zebra Books

A COUNTRY COURTSHIP

Donna Simpson

ZEBRA BOOKS
Kensington Publishing Corp.
http://www.kensingtonbooks.com

ZEBRA BOOKS are published by

Kensington Publishing Corp.
850 Third Avenue
New York, NY 10022

Copyright © 2002 by Donna Simpson

All rights reserved. No part of this book may be reproduced
in any form or by any means without the prior written con-
sent of the Publisher, excepting brief quotes used in reviews.

If you purchased this book without a cover you should be
aware that this book is stolen property. It was reported as
"unsold and destroyed" to the Publisher and neither the
Author nor the Publisher has received any payment for this
"stripped book."

All Kensington titles, imprints, and distributed lines are
available at special quantity discounts for bulk purchases for
sales promotion, premiums, fund-raising, educational or in-
stitutional use.

Special book excerpts or customized printings can also be
created to fit specific needs. For details, write or phone the
office of the Kensington Special Sales Manager: Kensington
Publishing Corp., 850 Third Avenue, New York, NY 10022.
Attn. Special Sales Department. Phone: 1-800-221-2647.

Zebra and the Z logo Reg. U.S. Pat. & TM Off.

First Printing: June 2002
10 9 8 7 6 5 4 3 2 1

Printed in the United States of America

*For Mick, whose unwavering support and understanding is
a constant source of joy and strength. Thank you.*

Prologue

"But, Mama, why can't I just stay here in Bath with you?" Though Miss Jane Dresden shuddered at the thought—Bath was dreadful, almost as bad as London, in her eyes—it was better than the alternative. Better than an arranged marriage to a coldhearted viscount from the equally frigid north, who was too lazy to seek his own bride and too prideful to enter the marriage mart. Well, let the man find some other sacrificial lamb; she had no desire to live in frozen dignity in some great ancient noble pile.

Mrs. Olivia Dresden, swathed in layer upon layer of soft knit shawls over a warm merino dress, reclined on a sofa, her thin, wasted face only registering exhaustion. Even though the elegant little room was overheated, with a fire blazing in the fireplace, she shivered. "Jane, dear, please, don't speak so loudly. It hurts my head."

Mr. Jessup chimed in, "Be a little more thoughtful of your mother, Miss Dresden. She is suffering more than she lets on, you know."

Jane shot a look of dislike over at the man who sat by Mrs. Dresden's head and periodically waved a vial of hartshorn under her nose. Jane's mother, a widow of many years, had come to Bath for her health only to find her decline. She now spent her days in her stuffy parlor, recumbent, a victim of her nerves, her stomach ailments and her aching head. Jane couldn't help but think that creatures like Mr.

Jessup, who leeched onto the ill, enabled women of delicate
constitution to decline so they could maintain their own
manner of living. He was a new visitor, relatively speaking;
Mrs. Dresden had just been introduced to him by a mutual
friend two weeks before, but he had spent long hours every
day since in the comfortable home Mrs. Dresden had rented
in Bath. Her mother, Jane feared, fed on the ready sympathy,
the murmured commiseration, and the male attention he offered. She was weary of his company but her mother delighted in it, so Jane could do nothing but note how
threadbare his jacket was, and how day by day his expensive
little trinkets—enameled snuffbox, gold toothpick case, jew-
eled quizzing glass—seemed to be disappearing one by one,
likely to a pawnshop.

"Mr. Jessup," Jane said, moving restlessly on her chair,
restraining with difficulty her own vigorous, healthy desire
to move, to walk, to do *anything* but sit a prisoner in this
overheated, overfurnished room. "My mother knows I
would do nothing to exacerbate her poor health, but I cannot
think that hartshorn under her nose is going to help a head-
ache!"

"Please, Jane, do not speak so!" Mrs. Dresden lifted one
delicate blue-veined hand to her forehead, and Mr. Jessup,
a veritable elderly tulip in fawn breeches and aqua coat,
shot Jane a look of malevolent triumph. He knelt at Mrs.
Dresden's side, pulled the bulkiest shawl up over her thin
bosom, and murmured in her ear.

"Jane, this is for your own good," her mother said after
a whispered conference with her admirer. "If I should pass
on, or . . . or if my circumstances should change in any
other way, I want you taken care of. You are only adding
to my burdens, dear girl, by your intransigence. Please, go
north with your aunt and meet Lord Haven!"

Jane sighed, exasperated, and sat back in the straight-
backed chair she had chosen as the only bearable seat in a
room filled with reclining sofas and overstuffed ottomans.

It was *her* life, and yet she seemed doomed to live it out as breeding stock for a titled terror who would likely despise her for her common tastes and low desires. All she wanted from her life now, at her almost unmarriageable age, was to retire to a cozy cottage somewhere in the country, somewhere where she could maybe have a little garden, with roses winding up the whitewashed walls. There would be a sunny kitchen overlooking an herb garden in her cottage; she would grow rosemary and thyme, sage and savory, and she could learn to cook!

The overheated room melted away as her vision clouded and the cottage appeared in all its simple beauty. It would be in a small village on a winding lane, perhaps in Oxfordshire or Kent. Her neighbors would be simple, hardworking folk who would take her to their collective bosom and teach her all the little ways of the village.

Or perhaps her cottage would be on a hillside somewhere, by a pretty silver stream in the country. The Cotswolds, mayhap. No neighbors at all. She would keep a gray tabby cat who would sit on the hearth and wink at her while she read a cookery book or kept her simple accounts.

Jane smiled mistily and plucked at the skirt of her plain but well-made dress. That was it; the country, and a cottage on a hillside. Then the garden could be as big as she wanted and she could grow vegetables among the roses and herbs among the daisies. Lost in her daydreams of pastoral perfection, she was startled when a cruel, hard-mouthed viscount strode into her reverie, demanding that she sit in his golden saloon and visit with the Duchess of Someplace-or-Other while netting a purse, needle-pointing a screen, and counting the family silver.

She shook herself. Perhaps she should not have looked up her proposed bridegroom's family lineage. The title, Viscount Haven, dated back hundreds of years to early in the Wars of the Roses, and the estate manor was even older, a

great cold, dingy pile that probably stretched a half a mile
along a desolate, brutal Yorkshire moor. And the many past
Viscount Havens had been hard, cruel men who had cared
for little beyond enlarging their massive estate and piling
more gold in their coffers. She shivered.

She was no silly goose, Jane thought of herself, and she
would not have assumed that the present title holder was
built along the same lines as his ancestors, but she had very
particular knowledge that led her to believe he was a shard
off the same flinty rock. And that was the man her family
wanted her to wed, and in Yorkshire of all places? That fate,
Viscountess Haven of cold and dreary Yorkshire, did not
accord well with her daydream of a warm and cozy cottage
and that most elusive and ephemeral of imaginings, a kind
and gentle man who would love her.

At that moment the pert maidservant who looked after
such things was answering the door—Mrs. Dresden claimed
not to be able to stand the bold accents of even the best
manservants—flounced into the parlor and said, "Lady
Mortimer, mum."

Lady Mortimer, Mrs. Dresden's older sister, surged into
the room as the maid slid out. She was a woman of fifty
years or more—she never admitted to more than forty-
nine—with black hair shot with iron gray and dark snapping
eyes. Her back was straight, her gait bold, and her mien
challenging. She wore black, in perpetual mourning for a
husband she had never much cared for when he was alive.
Lady Mortimer was born to be a widow, not a wife.

Jane's mother looked somewhat alarmed as she shrank
back under her woolen barrier, and Jane wondered, not for
the first time, if her mother was using this trip north as a
ruse to get Lady Mortimer out of Bath. Mrs. Dresden didn't
like her sister overmuch, it was true, but surely she would
not sacrifice her own daughter's happiness just to get rid
of her sister for a month? And yet she had supported Jane's
right to refuse to go until recently, when she had begun

siding with Lady Mortimer, who had arranged this match through an old school connection of her husband's.

Jane stood and nodded to her aunt. "My lady," she said, the only greeting the woman would acknowledge. Marrying a baron at a young age had infused Lady Mortimer with a sense of her own worth that only ever wavered in the presence of someone of higher rank. "We were just discussing why I think this trip to Yorkshire is not necessary." She clenched her hands together in front of her, uneasy as always in the presence of her stern and demanding aunt. One would think at her age, a grand and ancient twenty-seven, that she would have gotten over her childhood fears, but Lady Mortimer had taken a switch to her on numerous occasions when, as a child, she was inclined to mischief and frolics. The woman still unsettled her. She was everything the aristocracy was supposed to be—cold, contemptuous, and condescending. Jane had met innumerable "Lady Mortimers" in the ballrooms and parlors of London before her mother finally succumbed to her various ailments and moved them both to Bath for her health, and yet she had never learned how to handle them.

"Not necessary?" Lady Mortimer said, casting a belligerent glance at the meekly withdrawing Mr. Jessup, who was melting back into his deep club chair like a shadow. Satisfied that she had cowed him sufficiently, she then fastened her basilisk glare on Jane. "Not necessary to go to Yorkshire? You, niece, are seven-and-twenty, not seventeen. I would like to be informed where you think you will find a likelier candidate for husband than a well set-up viscount of wealth and property who seems to have no disabling diseases. I have gone to considerable trouble to arrange this, and his lordship is expecting us within the week." She turned her gaze to her younger sibling. "Sister, do you have someone else in mind? A better match than a wealthy viscount with considerable acreage and impeccable lineage? Mayhap you are hiding an earl, or a duke?"

"What?" Mrs. Dresden said, her eyes wide. She cast a glance at Mr. Jessup, and then squeaked, "No, I have no one in mind . . . no one."

"Then it is settled. We leave tomorrow, as planned."

Jane opened her mouth, then briskly shut it again. She sank back into her chair. The heat in this stifling room must be getting to her brain; she longed to throw back the curtains and open the window to let the early spring air flow in, but knew it would upset her mother. Besides, it would only be Bath air, not country air, which she craved more than chocolate bonbons or crème caramel.

Perhaps instead of seeing this enforced journey as a penance, she should view it as an opportunity, a chance to make her future what she wanted. She bit her lip. Did she dare? She must, if she wanted any kind of life for herself. "I will . . ." She took a deep breath, and said, all in one spurt, "I will go north and meet Lord Haven on one condition." She eyed her mother's hopeful expression and her aunt's wary one.

"I knew you would see reason, my dearest," Mrs. Dresden said, weakly.

"You have not yet heard my condition," Jane said. She pressed her knees together to keep them from quivering—she had never stood up to her family, especially not Aunt Mortimer, in her whole life, and so this was a new experience—and took another deep breath. "I will go north and have a look at Viscount Haven under one condition," she repeated. "If I decide after being there for two weeks that I cannot bear the man, then not another word will be said about it and I may come back here to Bath and live with you, Mother. Or . . . or I may buy a cottage in the country for us. Wouldn't you like that, Mother?" she said, a pleading note in her voice. "A sweet little cottage in the healthful country air, maybe in Hampshire or Oxfordshire? I . . . I would look after you, and we would have a garden and live in a little village where there would be nice folk, a vicar, and an apothecary?"

Mr. Jessup took Mrs. Dresden's hand and squeezed it, and the woman dimpled up at him, a trembling smile on her face. Jane watched the interchange uneasily. "Don't you think that is fair?" she prodded, thinking that she would race back to Bath the moment the two weeks was up, if only to pry the limpetlike Mr. Jessup's hand out of her mother's.

"I think that is fair, do you not think so, sister?" Mrs. Dresden murmured. Mr. Jessup whispered something to her and she nodded. "Though I think we should agree on three weeks or a month, to really give you children a chance to get to know each other."

Jane opened her mouth to object but Lady Mortimer said, "I think that will be adequate. I am sure that once Jane sees the exalted style in which the Haven household is run and the elegant manner in which they live she will be more than happy to ally herself with them."

It sounded like a treaty, not a marriage, Jane thought gloomily, hating the way her aunt referred to her in the third person, as though she were not even present. And yet what could she do? It was either this or the infamous Bath mockery of the London marriage mart, she realized, with elderly gents in frock coats or valetudinarian younger men as suitors, for her mother had made it clear that she would accept no other fate for her daughter than marriage. They had had the discussion many times and always it ended the same, with the seemingly fragile Mrs. Dresden saying that a woman's place was at a man's side, and Jane had better resign herself to it. It was amazing that the woman even agreed to Jane's terms, that she could give this one last try and then do what she really wanted.

But Jane knew her own heart. She belonged in the country in a little cottage with a minuscule garden plot, perhaps, and a few chickens to tend and a goat, maybe. She could learn to milk it, for she had read somewhere that goat's milk was more healthy than cow's for invalids. Her mother might finally get better, be able to move about and find joy in life again.

If she had been born of more humble origins it would have been so much easier, Jane thought, for even marriage, then, would not have been such a frightening specter. She would be able to marry an ordinary man with wants and needs like her own, rather than a blustering baron or minatory marquis who would expect her to hostess enormous parties, waltz at Almack's, tittle-tattle with the privileged ten thousand, all while she would be wishing them at the devil.

All she wanted was that snug country cottage. The husband was impossible, for what farmer of humble means would marry her, the granddaughter of an earl and niece of a baroness, as she was constantly reminded by her aunt? The man to whom she could imagine committing herself for life she had met only in her dreams. There she had seen him, noted the quiet strength in his face, felt the loving security of his strong arms. He would have no want or desire for an elegant female who knew how to net purses and dance the quadrille. All he would want was a woman to love him and take care of him.

She sighed and shook herself out of that delectable daydream. That was out of the question; she had already surrendered her hope for a marriage of love. She would settle for the cottage and a destiny taking care of her mother, a quiet retreat after a life spent despising London society and the Bath elite.

She straightened her back and dared to speak. "It is a deal, then," she said. "I will go to Yorkshire with you, Lady Mortimer, and I will give this viscount a fair trial as a possible husband." And would hate him on sight and reject him; that was the forgone conclusion. "If I decide against marriage, I shall come back here and Mother and I can choose how to proceed." Her mother gave a weak murmur of assent and Lady Mortimer nodded smartly. But for all that she had achieved her objective, she was uneasy about it. The ordeal was not over yet, and though she had no intention of marrying this hateful Lord Haven, yet, she had a sense that it would not be as easy as living out the three weeks agreed upon and then coming home.

But she would face each difficulty as it came. She had gained her point, for now. She would go to Yorkshire, meet the despised viscount, reject him, and then hasten home to her mother and plan her real future. She frowned at Mr. Jessup, who still clung to Mrs. Dresden's thin hand, but his answering expression was a sly smile that filled her with foreboding. She would definitely hasten home. Her mother was ever hesitant and always took more than a month to consider any new course of action. Jane would have enough time to head off any foolish whims her mother might have.

And then life could settle into its proper gentle rhythm. She could find the peace she longed for.

One

He was a big man, broad-shouldered and tall, but his shoulders were bowed as though with the weight of the world. He trudged up the muddy path, weary and down-hearted, but one look up, one glance at the welcoming light coming from the neat stone cottage and the curl of gray smoke from the chimney, and his heart lifted. Mary was there. Mary was there and she would have supper waiting, and the cottage would be warm and the baby would be sleeping.

His step lighter, he approached the cottage, kicked off his muck-caked boots outside the door on the stone door-step, and padded sock-footed through the door. The woman at the fire turned, giving him a smile that would melt a Yorkshire snowdrift.

"Gerry, you look *that* tired. Has it been a hard one, then?"

All the troubles of the day, all the weariness of long hours, conflicts, hard work with no appreciation, dropped away from him in the welcoming atmosphere of Haven Home, his farm. "Aye, that it has, Mary." He began to shrug out of his heavy coat and she came from tending the supper to help him, lifting the damp woolen coat off his shoulders and hanging it on a hook behind the door.

"Sit you down, then, supper's ready. Yer favorite, stew and dumplin's."

Donna Simpson

"Ah, Mary, you know the way to a man's heart. You're a rare gem."

Dimpling and blushing, Mary shooed him toward a low chair at the scarred table by the window. The glass was covered by the steam from the evening's meal, but there was nothing outside he wanted to see anyway. Cold, hard reality was outside. Burdensome responsibility, nagging harpies, uncooperative workers; all those were left outside the door. It was inside this little cottage that life started.

Mary dished up a full bowl of fragrant stew, making sure he had a large helping of the light and fluffy dumplings for which she was famous throughout the valley. Gerry knew he was a lucky man. Many would give much to have Mary cook them their evening meal, and he was the lucky sot who enjoyed the pleasure. He watched her as he ate; she dished her own meal up in a smaller bowl and sat down at the opposite end of the table, but then popped up again and served him a large tankard of ale and herself a glass of buttermilk. Finally she sat and stirred her stew to cool it some, nodding with satisfaction as she tasted. She was plump and still pretty, was Mary, even though life had not been easy, and childbirth the greatest challenge of all.

"The babe asleep?" he muttered around a mouthful.

"Aye, that she is," Mary said, after swallowing. She took a long sip of buttermilk, leaving creamy flecks on her upper lip that made him want to kiss them off. He licked his own lips and turned his attention back to his meal. "But if you're very quiet," she continued, "you can have a wee peek after yer supper."

"I'll not disturb her. I promise." They ate the rest of their meal in companionable silence. That was one of Mary's many attractions. She did not demand conversation, as did most of the women he had met in his life. He could be silent and she would not accuse him of being taciturn or moody. He could just be himself and it was good enough.

Finally pushing away from the table, his appetite sated,

he glanced around and as if she read his mind, Mary brought him his pipe. He seldom smoked, only while at his ease in front of the fire at the cottage hearth, but tonight he needed its subtle comfort. His large hands circling her waist, he pulled her down into his lap, where she landed with a soft "oof" expelled in her surprise. He kissed and nuzzled her ear, but she pulled away from him and stood, facing him.

"No, me lord, no." She twisted her hands in her apron and her soft features showed her unhappiness. She took a deep breath and said, "Lord Haven, you an' me bin friends since childhood, but you be the lord o' the manor and I am just Mary Cooper, widowed farmer's wife. An' I told you there would be none o' that. It is not fitting, and I will be no man's whore."

He flinched, for the verbal slap hit him hard. He never meant to make Mary think that was his intent. It had been the impulse of the moment, the whim of the instant. "Mary, I am sorry. You know . . . I *hope* you know I never meant to make you feel uncomfortable. I guess I got carried away with the playacting." With a deep sigh of regret he stood and laid the pipe down on the table. He knew from past experience that all comfort would be gone now. His miserable error had reminded Mary of the gulf that separated them, and how this little homey scene would be perceived if it were known that the widow Mary Cooper was entertaining the master of Haven Court, his lordship, Viscount Geraint Walcott Haven, family name Neville, descendent of the ancient Earl of Warwick and relative of the current earl. He surrendered to the inevitable, feeling the mantle of his unwanted rank and power slipping back onto his broad shoulders. "I will be going back to the house now." He could not meet Mary's eyes, for he knew he had made her uncomfortable. "M'mother will be looking for me. Kiss the babe once for me, will you?"

"That I will, Lord Haven."

"Gerry. You used to call me Gerry when we were children, Mary. And just now you did the same."

"But we're not children anymore, me lord." She stiffened her back and shook her head, gazing at him with sad eyes. "Not for many years now. 'Twas my mistake to call you that when you came in tonight. I would have both of us remember who we be."

Haven moved to the rugged door and shrugged himself into his coat. He opened the door and pulled his boots onto the mat just inside and slipped his feet into the sodden leather, grimacing at the cold dampness. Straightening, he glanced over at her hesitantly. "I may come back again, mayn't I? For dinner? Sometime soon?" He held his breath while Mary, looking undecided, watched him. "Please, Mary," he said, humbly. "I'll not forget myself again, I promise. The childish playacting is over. We are just friends; I know that." Sometimes he felt that the comfort and warmth of this little cottage and the companionship of its inhabitant, his old friend Mary Cooper, was the only piece of his life that made sense, the only part that felt real and wholesome.

"Aye, that you may." The baby whimpered in her sleep and Mary retreated to the cradle in the corner near the fire. She fussed a moment, pulling a blanket up over little Molly, but then looked back at her friend, her childhood companion. "It is yer own property and I canna stop you, after all. But do not be thinkin' it means anything beyond friendship, Ger . . . Lord Haven. I want *no* man in my bed, not with Jem so recently gone above. And when I do—*if* I ever do— it will be marriage, and to someone of me own station in life. I'll not have you misunderstand me."

Her tone left no room for argument; her words were final. If he was realistic, he knew she was only telling him the truth as the world outside the cottage door would see it. He was the lord of Haven Court, the hereditary holder of one of the largest estates in Yorkshire; when he married—*if* he married—it must be to a woman who could fill the position of viscountess, as grim as a marriage contracted under those terms sounded to him. As he stood there in her doorway he realized that he had not told Mary of the overtures made on his behalf in aid of that aim, and decided then and there that there was no point in telling her until there really was something to tell. He already knew that the young lady being courted on his behalf was not going to be to his liking; he had seen a miniature of her and a more pinched-face, sour spinster he had never seen.

Ah, well, he might just marry her anyway, just to shut everyone up. What difference did it make? He was never going to find the woman of his dreams; that fantasy of cuddling a loving and welcoming woman in his arms and bed within the bonds of wedlock had died years before. It seemed he might have to settle for a marriage of convenience or none at all. And it could not be *no* marriage. He owed his title its continuation, or so his family told him time after time. Mary moved toward him and put her hand on the door, as if hastening him out.

"I understand, Mary. I really do." He put his hand on her shoulder and squeezed, but let it drop with no further caress. Mary was his oldest and dearest friend, the playmate of his childhood, and he would not hurt her for the world. Her husband, Jem Cooper, had been a good man and a good tenant and his death had hurt Mary deeply. Though she spoke of it as recent, it was more than a year now. The poor man had not even lived to see the birth of the baby he had made with his wife.

Haven stepped out the door into the crisp late-March air and breathed in deeply, readying himself for the walk back to the house. The door closed softly but firmly behind him and he heard the latch fall into place and the bolt snick. Mary was shutting him out of her life a little more every time he slipped and moved to kiss or caress her. He must not let that happen again. Not for the world would he make her uncomfortable in her own home.

He paced down the path, the cold wind whipping red into his cheeks as he steeled himself for what lay ahead of him at Haven Court, his true home. The journey to his estate and back to his true identity, that of Viscount Haven, lord of the district and most prominent aristocrat for miles around, was more mental process than physical, and he spoke to himself sternly as he went.

Now, Haven, you have a houseful of women, it is true, and more expected, but that is no reason to run away. He walked up from the farm across the long moor as the sun bid its final adieu to the Yorkshire hills, coloring the sky in shades of porphyry and cobalt, strings of kohl lining the streaky clouds on the horizon. *They cannot plague you if you do not let them. Their nattering and gossiping must not drive you to hide away in your library again, nor must you let them nag you into actions you do not want to take.* He walked on, but his pace slowed. "Mph," he grunted. "Easier said than accomplished, my cowardly lad," he muttered out loud to that self-righteous, priggish voice in his head. A grandmother, mother, and two sisters meant he was the only male in the house who was not a servant. He was outnumbered and outtalked, harried and nipped at like a bear baited by dogs.

The shadows of the scattered ancient oak trees, planted in this barren landscape almost two hundred years ago by one of the early Viscount Havens and bent and gnarled by the insistent wind that swept down the moor, grew longer and then faded into a uniform darkness. He followed a low stone wall, climbed the final hill, skirted rocky outcroppings, and strode over the rise, then stood on the prominence, gazing down at Haven Court, the ancestral home of Viscount Haven for over three hundred years since the first Viscount Haven was created. It was a priory before that, stretching back to its first years as a Catholic retreat built shortly after the Norman Conquest. It was a lovely home, he supposed, from the original square, turreted section, to the long, low additions, two of them, that held more modern rooms along with the kitchens and servant quarters. Visitors always congratulated him on the beauty of the old gray walls covered in ivy and the three floors of windows, blazing with light now in the early spring evening. Just beyond Haven Court was the dower house, Haven Wood, where his grandmother nominally made her home, though she was at the Court more than in her own home.

He shrugged. He preferred the Haven home farm cottage, with its snug dimensions and low ceilings, but if he dared say that his mother, grandmother, and sisters would ring a peal over his head as usual, so he would keep his silence.

He picked up his pace again, determined anew to take control of his distaff relatives and exert his authority as master. When had he lost that control? Had he ever had it? And did it matter? He suspected that he never was the "master of the house" in its true sense. Perhaps it was too late. If he married, would that make one member of the household for his side, or would his wife join the women against him and make the harrying that much worse? He supposed he would not know until he met the prune-faced Miss Dresden, his proposed bride.

He entered through the high Roman-arched doorway into the great hall, a part of the turreted old section, to find the manse a buzzing hive of activity. Servants rushed back and forth up in the gallery and on the main floor, their footsteps echoing hollowly in the high-ceilinged room; a maid carrying a folded shawl and stoppered bottle pushed past him. Somewhere a woman wept. *Hmm, in the drawing room,* Haven thought. The weeping changed to a wail. He frowned and moved toward the sound. Though his instincts were to shrink away from aristocratic female sensibility, womanly pain aroused all his protective instincts; he could not ignore it. He entered the drawing room to find a middle-aged woman weeping, attended by his mother and eldest sister, Rachel.

His mother looked up from her seat by the troubled female, her lips pursed and frown lines etched deep on either side of her mouth. "Haven! *Finally!* Why were you not home two hours ago? You *knew* we had company coming."

How could he tell her that was the very knowledge that made him delay his return home until the last possible moment? The maid he had seen rush by him in the hall was draping the woolen shawl over the woman's arms, aided ineffectually by Rachel.

"I did not think my absence would cause such a commotion," he said, only half joking. The woman set up a new wave of bawling, reminding Haven forcibly of a sheep in prenatal distress.

"Do not jest," Lady Haven said over the racket. "Lady Mortimer is very much upset. Her niece is missing! Just imagine, the girl went missing at the last stop, an inn some miles from here down the Derbyshire road."

"Went missing?" The hesitant farmer was gone in an instant and the authoritative Lord Haven was very much in evidence. His dark blue eyes, rimmed by thick lashes, snapped with command as he stepped forward, knelt on the rug, and said, "Lady Mortimer, what does my mother mean by 'went missing'? Where is Miss Dresden?"

His tone brooked no argument and the older lady pulled herself together, sniffling into her handkerchief for only a moment longer before saying, "It was at that wretched, *wretched* inn. My niece went down to the kitchen to bespeak another pitcher of hot water—we stopped there late this afternoon to refresh ourselves before making our entrance to Haven Court, you see—and when she was so long I called the maid, but she didn't know where my niece was, and so I called the landlord's wife and she did not know where Jane was, either, and then I called . . ."

"Enough!" He stemmed the tide of her rising hysteria

before it took hold of her again. "Was there any sign of her?"

His deep voice acted like a pitcher of cold water dashed in her face. She pulled herself together—he had the impression she was not normally a scattered kind of female—and said, "No, there was no one who had seen her, but a stable lad found th—this slip of paper on a nail in the stable."

She handed him a crumpled bit of paper that was much stained with her tears. Haven read it and frowned. *"The girl is ars,"* it read. *"If you want ta see her agin, then do as yer told. We'll contact yer."* He shook his head. Ransom? Was this a kidnapping? But something about the note—He turned to stride from the room but before he did, he moved back to Lady Mortimer and put one hand on her shoulder. "My lady, do not worry. I will find Miss Dresden, I promise you that, and I will ensure that she will be unharmed. I will punish whomever is responsible for this deed, too. He will feel the sting of the lash, or worse."

As he strode away he could hear his mother's harsh voice crying out, "Haven, you have left a trail of muck on the Aubusson! *Haven!* How many times . . ."

The full moon rose above the Yorkshire hills and Mary Cooper rocked her baby as it suckled. As she rocked, she sang an old lullaby that she remembered from her own childhood; *"Sweetly sleep, my babe, my own, your da will protect you and keep us from harm."*

But he wouldn't. She stifled a sob and cleared her throat, concentrating fiercely on her blessings to counteract her melancholy. She had many blessings and knew it. Ah, but it was hard not to think of what could have been. At this time of the evening, the quiet, soft time of crackling fire and warm darkness, she thought of Jem and missed him, thinking that if he were here he would be sitting by the fire whittling something, for his hands were never still. He could not read or write, but neither could he abide laziness, which was why Lord Haven had kept him as the home farm manager for so many years. Jem had been a fair bit older than she, but a more loving husband she could not have wished for. He was not handsome in any sense other than 'handsome is as handsome does,' he was intelligent but not learned, gentle but not genteel, and he was her husband. He was as unlike Gerry as could be, she supposed, and yet like him in so many important ways. Having Gerry as a childhood friend had taught her what she wanted in a man and husband and she had found it in Jem.

Lord Haven. She rocked the baby and thought about her childhood friend, Gerry, now the grand and powerful viscount, Lord Haven. She worried about him, for the carefree boy he once was had been replaced by a rather dour, hardworking, but cynical man. Not that that was his natural demeanor. Around her he was a gentle and considerate friend, but his reputation in the village was of a hard man with little to say.

As a youth he had not been sent to school as perhaps he should have been. His father was a weak man under the thumb of his powerful wife and strong-willed mother; they both wanted Gerry home, so he was schooled by the local vicar. But there came a time when it was appropriate for the Haven heir, Baron Lesley as he was then, to go to London and take part in the usual entertainments of a viscount's son. He didn't want to go, but he went. The tales he brought back from that far-off mythical place, a place of great lords and ladies, brilliant ballrooms and the tonnish elite, were stories of frozen ladies with perpetual sneers on their handsome painted faces, and of ridicule suffered by the cloddish country lad who had no experience of aristocratic females and all of their wiles. After three Seasons, and upon ascending to his father's title, he refused to return except for the necessary business he must occasionally tend to in the south.

And he resolutely refused to wed or even think of marrying any of the young women thrown at him as the holder of an illustrious and ancient title. He had a multitude of reasons. Those young ladies were steeped in artificiality. They were cold and frivolous, heartless and soulless. They were stupid or vicious or inane. It was always something.

Mary looked down at the sleeping baby in her arms, thankful once again that she had at least the child to remember her husband. Gerry should have that, a wife he could love, children. He deserved a family; he would make an ideal husband and father, for beneath the hard, handsome exterior—whether he knew it or not he was a fearsome sight when in a towering rage, every inch the austere, callous lord of the manor—was a heart as soft as mallow. Take this cottage. Her snug little home should belong to the new manager of the Haven home farm, but Gerry would not hear of her being tossed out with her baby from her marital home after her husband's death. Instead he had built a more modern cottage with larger barns for the new manager. She was grateful, for though the cottage was isolated it was her home and had been for the seven years of her marriage. Lonely it might be at times, but it held all of the fond memories she had of her husband and their life together and she could not let go of that yet.

She knew the townsfolk were talking. It was thought strange that Lord Haven let her stay in the remote cottage even though she had no right to it now and did not work for his lordship. Her daughter had been born a long seven months after Jem had died, and she knew there would be those who would look askance if they knew the frequency with which Gerry ate his dinner at the cottage. The only reason people did not know was the relative isolation of her snug home. It was nestled in a valley among the moorland hills that undulated across the county, and she seldom saw a soul other than Gerry for weeks at a time. She spent her days tending her garden, spinning wool, and caring for

her baby. If they knew the many nights he stopped at her
cottage for dinner, spending hours sometimes by her fireside, there would be whispers and pointing fingers. But she
could not turn away her friend, not when his heart was as
sore and lonely as she knew it to be.

It all came down to the same thing in the end. Gerry
needed a woman, a wife. And it would never be she. There
was a chasm between them of class and education and interest. And besides, the only emotion she felt toward him
was a warm friendship, as if he were the brother she had
never had. And he didn't really love her; she knew that. He
mistook the warmth of their friendship, the ease of companionship, for love. And that was only possible because
he had never been in love before, never known the sweet
madness of the soul that overtook a man in love.

There was a sound outside and she looked up, alarmed.
The wind was up, whistling around the cottage like a spirit
in turmoil. The old ones would call it a "thin" or "lazy"
wind, a wind that cut right through you, being too lazy to
go around.

The bang was repeated and she hastily pulled her dress
up over her shoulder and carried the baby to her cradle.
Pulling a shawl over her shoulders, she headed out the door.
It must be that pesky barn door again! She had meant to
tell Gerry about it, but had been distracted by his unwelcome advances and had forgotten to tell him that the latch
was broken.

The wind was whipping up and the tree near the well
was bending almost to the ground. She pulled the shawl
closer about her shoulders and hastened across the damp
yard, struggling against the blast of wind that stormed up
over the moor. A fine misty rain was coming down again,
cold on this March evening. Before she even made it to the
barn it had turned into a drizzle. The snow had just disappeared, but now with this needle-sharp rain pelting down
it felt just as cold as January.

Through the darkness she bustled and grabbed the swing-ing door to pull it shut, but thought she should really check on Esther, the aging milk cow, before going back to the warmth of the cottage. The rain could have blown in on the poor beast and she could not bear to go back in if she thought Esther was cold and wet.

Poor old girl, Mary thought, patting the bovine flank. But no, she was not wet, nor did she seem anything but the contented—wait, what was that?

A noise in the corner of the tiny barn drew Mary's at-tention. There was movement, and she wondered if Lally, the very pregnant barn cat, was ready to bear her litter. Letting her eyes adjust to the darkness, she crept to the corner that the noise had come from and gazed over the wood barrier into the empty stall that used to belong to Jem's old nag.

And there, shivering in the corner of the stall was . . . a girl. Or rather, a young woman, dressed in the garb of a serving girl or kitchen maid. And . . . *oh my,* Mary thought. Her clothes were torn and she was weeping.

TWO

"Haven, what are you going to do?" Rachel put her fists on her slim hips and stared down at her brother, tapping her slipper-shod foot on the floor.

"Yes, Haven, what are you going to do?" Lady Haven joined in with her daughter's harangue as her son, back from a long night and day of searching for his missing bride-to-be, wearily dropped into a deep leather chair in the study. "Lady Mortimer is beside herself! It has been almost a full day and still you have not found the girl! What *have* you been doing?"

"Yes, what have you been doing instead of finding poor Miss Dresden? Out hobnobbing with the hired help again?" Rachel said, a nasty expression on her pretty face.

"Leave him alone, Rach. He's dead tired." Pamela, a pixielike girl of nineteen with brown hair she persisted in calling "dung-colored," followed her sister and mother into the book-lined, wood-paneled room. She moved around behind her brother's chair and massaged his shoulders as she chastised her sister. But she said not a word to her mother.

"It's all right, Pammy," Haven said, running a hand through his thick sandy hair and using the other hand to cover his youngest sister's, where it rested on his shoulder. He had thought a retreat to the library in order the minute he came into the house, but it was not to be a sanctuary.

He was doomed to have the women in his family follow him even into his den to torment him.

"Do not use such low language, young lady," Lady Haven said, waggling her finger at Pamela. " 'Dead tired' is an abominable colloquialism. And do not be so familiar with your brother." She reached out to smack her youngest daughter's hand, but since it was snatched back quickly from Haven's shoulder, the blow struck the viscount instead. His jawline firmed, but he said nothing.

Rachel, a young lady who normally exhibited exceptionally correct behavior, stuck her tongue out at her younger sister as Pamela clutched her hands, rough from riding without gloves, behind her back.

"Rachel," Lady Haven snapped, catching sight of that extremely unladylike expression of dislike from sister to sister. "If you are to be a role model for Pamela you must not behave like a hoyden; you are three-and-twenty, not nine. Have I not raised you better?"

"No you have not, Lydia, you have spoiled them terribly." The new voice was that of the ancient and terrifying Dowager Lady Haven, the eighty-year-old matriarch. She moved into the room, stiffly upright despite her use of a cane. "Ever since my son died they have had no discipline at all. Since long before he died, I should amend, since he was little better than a cat's-paw. In my day they would have been wedded and bedded five years ago and have babies by now. And before that they would have been in the schoolroom with a backboard strapped to them for twelve hours out of the day. Rudeness would have been treated with a switch on the backside."

"Mother," Lady Lydia Haven said stiffly, "this is a new age and a new century. We do not treat our children like slaves."

"No, you raise wretched little heathens, no better than snorting piglets rooting in a garbage heap."

Haven sank deeper and deeper into the buttery soft

leather of the chair, letting their voices seethe and bubble around him like the hissing and chuckling of a boiling cauldron. Women! He was plagued and beleaguered by women! And how they could talk—without ceasing, sometimes. What they found to talk of he did not know. At times it seemed to him that they just liked to hear the sounds of their own voices *endlessly.*

He rubbed his tired eyes as Rachel and Pamela joined in the squabble, one on his mother's side and the other on his grandmother's side. It had been such a long night and day, almost twenty-four hours of ceaseless movement, riding and walking and searching. Miss Jane Dresden, for all he could find out, had descended the back stairs of the Tippling Swan in Lesleydale into oblivion. She had disappeared not only without a trace, but without a sound or sight from any living creature. He had questioned. He had badgered. He had annoyed, harassed, interrogated, and bullied everyone in the village and on the outlying farms within a radius of three or four miles, but no one had seen her, nor had they seen any men unknown to them.

Who would have kidnapped a girl of obvious quality from an inn? He leaned his head back, closed his eyes, and shut out the rising voices around him. Where *was* she? The landlord of the Swan swore that she never did arrive in the kitchen on her supposed errand for hot water. Somewhere, then, on the journey from the upstairs bedchamber to the kitchen at the back of the inn, she had been taken. Accosted, presumably, by the villains who had seized her.

The thought of any female alone and frightened, held captive and possibly unspeakably tormented by brutal men, launched him out of his chair again. This was *his* domain, Lesleydale and all of the outlying farms and properties, and no woman should have cause for fear in his part of Yorkshire. Silence fell among his distaff relatives and various shades of blue and green eyes stared at him.

"I am going out again. I swore I would find Miss Dresden and I will." He didn't even recognize his own voice, so hard and sharp it was. It echoed off the green-painted walls and almost rattled the wood paneling.

The ancient dowager nodded brusquely and rapped her cane on the marble floor. "We know you will, Haven. We have no doubt in the world of that."

"Well, I do." Lady Mortimer, speaking up from the doorway, glared at the viscount, dark brown eyes snapping with anger. "It is a proof of the laxity of his lordship that there are the kind of brutal cutpurses in the neighborhood that would do such a deed, feeling themselves safe from capture!"

"Do not say that about Haven," Pamela cried, ever on the defense where her adored older brother was concerned. "He is a good landlord and well respected around here. It is not his fault if some dastardly hedge-birds followed you from Bath and nabbed that addlepated nodcock of a niece of yours!"

Lady Haven groaned and rushed to Pamela, smacking her on the back of the head while Lady Mortimer moaned and dropped into a chair. "What did I tell you about that hideous cant you picked up in London?" Lady Haven screamed. "And how could you insult our guest—Ellen, *Ellen!*" Lady Haven shrieked out the door to a maid passing by. "Get the smelling salts again. Lady Mortimer is overset."

"Not overset," Pamela grumbled. "Dicked in the nob, if you ask me."

Haven, struggling to hide a smile, gave Pamela, his favorite sister, a sympathetic look and a shrug. His amusement died in the face of the certainty that Lady Mortimer had a right to her resentment. He strode out of the room, tossing back over his shoulder, "I will find her. I said I would and I will."

* * *

Mary, sitting in the settle by the hearth with Molly on her lap, gazed worriedly at the bed in the corner. The girl had slept all through the night, waking just once during the day, and then only briefly. If only Gerry were here! She didn't know what to do. If the girl was sick she should see at least the apothecary, but that would necessitate Mary getting dressed against the cold spell that had swept over the moors and getting the baby bundled up—she could not leave Molly alone with a sick girl, certainly—and walking the four or five miles over the hills to Betty and James Johnson's farm, the new home farm. She would have to do it, she supposed, if Haven did not drop by sometime within the next hours.

But just as she came to that conclusion the girl stirred, opened her eyes, and struggled to sit up.

Mary watched her carefully. "Are . . . are you all right, miss?" The girl was clearly of some quality—her looks and fair skin and soft hands denoted that—and yet her clothing was that of a serving wench or kitchen maid. And her dress had been torn at the bosom, with the bottom ragged and much of the skirt muddy. Mary vacillated between being sure the girl was of the gentry, at least, to thinking she was perhaps just a maid who had more presence and beauty than others.

"Where am I?"

Her voice was clear and well modulated. Gentry, Mary decided. No matter what the clothes looked like, this girl *must* be of the gentry. Perhaps down on her luck, or . . . or deserted, mayhap?

"You are in my cottage on the moors, miss. I am Mary Cooper, a widow, and this is my baby, Molly." She held up her little girl—Molly cooed happily and giggled, waving chubby wee fists in the air—and watched the young woman's eyes light up as if candles had been lit behind the luminous gray orbs.

"Oh," she breathed on a sigh. "She is precious!" She moved to sit on the edge of the bed and a smile touched her lips, curving them upward in a bow, but the movement was too hasty. She put one hand to her head and closed her eyes for a moment; but if she was faint, it passed quickly. She took a deep breath and looked up again.

"You haven't eaten, likely not in a day or more, miss. Will you take some broth from the mutton stew? It is nourishing, but won't be hard to take down if you're still not in decent fettle." As the girl nodded, Mary shifted Molly to her hip and got up to fill an earthenware mug with the steaming, thickened broth. She brought it over to the bed and handed it to the girl, noting the pale, soft hands, free of calluses. Gentry, most definitely. But who was she? And what was she doing in the barn? She had so many questions but the girl looked weak still, and Mary did not want to keep her from her nourishing meal.

But surely her name would be a start. "What is yer name, miss?" Mary asked, sitting back down on the settle by the fire. She moved Molly to her lap again, and the baby coughed once and sneezed, rubbing her tiny nose with one pink fist.

Her gray eyes wide and startled, the young woman stopped drinking and bit her lip. "My n—name?"

"Yes," Mary said, patiently, wiping her daughter's nose with a cloth. "Yer name. Drink up, though, miss. It'll warm yer insides."

"I—" the girl paused and took another sip. Her gray eyes watchful, she said, hesitantly, "My n—name is . . . is J—Jenny."

"Same name as me young cousin!" Mary said, with a reassuring smile. Why the girl was so afraid of divulging her name Mary could not imagine, but perhaps she had her reasons. Or it could be that the hesitation was just the lingering effects of her ordeal. "She's a lady's maid in London, is me Jenny. Finish yer broth, then, Jenny—if'n you don't mind me callin' you that—and then get back under the covers." Molly yawned hugely and Mary decided her little one needed some sleep, too. She put her in the cradle and pulled

the soft, hand-knit coverlet up over her. She then moved to
stand beside the bed and gazed down at her new charge.

"You are so kind," the young woman murmured, finishing
the last drops of the broth and putting the mug in Mary's
outstretched hand. She gazed around the cottage with avid
eyes. "What a lovely home you have," she said, snuggling
under the covers and pulling them up over her shift. With a
start, she looked down at her underclothes, but she did not
seem shy at all. Her eyes touched on her dress hanging clean
and drying near the fire. Mary had repaired the rip at the
bosom with her neat stitches and no one would be able to
notice unless they were closer than they ought to be.

Mary watched her for a moment. Lady's maid or lady;
which was she? She could just ask, but it was enough for
now that Jenny seemed to be healthy, if still tired. There
would be time later to settle the mystery of who she was
and how she came to be in Mary's barn in the middle of
the night. "Thank you fer the compliment," Mary replied,
gazing around her snug cottage. "Molly and I like it."

"May I hold her, your baby?" the young woman murmured.

"When you awaken again," Mary said, smiling as she
watched the gray eyes drifting closed.

"But I am not in the least bit sleep—"

In the same dream she had been having for ten years or
more now, Jane dreamed of arms around her, holding her
close. She relaxed back and felt the hard wall of a man's
broad, sturdy chest. She was cradled in warmth and love
and security, and a deep voice murmured comforting words
of devotion. His breath was warm and tickled her ear, but
instead of giggling she was inclined to surrender to the
rising desire to turn over and kiss the lips that would be
waiting for her, wanting her.

In a moment, she thought hazily. There would be time

for that in a moment. She was in a little cottage again, only usually all she could see was the fireplace. This time she could see the smoke-stained stone walls, the bare wood rafters hung with bunches of herbs and dried flowers, the scarred wooden table and chairs near the window, and she noted the rush baskets full of apples and the strings of dried fruit. She could smell the smoke of the fire and the rich scent of mutton stew, and clothes drying near the hearth. The mantle held rough pewter candlesticks and there was a settle near the fire made of stripped willow branches, a settle made for two, covered in a handmade quilt of simple pattern. And a cradle fashioned by hand, with a baby in it on the stone hearth.

She awoke with a start. A . . . a baby?

It was dark and she was disoriented at first, but then she remembered. She remembered a plump, pink-cheeked woman named Mary, enough like her in many ways to be her own sister, and a rosy baby named Molly, and a delicious cup of broth flecked with herbs, rosemary, and thyme and wild savory. Propping herself up on one elbow, she saw, by the dying glow of the fire, the woman, Mary, asleep sitting up, her hand in her cheek. The cradle was near the hearth at her knee.

This place felt strangely like home. Jane relaxed back, happy now that she knew where she was. It was as if she had dreamed this place, this cottage and this life, into existence, it was so much the life she had imagined as she lived her stuffy existence in London and then Bath. Every detail of the cottage—the clean scent of linens drying by the hearth, the heavy, hand-hewn rafters, and the homey, woven rag rugs on the floor—seemed precious and perfect.

But the moment she told Mary the truth, that she was Miss Jane Dresden and that she was—practically—the betrothed of the hard and haughty Lord Haven, the woman, whoever she was, would have no choice but to send for her aunt, Lady Mortimer, and she would have to go on to Haven

Court. She didn't know exactly where she had wandered to in the dark and frigid night, but it could not be so far away that the woman who owned this cottage would not have heard of Lord Haven and his resentful temper.

Jane turned onto her side and stared over at the faintly glowing fire. Embers popped and fell in a shower to the floor of the grate and Mary moved restlessly. Jane just could not go to the viscount's home now. She had fled into the night to avoid that fate, a loveless marriage; she considered the agreement she had made to seriously consider Lord Haven as a groom to be irrevocably broken, torn asunder by the treachery of some of the participants. Things were different now and she must decide what she was going to do now that she had been cut adrift from her old life, partly by that treachery and partly by her own precipitate actions.

With any luck she was many miles away from Haven Court, though she thought she might have lost her way in the darkness. She shivered as the memory of that long night of wandering, scared, cold, lost, and wet, came back to her. How lucky she was to have wandered here, into the safety of this snug heaven. But what was she going to do? Where was she going to go now that her life was in a state of turmoil?

Would it hurt, an insidiously meek voice said in her head, *to just be "Jenny" for a few days, until you get your bearings and figure out what you want to do? You told her your name was Jenny,* the voice whispered. *Just keep being Jenny, runaway maid, perhaps, or turned-off lady's maid.*

She lay back and stared at the rafters and into the mysterious darkness above. She could hear the wind sough outside the window, and the panes rattled in their frames. It seemed to her that she was some distance away from any habitation, for she had wandered long and far. But she could not be certain. For all she knew she could be just the other side of the river from Lesleydale! She would have to find out from her hostess. Much depended on that, for if this woman heard in the village about the missing Miss Dresden—there must, by now, be a stir about her disappearance—then she would know immediately who her house guest was.

Jane felt some compunction about involving the widow Mary Cooper in her disappearance, but with a bit of luck she would be able to disappear again before the woman was too deeply involved. As for herself, she felt no guilt at all about the way she had left the inn. She was in Yorkshire under protest and now she did not think she owed anyone anything, least of all the hideous Lord Haven, as he had become in her imaginative brain.

Not without reason. In her own secret investigation of this man she was being matched with she had spoken with one lady who had met Lord Haven in London, many years before. She remembered him well as a graceless, bumbling, plain, dour, mean-tempered oaf with no intelligence and even less conversation. Others Jane had spoken with were marginally more polite—they called him stern, unyielding, practical, quiet—but it all supported the image of the viscount as dour and humorless. And that was who she was to marry?

Squeezing the pillow, agitated, Jane tried to relax, but bitterness at her ordeal overwhelmed her. Oh, but no, her aunt and mother had said; she was to make up her own mind. If she didn't want to marry him, why, she could just walk away and go live in her little cottage, just her and her mother. That had been her understanding, the only reason she had reluctantly agreed to this trip.

Ha! It had become plain on the journey north that her aunt had no intention of living up to her end of the bargain, as Jane had understood it in Bath. It had become increasingly clear that she would be bullied and harried into it, and not just by Lady Mortimer but by the viscount, too lazy and proud to seek his own wife in London, and by his mother, whom Lady Mortimer knew from her own long-ago London Seasons and whom she described, in terms Jane *could* not like, as someone very like herself.

Jane would marry Haven, she had been informed, or Lady Mortimer would know the reason why.

It was her worst nightmare; Jane would be immured in this harsh, desolate, sheep-filled country with a miserable husband and likely a dozen babies in as many years. It was not that she did not want children; she did, desperately, but not at the price of being bedded by a humorless, emotionless giant of a man in a cold, dreary castle in the farthest reaches of England.

To counter that, she had her dream husband. She wanted a warm man, a soft-spoken, loving, kindhearted man who would care for her and with whom bearing children would be an endless joy. She wanted the cottage in her dreams and a fireplace of her own, with a man who would cherish her, not see her as a decorative ornament for his fastidiously decorated palace, or a brood-mare to satisfy his family's requirements.

Mary murmured in her sleep; Jane watched her hostess shift restlessly in her uncomfortable slumber and thought about her current situation. It was a series of unfortunate happenings that had resulted in her precipitous flight from the inn. She had been unhappy coming up to Yorkshire, yes, but she could have withstood all of her aunt's nagging, could have fortified herself with the knowledge that if she just held to her convictions she could ride out Lady Mortimer's anger and that of Lady Haven, and return within the month to Bath and her mother's side. But one letter had changed all of that rosy wishful thinking, that gauzy dream of a life of her own choosing.

The fateful missive had caught up with them at the inn in Lesleydale; it had been posted from Bath only two days after their own departure. And now, with a few hastily scrawled words, all of her hope was dead; confused, unhappy, frightened, she had made her heedless plans and fled.

Perhaps she would not have been so reckless as to run up into the moors alone—that had not been her plan—if she had not been accosted by those drunken louts in the stableyard, and had her dress torn, and . . . she hid her face in the pillow under her head. There was no avoiding the truth. She had made a mess of everything, losing even her meager reserve of money and her precious pearls in her idiotic flight. What was she going to do? Where could she go?

Perhaps being "Jenny" for a few days would give her time to think. Claiming that name was an inspiration, for it really was hers, in a way. Her old Scottish nanny had called her that for all the years of her youth, and the name held fond associations. She had been Jenny to her own dear Nanny Biddy, and "Jenny" she could still answer to.

All she needed was a little time. She had to decide what she was going to do now that she had broken away from her family. She felt not an ounce of compunction for the alarming note she had made up on the spur of the moment. If it frightened her aunt, then good! The wicked old harridan deserved it. But Jane did not, deep in her heart, think that her aunt would be frightened for her. Annoyed that her scheme was not going to come off as expected, perhaps, worried for the family's reputation certainly, but not truly concerned for her niece's well-being.

As the dim light of morning filled the tiny cottage and the baby stirred, Jane, curled up under the warm woolen blanket, made her resolution. She would stay here for a few days with this kind-faced woman, Mary, and her adorable baby, in this delightful cottage in the Yorkshire hills, and then she would disappear again. She still had a little money tucked in her stocking. She would either travel on the stage back to Bath and confront her mother, or she would go up to Morag's—Nanny Biddy's niece and Jane's old friend—home in Scotland. North or south; within the next few days she would decide literally on the direction of her life.

Three

Haven, having escaped from the Court and its pervasive atmosphere of blame, found refuge at the Tippling Swan and sat in a corner of the smoky, low-beamed drinking room of the inn. It was very late, past midnight or later, and yet all around him the raucous voices of men eddied and flowed like a muddy stream, swelling on the tide of a joke to a boozy wave of laughter. Joseph Barker, the innkeeper, brewed a dark lager that was the pride of the parish, and most of the men present gulped back great drafts from hammered metal tankards.

As he scanned the crowd Haven wondered, was one of them a kidnapper, maybe worse? He cast his piercing blue gaze around, lingering on Burt Connor, Georgie Robertson, Artie Davies, each man in turn, but there was not a one of them he thought would descend to such depths as kidnapping a female. It just did not seem possible that one of these men, or more perhaps, for abduction was rarely a solitary crime, had strayed so far from the law as to take an innocent girl of good birth for ransom, a demand that had not yet been followed up. The note had said a demand would follow, but so far, nothing.

He motioned through the thick air for the landlord; Joseph Barker was a bulky, surly sort who gave him an unpleasant look but, grumbling, joined him. The man turned one of the sturdy wooden chairs around and straddled it, rolling his shirtsleeves up over meaty forearms.

Haven leaned across the battered wooden table and said, "Are you certain, Joseph, that you neither saw nor heard anything the day Miss Dresden disappeared?"

"I towd ya, me lord, I hain't seen nuthin'." Barker narrowed his eyes, squinting through the smoky air. "An' I'd be beholden to ya if ya wouldna' make like I did."

"I didn't, Joseph. I am just trying to get to the bottom of this. She and her aunt were here, and then the girl disappeared. Do you remember Miss Dresden?" Haven raised his voice over another wave of laughter.

With a leer, the landlord said, "Right enough, me lord. Never forget a pair like 'ers."

Haven frowned. What the hell did that mean? "But you never saw her come down?"

"Not arter her an' the auld besom, her auntie, went up t'stairs, nup."

"So you have no idea what happened to her? You saw no one suspicious, nor . . ."

With a sigh of exasperation the landlord grunted. "Don't rightly know, me lord, what I ken tell ya that I hain't already tol' ya!" His words were muttered with a belligerent tone. "An' anutter thing, me lord. Yer makin' the fellas a mite anxious, like, an' . . ."

Haven sighed deeply as he listened to Joseph's unhappy reproaches. The landlord's words held some merit. The viscount was being cast unpleasant looks in a place where he had been used to be honored. The men around Lesleydale might hold he had little to say for himself, but what little he did say was accounted to be sensible and just. Now, after his insistent questioning, they were grumbling that he was casting them all in a suspicious light. Not a man among them would stoop to snatching an innocent maiden, they muttered, and for the lord of the manor to be saying they would—

In short, it was making for an unpleasant time. And yet
what else could he do? Miss Dresden was in his part of
the county and he felt a duty toward her, though she had
disappeared before ever she got to his own door. Even if
he did not feel that tug of responsibility, a young woman
missing, in his parish? He was bound, by all his ties to the
land and the people, to set this right. She had gone *somewhere,* for he had no belief in the supernatural. Flesh and
blood women did not just disappear. "I know, Joseph," he
replied, cutting off the innkeeper's litany of complaints.
"But think—have you seen any strangers, even anyone who
was vouched for by someone else?"

The man frowned, scrubbing his scruffy chin and folding
his meaty arms over the back of the chair. "Yuh ast me
that afore, me lord. Carn't say as I hev. I'll ast the missus.
Again. But seems ta me yer lookin' in the wrong place. I
don't 'low that kind o' foolishness at my inn, you know.
P'raps at the Dog's Hind Leg," he said, naming an infamous
hedge tavern on a back road.

"But she disappeared from *here,* Joseph, we cannot get
past that."

The landlord grunted and stood. "Don't mean t'were
someone from here who done it! Could ha bin summat as
follered her from Bath!" He turned and retreated to the bar,
where a barmaid stood waiting for him to draw her a tankard of his dark and bitter brew.

"Haven! How goes it, my friend?"

Twisting in his seat, Haven was relieved to see Colin
Varens, a local baronet, who, though a few years younger
than he, was a sensible man with a cool head. Sensible
except in that he was in love with Rachel and had been for
four years. Haven thought the man could do much better
than his contrary, flirtatious, impetuous sister. In fact, Haven suspected that Pamela, younger than her sister by three
years, was well along in the way of being head over ears
for the baronet, who was not accounted a handsome man,

nor fashionable, but had an open countenance and pleasing expression. But Colin only ever saw Pammy as a child; her slight frame and boyish slim figure made her look more thirteen than almost twenty, though her thoughts were often surprisingly deep and her spirit gallant.

"Colin, good to see you. Didn't expect to, this late of an evening." Haven stuck out his hand and the two men shook.

Varens turned the chair around and sat in the seat vacated by the innkeeper, frowning. "What is this nonsense I hear about someone being kidnapped from the Tippling Swan? My estate manager was full of some wild tale. I told him he was out of his mind, but he insisted."

"It is true, unfortunately," Haven said. He glanced around and lowered his voice, for with the meeting of the two most prominent men of the parish the room had grown quieter, and there was an uneasy feel of resentment in the very air they breathed. It was damn uncomfortable, but there was nothing he could do about it at this juncture. Once the mystery was solved things would return to their normal even tone.

"As I said, it is true." He explained about the disappearance of Miss Dresden, and the measures he had taken to recover the young lady. "I have searched my own property—most of it, anyway—and ridden over every back road I know of these past thirty-six hours or more. No one has seen her, nor anyone who could have kidnapped her." He scrubbed his hands over his face and dug at his raw eyes. He was exhausted and would need some sleep soon. "It is a mystery and I am not overfond of mysteries, especially when they concern me or my family."

"And do you think everyone is telling you the truth?" Varens asked. He glanced around the room, and some of the men who had been staring at them with menacing expressions resumed their determined drinking. Varens was known to be handy with his fists and not above a fight with the yeoman class.

"I have no reason to think otherwise," Haven said. He stared at his younger friend, wondering if he was intimating that there was deception in their midst, and then glanced around the room, relieved to see that the men were now ignoring them. "What are you saying, Colin?"

"Nothing, truly, Haven. I am just casting around for explanations. It all seems so . . . unlikely. Kidnapping, here? I *have* heard something you ought to know, though," he said, his plain face set in a grim expression and his eyes serious. He leaned across the table and lowered his voice. "I don't know if this has any bearing on your case, but my stable manager said that the other day, the very day you say this Miss Dresden disappeared, I believe, he was coming out of the back door of the Swan to relieve himself and he saw two men jostling with a barmaid or some such female. When he shouted, they let go of her and she ran off."

"She was a barmaid? How did your man know?"

Varens shrugged. "I assume it was the way she was dressed. He said 'barmaid' not 'lady,' so it must have been her clothing that led him to presume her status."

"I am not looking for a barmaid, Varens, though I thank you for the thought." He was disappointed that after the buildup it should turn out to be something so mundane as a barmaid being roughly handled. That happened all too often. "Miss Dresden is a young lady of the gentry, Varens, granddaughter of an earl. She would hardly be mistaken for a barmaid." He thought of the miniature he had seen of the lady, her face pinched, her expression haughty, and added, "No, most definitely Miss Dresden could not be mistaken for a barmaid. And, too, Lady Mortimer was very clear about her clothing. She was wearing a coach dress of brown sarcenet and a pelisse of the same fabric. And the situation is different, too. Miss Dresden was abducted; she would hardly be grappling with a drunkard in the stable yard."

"You're right, of course," the younger man said, leaning back in his chair, at his ease. The barmaid brought him a tankard of ale with a flirtatious swish of her skirts, but Varens did not seem to notice. He never had been in the petticoat line, saving all of his adoration for Rachel. "But I hate to think of any one of our neighboring men doing something so base as to kidnap a lady! How is your sister taking this?"

Haven shook his head. Always, Sir Colin thought of everything in relation to how Rachel was faring. "My dear sister is made of sterner stuff than you would think, Varens." He did not need to ask which sister his friend meant. Varens never considered Pamela unless he thought to buy her a sweetmeat in the village, or talk to her about horses. "But why do you not come over tomorrow and see for yourself?"

Gloomily, Varens sighed. "I would, but Miss Neville would likely hide away in her room, as she has done the last three times that I have called."

"I can order her to come down and greet you," Haven said, anger rising at Rachel's obdurate refusal to see that Varens was eating his heart out for love of her. Why was it women did not know how to value an honest heart, even if it beat in the chest of a man with a homely face, but would rather see a dandy in canary overcoats and no heart to speak of? "But," he said, forced to honesty, "she likely would not comply."

"I would not have her ordered to see me," Varens said. There was an expression of ineffable sadness on his face. "I know you think me a fool, Haven, for my feelings—"

Haven protested, but Varens put up one hand and continued speaking. "But I see something in her, something fine and noble and . . . I cannot explain. Someday, perhaps . . ." He fell silent for a moment, gloomily staring at the floor. "Why can women not be rational, like men?" he blurted out. "I do *not* understand them. Before she first went off to London, Miss Neville was very pleased to call me her friend, and I even thought there was a preference there, a . . . a softness. But ever since her first Season . . ." He broke off and stared through the smoke at the bar.

Haven sympathized, but thought it wisest to remain silent. However much he believed that Varens was an excellent match and that Rachel was a fool to let him slip away, he could not help but think that it was best for both, if there was no preference there on her side, that they should not see each other. His sisters had both been exposed to London society, but their Seasons had been spotty due to a couple of deaths in the family that had forced them to withdraw for a period of official mourning. Rachel had only had enough exposure to London society to know that she wanted more, *much* more, and would settle for no beau who did not share her enthusiasm for the ballrooms and parlors of the elite.

Varens despised London, and his means were not such that he could afford to indulge a wife who wished to make her home there. If only he could see Pamela's preference for him and fall in love with *her*. She relished the country and horses and loved Sir Colin's estate, Corleigh, as a second home. She had made a friend out of Colin's odd sister, Andromeda, and ran tame in their house when she visited. It would please Haven greatly to have his favorite sister and his best friend make a match of it. Unfortunately, Pamela seemed destined to forever remind Colin of a particularly pleasing puppy. He liked her, found her amusing, but did not think of her as a flesh and blood woman.

"Why are women so very impossible to understand?" Varens said, finally, after a period of brooding silence.

Haven shrugged. "Not all women are like Rachel." He thought of Mary, and her calm goodness, her sweet-tempered naturalness. Then he thought of all he had heard of Miss Dresden, her perfection of genteel manners, her rigid propriety. Lady Mortimer had sent a miniature ahead when the two families had first started negotiating, and the lady in the portrait was a pinched-faced, sour-looking spinster if ever Haven had seen one. It would not do. He had been seriously considering the match, knowing the duty he owed to his title and his ancestry. The title had descended directly through seven generations, with no oblique movements to sully the line. He must marry and produce a son. But surely Miss Dresden was not his only choice? He had thought he was resigned to it, but now he did not know.

"If only we could marry wherever our hearts took us, Varens. If only."

The other man gazed at him shrewdly, and said, "You are thinking of Mary Cooper, are you not, my friend?"

Haven frowned. "Not—" He shook his head, confused, as always, as to what he felt for Mary. Sometimes he thought he loved her, but she had told him on more than one occasion that what he felt was friendship and familiarity, mixed with male need. He respected her opinion and thought that she was quite likely right. It had been a long time since he had made love to a woman, and Mary was very pretty in a country fashion, but surely if he was in love with her, he would be sure of it. In any case, she evidently felt nothing more for him than friendship, so the point was moot.

"We are an unprosperous pair of lovers, are we not, Haven?" Varens rose from his chair and stretched his lean body. "I must be on my way. I will see what I can find out about Miss Dresden's disappearance. I am appalled that a lady would suffer such a fate as abduction in our neighborhood."

"I thank you for your aid, my friend." The two men clasped hands warmly and Varens left, the smoky air swirling about him as he strode through the taproom. Haven was about to follow him out but noticed the landlord berating a young potboy in the entrance to the kitchen. The young-

ster had something in his hand, but the landlord snatched
it from him and shook him by the shoulder, then pushed
him off toward the kitchen.

"What goes on, Joseph?" Haven said, approaching the
landlord. It was very late. A youngster that age should not
still have been working.

"I caught the wee wretch sneakin' back in from outside;
escapin' his dooties, he were! Should be in his bed under
the kitchen work table, restin' up for his work on the morrow instead of out in th'moonlight. Prob'ly poachin' rabbits,
the scalawag! Won't stand fer that, I won't. An' then . . ."
Barker looked down at his meaty fist and what was clutched
within it. "Me lord, look at whut he had! Sed as how 'e
found it under a cart in the stableyard."

The landlord held out his hand and glowing in the dull
light from a lantern in the hallway was a double string of
perfect pearls. They spilled from his grasp and hit the floor
with a clatter.

Four

Mary sat at her spinning wheel and paddled the foot treadle evenly. The comforting clunk-clunk and whir of the wheel was already a lullaby to her little baby. But as it happened, right that moment little Molly was not sleeping, she was laughing as Jenny tickled her under the chin. The girl had a natural hand with babies, though she claimed she had never even held one, much less taken care of one, before Molly. If that was true, then she must have a natural affinity for the wee ones. Molly, who sometimes fussed with strangers, had stared up into Jenny's gray eyes that morning and cooed immediately, breaking into a delighted chuckle, something she only ever did for her mother and for Gerry.

But who was Jenny?

Throughout the day, with Jenny gaining strength, the color coming back into cheeks naturally rosy, they had spoken at length. Mary had finally asked, gently but without equivocation, who she was and how she came to be in the barn so late at night. She was not wholly or even partially convinced that Jenny's answer was truthful.

She claimed to be a lady's maid trying to get home to Scotland. Nonsense. She was most definitely not Scottish, and Mary did not think she was a lady's maid. The young woman explained that she had gone for a walk to stretch her legs while waiting for the stage to change horses, but got lost and wandered in the wrong direction. It did not sound likely or even possible, and yet, for all that it sounded like a lie, Mary was loath to push her. There was a thread of weariness in the young woman and an undercurrent of desperation and confused misery that called out to Mary's maternal instincts, even though Jenny was close to her own thirty years in age. And there was that torn dress. She gazed at her own neat stitches, so nearly invisible at the bosom of the dress. No, she would not push Jenny for an explanation just yet.

Mary removed a filled bobbin of fine wool from her spinning wheel and started a new one on the spindle. "Molly likes you," she said, quietly, watching the intimate scene.

"And I love her," Jenny said, a trembling in her sweet-toned voice. She lifted Molly up and the baby flailed her feet in the rhythmic stamping motion babies do before they learn to stand and walk.

Mary pushed the treadle, starting the wheel and moving the basket of unspun wool closer to her feet. She paddled evenly, the steady speed keeping the thickness of the wool constant. How the work flew along when there was some-one to converse with, and when Molly was being looked after! She watched the two on the hearth. Seeking more information about the mysterious young woman, she asked, "Would you like to have a babe of yer own?"

"I would." Jenny bounced Molly up and down on her lap and the baby's giggle rang out in cheerful peals, her dusky curls bouncing and jouncing in rhythm. "But one needs a husband first, and I am not so sure I want one of those. They seem entirely more troublesome than babies."

So not a runaway wife, which had been one of Mary's conjectures about the young lady who sat in the stripped willow settle. The uncertainly in her voice had been too honest, Mary thought, and yet perhaps the girl was just a brilliant dissembler. How difficult it was to keep to her resolution not to pry just yet. She should be ashamed of her curiosity, she supposed, but she had so few visitors, and never one with a mystery accompanying her. "Ah, a husband is a change, to be sure. But where there be love, there be givin' an' takin'. My Jem had precious little notion how to go on with a woman in the house, at first. He had bin used for years to doin' fer himself, and it took near a year after our weddin' a'fore he would remember that I was there to make his tea and sew his buttons."

"What was he like?" Jenny asked. She cradled the baby in her arms, her quick eyes having seen the little girl's huge yawn and the fists that she rubbed in her eyes.

"Jem was the gentlest soul I hev met, save one more I could name. Some men be gentlemen in name only, and some are 'gentle men' down t'the soul. My Jem were one o' those, though he were only a farmer with no education to speak of. I . . . I wish he had lived to see Molly. What a pa he would ha' made!"

Jenny's expression, full of quiet empathy, made Mary realize how alone she had been for these past months since Molly's birth. She had missed the company of other women, the instant bond of understanding. It was how she knew that whoever Jenny was—whether she was in trouble and fleeing, or just who she said she was, a lady's maid out of work and on her way north—she was a good person, someone she could trust with Molly.

Conversation flowed on. *Lord, she had not talked so much in a year,* Mary thought. But with Jenny there was an easy exchange, a quick and happy chatter, the type of talk that soothes a woman's soul. It was one thing Jem could never understand, why women liked to talk so much, and about trivialities sometimes, something as simple as the new waistline in dresses or the funny thing their child said that day. Never having been married before in his forty-four years, Jem was constantly puzzled by Mary's need for conversation. Being with his wife was a complete change from the long, drawn-out silences between him and his cronies at the Tippling Swan, punctuated only by a dry observation of the weather, or a comment on how their stock went on.

But everything sped by so much quicker when there was conversation! Here she was with another full bobbin of wool spun already, and it was almost time to make lunch. A knock at the door made Jenny jump, and a worried look crossed her pretty face.

"Who could that be?" Mary said, cheerily, though she had a hunch who it was. She didn't have many visitors.

It was Haven, just as she had suspected, and he looked harried and tired. But Mary had seen the fear in Jenny's eyes and thought it might be best for the time being to turn Gerry away. She glanced back over her shoulder and slipped out the door, placing one hand on Gerry's chest and pushing him ahead of her.

"What is it, Mary?" he said, frowning. "Molly asleep? I'll not bother her, you know that."

"It's not that," she said. She crossed her arms over her bosom. The wind was chilly and the shade from the cottage, despite the brilliant sunshine that beamed down, was still wintry. March was often an unkind month on the moors, but thank the Lord it was almost over. "I . . . I have company."

His eyes widened, but then he shook his head, puzzled. "From almost any other widow in the world I would think that meant you had a gentleman caller, but I know you better than that, Mary."

"Gerry," she said, severely, "I canna believe you even thought that fer one bare second, and do not say you didn't, because you did!"

Shamefaced, he admitted it had crossed his mind despite his words to the contrary. "But it was just a fleeting thought and I didn't entertain the notion for more than a few seconds, Mary, truly. Now who is this company that I may not see?"

They had never had secrets from each other, and she knew that his persistence was just a failure to recognize his old friend's right to a life that did not include him. It was frustrating at times and she knew eventually, when and if she ever decided to have gentlemen callers again, it would be awkward. But what was she going to do in this instance?

Mary took a deep breath and prepared to do something she had never done in her life, particularly not to Gerry, and that was lie. But what else could she do? It was not that she did not trust him with the truth; if the girl had been abused or was in physical danger from someone there was no one she would rather confide in than Gerry. But he was a man, and if it was a case of not actual abuse but just a runaway bride, he might see things differently. There was *something* the girl was hiding, something that haunted her, but until Mary knew what it was—"It . . . it is my Cousin Jenny." It was the decision of an instant, to claim the girl as kin. And if she was ever going to back out of that falsehood, it had better be now. She dithered on the edge of saying she was just hoaxing him.

"Any cousin of yours is a cousin of mine, you know that, Mary," Haven said, and pushed past her into the cottage.

She wanted to be angry at him, but she knew that he simply did not recognize that there would be any reason why his old friend would deny him the door. Mary followed him in, swallowing nervously. What had she done? Lying to her oldest friend in the world, and all for a girl she did not even know! Well, now it was done. In for a penny—

Haven was prepared to see a plain girl, for so Mary had always described her cousin, Jenny, so when the girl at the fireside turned he was struck dumb, the breath sucked out of him as if he had been dealt a blow to the chest. She was the loveliest creature he had ever seen, plump and pretty, with glossy dark curls that cascaded down her back, restrained only by a bit of dark blue ribbon. Her lips were the color of cherry blossoms, a soft pink that stirred something deep within him, a dormant desire he had thought devoted only to his oldest friend in the world, Mary. And her eyes . . . he moved into the room as if on wooden legs, barely remembering at the last moment to yank off his cap.

The girl had looked away again, an indescribably enchanting expression of shyness and sweetness his last impression before she hid her face, holding the baby up and staring into the hearth.

"Even if I had not just been told," he finally said, finding his voice, surprised at how it croaked, "I would know you for a relation of Mary's." He had the strangest impulse to fling himself at her feet, there and then. He swallowed hard, restraining his impetuous urge. "So you are her cousin, Jenny. I have heard much about you, but nothing I have heard did you a bit of justice."

The girl cast one wide-eyed look past Gerry to Mary, who stood still by the door, then glanced away again, speechless. Her sweet shyness entranced him and he moved closer to chuck the baby under her dimpled chin. "There, Molly, your old friend Gerry has come to visit. Gerry . . . uh, Gerry Neville at your service, Miss Jenny."

Mary shut the door, closing off the cool breeze that eddied into the warm cottage, and she filled the kettle from an ewer of water on the table. "I'll make tea," she said, her voice tight and brittle with some kind of tension, "and some lunch. Can you . . . can you join us, Gerry?"

He breathed a sigh of relief and cast her a grateful glance. So Mary was not going to insist on any "my lording" or "Lord Haven-ing" right now. He had not expected such forbearance. But her cousin, a lady's maid, he believed, from past conversations, would stiffen in the presence of a viscount and she was shy enough as it was. He tried to will her to look his way but all he could see was the rose blush of her smooth cheek. "I'd be glad to, Mary, if it won't be putting you out." This was what he needed after the turmoil of the past two days, he thought, sitting down on the hearth and gazing up at Jenny and Molly. He moved slightly and caught her eye.

Gray. Yes, her eyes were definitely gray, but never had he thought that color to be so soft and warm, like . . . like the breast of a mourning dove. And somehow familiar, as if he had seen them somewhere before, but not really—he shook his head. None of that made a bit of sense and he was not a fanciful man. She had turned back to him and his gaze fixed on her lips. Her voice now; would it be harsh and grating, or affected and nasally, or velvet-soft and sweet-toned? Her eyes were wide and curious. Conquering her shyness, she caught his gaze and held it, as if she were trying to read his soul.

"Have you ever been to Yorkshire, Miss Jenny?" His voice came out tight and still croaky. He cleared his throat.

"No, never."

Soft. Toned like the highest bell in the church carillon, with a sweet note in it and yet clear. "I—I hope you like it here. Perhaps you would like to make it your home."

"Oh, I . . ." She shook her head and her dusky curls tumbled over her shoulder. "I don't think that will be possible."

How did she get such a genteel speech, he wondered. His mother's and sisters' maids tried their best to emulate upper-class speech, but it was usually a poor copy at best. But Jenny spoke like a . . . no, not like a duchess. The only duchess he had met talked like a stableboy. So, like Mary, whose speaking was above her class somewhat. That well-bred speech must run in the family. And yet Mary still had the mannerisms of her youth, the Yorkshire inflections. Jenny's was more refined, even. "Well, Miss Jenny, I'll leave that up to Mary to try to convince you."

How natural her childhood name sounded on his tongue, Jenny thought, examining his face with growing interest. And how handsome he was! She had not expected a country gentleman to be so . . . so good-looking, in a bluff, brawny way. He was a broad-shouldered, strong-looking man, with thick light brown hair that fell over his brilliant blue eyes. From his dress and manner she would guess him to be some sort of superior farmer; perhaps he had his own farm. Her customary shyness around gentlemen waned as they took turns holding Molly and playing with her, as Mary made lunch. She could see her new friend darting worried glances over at them and she knew what was bothering her. Mary must have told him that her unexpected guest and her cousin Jenny were one and the same person. She had felt from the start an empathy from Mary, a delicacy. She had not probed for her story and accepted without question what Jenny had told her, which was just that she was a lady's maid and was going north to find a new position near her cousin's home.

That she did not fully believe her was clear and yet she had misled her friend, giving Jenny time to take a breathing space. She was grateful. In time perhaps she could explain, but for now she was just grateful for this respite from her own world.

As time passed, Gerry decided that Jenny's resemblance to a lady of his own class was merely superficial. Her voice was lovely, her movements graceful, but her talk was more honest than the young ladies he had met in London, or even in his own district at local assemblies. She did not flirt, nor did she simper. She asked intelligent questions and listened to his answers, not flinching when the subject matter was not quite fit for a lady.

In other words she was perfect, and he was smitten. He hardly knew her yet, but already he felt more at home than he ever had with any lady outside his family or other than Mary.

Why couldn't Miss Jane Dresden have been like this girl? He had never met the lady in question, but her manners and personality had been described to him; she was, he had been told, a perfect pattern card of what a *lady* should be.

That meant, in his estimation, prim, proper, careful, unnatural, fussy, prudish—everything that this girl, Jenny, was not.

He turned away from the thought of the unfortunate Miss Dresden. The knowledge that she was out there somewhere, alone and scared, plagued him night and day. But he had spent the last two days looking for her; surely he was entitled to this brief recess from worry! He really did not know what he could do that he had not yet done. He sighed and stared into the fire. At that moment Mary called them to the table.

As they ate cold mutton and homemade bread with honey, Haven wondered how to ask Mary if she had seen or heard anything to do with the missing girl, without revealing himself to be the viscount. He had meant to bring up the topic immediately, but had been distracted by the addition to Mary's household. He glanced up. At the sight of Miss Jenny's tongue delicately licking a drop of honey off her fingertip, he felt his groin tighten and swiftly looked away. It had been a year or more since he had allowed himself the relief of a convenient woman, and for most of that time he had forgotten about his physical needs, burying himself in exhausting work. He must distract his mind from the delectable sight of Mary's younger cousin or he would not be fit for company.

He cleared his throat. Better to talk about his troubling search for Miss Jane Dresden. Surely he could just mention it in a general way, without identifying his reason for being involved. "Mary, I near forgot. There has been a spot of trouble in the village, at the Tippling Swan. I am perplexed, I will admit. I meant to ask you if you have seen or heard of a young la—"

At that moment Mary's cousin's plate slipped sideways for some reason, and her bread went flying onto the floor. "Oh, no," she cried. "How clumsy!" In her quick move to pick it up, her mug of buttermilk tipped, sending a stream

of the creamy beverage over the scarred surface of the table
and down onto Mary's pristine floor.

Gerry hastened to pick up her bread, tangling hands with
Miss Jenny as he did so. Mary swiftly grabbed a rag and
started sopping up the buttermilk. In the ensuing laughter
and chatter the baby awoke from her nap and started wail-
ing, meaning it was time for Mary to feed her. He glanced
at Mary settling into her chair by the fire with Molly, and
turned to her cousin. Picking up his cap, a disreputable hat
he used for his farming chores, he twisted it in his hands
and said to Mary's guest, "Miss Jenny, would you do me
the honor of walking with me? If you haven't been to the
area before, I would be pleased to show you around."

"I never have been this far north," she said, shyly. She
looked over to Mary. "Do you think . . . should I—"

"Go on wi' the two of you," she said with an understanding smile. "Gerry, show her the Lesley."

Gerry felt his heart pounding as he opened the door for
the young woman. He was aware, as he never had been in
his life, that he felt something for Miss Jenny that no other
woman had inspired. But he hardly knew her! Had he created her out of some deep desire in his own soul, or was
she what he hoped and thought she might be? She advanced
down the path ahead of him, pulling her shawl up over her
shoulders, and he admired the sway of her hips under her
simple blue dress. Miss Jenny was, to his mind, an amalgam
of Mary's simple honesty and charm, mixed with her voluptuous and natural sensuality, but with a dash of, for lack
of a better term, "essence of lady" thrown into the mix.
She was utterly enchanting, everything from the top of her
lovely brown curls to the tip of her small feet, and she took
his breath away.

"Shall we follow Mary's orders and take in the sights of
the Lesley?"

"I would be delighted," she said, taking the arm he held
out for her as naturally as if they were in Hyde Park of a

London afternoon in the Season, ready to stroll along the Serpentine.

Just the touch of her arm tucked tightly against his side sent a thrill racing through his body. And yet it was not just her physical effect on him that he was astonished by. He had met girls who attracted him before. There had been a barmaid in Lesleydale that he had been mad for and had lusted after. But she had been a forward lass, taking him by the hand one night and leading him to her tiny closet up the stairs. They had carried on a liaison for a few weeks and her lusty lovemaking taught him much, but such forward ways could not inspire love in him beyond the physical. And he had known that the girl would easily move on to another lover after he parted ways with her, as she had done with her last lover, and would do with her next. Since then he had found comfort in the arms of many a barmaid, and once or twice a voluptuous widow in the village.

He felt that same pulse of physical attraction for Miss Jenny, but there was a difference. It would never be with her, he knew already, a quick tumble between the sheets, no matter what her class. A swell of resentment coursed over him at the fanciful whims of fate. She was a lady's maid and he was a viscount; there could never be anything for them beyond this, this walk in the brilliant spring sunshine.

And so, he admonished himself, he must enjoy what he could and not resent what he could not have. It was a waste to walk with this lovely girl and brood over what could never be for them: marriage, children, a little cottage like the one they walked away from this moment. Grieving over the vagaries of life would not change a thing. He smiled over at her. "I shall show you the natural wonders of Yorkshire and hope to convince you that it is, as I believe, the most beautiful place on earth."

From the cottage door Mary watched them. What had she done? She was lying to both those poor idiots and she did not know why. Or, if she was honest, yes she did. She had lied to Gerry about Jenny because of a look of fear and wariness in the girl's eyes. She was hiding from something or someone and it was Mary's instinct to shield her, even from the gentle probing of her old and dear friend, Gerry. As Mary's cousin, no one would look at her twice.

And she had lied to Jenny, or at least omitted to inform her that this was his lordship, Viscount Haven, because she had caught the mute appeal in Haven's eyes the minute he had seen the beauty at Mary's fireside. She had never seen Gerry so happy as he was the moment he had offered to be a guide to Jenny and held the door open for her.

It went against the grain to lie to anyone, least of all her dear childhood friend, but it was done for better or for worse. How would it end? And who *was* Jenny?

Five

The day was brilliant with sunshine, but chilly, with a swift wind that caught at her hair and lifted it, tumbling it into confusion. They walked down the path away from the cottage and Gerry rushed ahead to unlatch and open the gate for his companion. She smiled shyly up at him, her bashfulness returning now that they were alone. She looked to him as to the direction they were to take, and he offered his arm once again. Pink rose to her cheeks as she took the proffered arm and allowed him to guide her to the west, along a beaten path that led up over a high moor and down into the valley of the Lesley.

He looked down at her feet, admiring the flash of shapely ankle he saw as her skirts swished with each step. "Are you . . . will your shoes stand the walk, Miss Jenny?" What a dolt he must sound!

She nodded.

He pondered what to say, what to talk about to bring her back out of her shyness. But the feel of her close to him was sending his senses reeling and he feared he would not be able to string five words together into a sensible speech. As they strolled in silence, the wind whipping pink into her cheeks, he battled his growing attraction to her. This was ludicrous, to become so enamored of a girl with whom he could have nothing more than this day. And on what was his infatuation based? A few words, a look, a sweetness of expression?

T'would never do, and he knew it. His common sense acted like a cold rain, slowing his pulse, cooling his fevered brow.

He took a deep breath. He would treat her like the new friend she was, as he would any relative of Mary's. "Have you ever seen a shepherd round up his flock?" he asked, cheerfully.

She shook her head. "I . . . no, I have not, Mr. Neville."

"Could you not call me Gerry?" he asked, pleaded, almost.

"Oh, I don't think—"

"Please." He turned her to face him and took her gloveless hands in his. They were small and cold, and he rubbed them, trying to warm them. "I am practically a brother to Mary and you are Mary's cousin. Can you not think of me as kin—well, not as kin, exactly," he stammered. The way he felt about her was not cousinly and he did not want her thinking of him with that much ease, no matter what his resolutions concerning her were. "But just as near-relation? And call me Gerry?"

"All right," she said. She looked around her, and said, "This countryside is so beautiful, wild, and free! I always think that we were meant to live like this and not in stuffy houses in a great city!"

"I agree. There is nothing like the open country. Did your mistress live in London most of the year?" he asked, as they strolled, arm in arm, up the gentle rise following the footpath.

He felt her start. Perhaps her last employment was not pleasant; he hoped he had not raised an unhappy subject. She nodded, but remained silent.

"You didn't like it? Living in London, I mean." He felt her shudder.

"I hated it," she said, her voice trembling with emotion. "I despise London. It is dirty and smelly and noisy, and the people are rude. And Bath is little better. It is full of painted old men and ill-tempered dragons with unhappy young girls they try to foist off on those painted old men as brides."

He chuckled. "I see we agree on some things, London in particular."

"You have been to London?" she asked, surprise evident in her voice.

Damn. He felt her curious gaze on his face and looked down at her. If he was the gentleman farmer he was pretending to be, he would not likely have made that trip; none of his employees, other than his personal servants, had. This lying business was more difficult than it should be. Or perhaps it was meant that way, to catch sinners such as he. "I—yes, I have been, once. On business. For my—for . . . for his lordship." Damn, but that sounded awkward. And yet if he were truly the farmer he was claiming to be, it would come easy. How ingrained were the habits of command, and he had not even realized it! Perhaps he was more viscount than he knew, accustomed to the position of power he held in his community.

"Oh. You . . . you work for the . . . the viscount, I suppose."

He didn't answer. Let her assume what she would, he would not add to his considerable deceit. They came at last to the top of the rise; below them was the broad spreading valley through which the Lesley wound, numerous trickling gills fed by the rains of two days before quivered in silver flashes down the verdant hillsides and joined the river. They stood together for a moment.

"It is truly breathtaking," she said on a sigh, gazing enraptured at the brilliant emerald hillsides that rose to meet the azure sky. The valley through which the Lesley wound was below them, with groves of trees delineating its path. "You know, I have never been this far north. We hear, in the south, that the north is wild and desolate and cold and . . . and treacherous. I was a little afraid coming here. But it's not fearsome, it's beautiful!" She spread her arms open wide and turned in a complete circle. "How free I feel! And how . . . how happy!"

His heart did a wild cavort in his chest at the awe and gladness in her voice, and all of his good intentions, all of his sensible resolutions, tumbled away. She was utterly en-chanting, and it was not just the voluptuous freedom of her movements and her buxom loveliness, not just the way the wind tumbled her curls and her smile curved the sweet bow of her lips, it was the gay laughter in her voice and the delight on her face. It was the wonder with which she wel-comed Yorkshire into her heart. One would almost think she loved it as much as he did!

Oh, to be the simple farmer he was pretending to be! They had not known each other two hours yet, but he felt a tenuous thread of connection that was thickening, binding them in a mutual appreciation of the simple joys of his home county. What he would not give to be able to deepen their friendship, courting her openly, falling in love minute by minute and hour by hour! He watched her, eyes closed, deeply breathing in the clean, fresh Yorkshire air, and thought how he would, if he could, plan ahead to a life that would consist of simple vows in the village chapel and a cottage near the Lesley, children and home and work. It was a humble dream, perhaps, but what more did a man need? What was there beyond that, a good woman to plan for, to work for, to . . . He swallowed, squash-ing back his delightful daydreams.

Jenny glanced up at her companion. He was staring at her and she caught her breath at the yearning expression on his open countenance and in his brilliant blue eyes. If only, if only—Inwardly she sighed at the idiotic playacting she was taking part in. Mr. Gerry Neville was a farmer. A superior kind of gentleman farmer, it seemed—in fact he must be distantly related to the viscount, for they shared a family name, Neville—but still a farmer and the hired worker of another man. And she was the granddaughter of an earl, niece of a baroness, with a family line that was titled in many different directions. If he knew he would back away from her as if she were carrying an infectious disease, such were the barriers between the classes.

But though there could never be anything more between

them than a passing friendship, there was this moment and this day. There was the glorious sun warming her face and the clean breeze sweeping up from the Lesley and the lush grass beneath her feet, softer than the thickest Aubusson carpet. She swore to herself that she would enjoy this day for what it was, a respite from her life, before planning what she was going to do, where she was going to go.

"Tell me about Yorkshire," she said. He took her hand in his as naturally as if he had done it a thousand times, and yet she knew she would always remember that first touch and the way her fingers twined around his, callused but gentle as they were.

"Yorkshire." He cleared his throat. "Yorkshire is the largest county in England—did you know that?"

"Every schoolgirl knows that," she chided, and only realized her mistake when he slued a curious glance in her direction. How would she, an unschooled maid, know what every schoolgirl should know? "I m-mean by that, every child who has ever looked in a book. I was . . . was lucky enough to have an educated mother."

"Yes." There was silence for a moment, and she thought by the intent look on his face that he might pursue her education further, but he returned to the subject at hand. "Well, Yorkshire *is* the largest county, and all those prissy London folk who damn it as wild should thank us, for we provide more mutton for their table than anywhere else in England. And what many people do not know unless they are dealers, we are the foremost producer of horses for stable and carriage. Many a horse for auction at Tattersall's has been bought first at York."

They walked on hand in hand, down the long, slow descent on a diagonal pathway. As she listened, Jenny wondered idly what her aunt had told them when she arrived at Haven Court, and how the fearful Viscount Haven was behaving. She slanted a glance at her amiable and gentle companion. With his open countenance, ready conversation, and cheerful expression, he was the opposite of everything she had heard of her proposed bridegroom. She wondered if the viscount was even now storming about his castle like a thwarted child at Christmas, or was she setting her own charms at too high a price? Maybe he was as relieved that she was gone as she was to *be* gone. Or perhaps he had not even noticed that she was not there, so wrapped up in his own business that the failure of one prospective bride to show up was a minor nuisance. Maybe he had a string of them lined up, to be paraded past him like prospective servants at the mop fair. She almost giggled at the image.

That he would be worried for her was out of the question. The Viscount Haven she had heard of in London was a cold-mannered, dour, and unpleasant man, with all the charm and personality of a whelk and about as much conversation. She glanced up at her companion. Not like Gerry, who had played with a little baby and brought a smile to infant lips with his faces and burbling noises, and who now was smiling at her as he told her some amusing detail of Yorkshire life.

"I am intent on surprising you somehow about my county," he was saying. "Did you know that . . . let's see . . . that . . . ah." His expression grew serious. "Ladies like romantic stories. I have one for you. It is said that during an outbreak of the Wars of the Roses a Lancastrian maiden, in love with a York supporter, was kidnapped by her lover and brought to our own little village of Lesleydale where the two plighted their troth." His face shadowed for a moment as he spoke of the kidnapping. He frowned, but then shook his head and continued his tale. "Anyway, the Lancastrian maiden's father, irate at the abduction of his daughter, came north through the worst of the fighting and demanded his daughter back."

"Did he get her?" Jenny asked.

"No. The girl proclaimed her affection for her Yorkish husband and her determination to stay with him. She loved him too much to ever give him up. So the father—I have often thought he must have been an affectionate sort—

stayed and pledged fealty to the York cause, just so he could stay close to his beloved daughter."

Jenny sighed. What love that proved for a daughter! How would things have been different in her own life if her father had lived? She remembered him only vaguely as an affectionate man, quiet, hardworking, and loving. But her mother had always complained about how she had come down in the world by marrying him, and Jenny wondered if she had been so openly bitter during her father's life. "That's a beautiful story," she said, sighing happily. "It is true, ladies do like a love story."

"Romantic," he agreed, grinning and taking her hand again. They walked on. Though the Lesley had appeared close at the top of the moor, there was really a long series of hills and dales between them and the river still.

Her pleasure died for a moment, remembering the awkwardness back at the cottage earlier. His talk of kidnapping and abduction had brought it back to her. Gerry had been about to tell Mary about the missing Miss Dresden, she was certain. It was only her own quick, purposeful clumsiness that had deflected the conversation and stopped that line of talk. But it could only be a momentary reprieve. There would come a moment when he would be alone with Mary and would ask her if she had seen a girl, a stranger wandering the moor, or if she had heard of such a creature, and then Mary would know who she was and be forced to turn her in. It was coming and perhaps as quickly as that very afternoon, when they returned from their walk. And then she would be forced to deal with the viscount and her aunt and the whole mess she had made by running away so precipitately.

She took a deep breath of clean, crisp air. But she would not brood; instead she would enjoy the moment. The Yorkshire countryside was a delightful surprise, the undulating swells of the grass-covered fells a welcome sight to eyes that had only ever experienced the closed and somehow smaller landscape of the south. "What is that?" she asked, shading her eyes and pointing at a far building that huddled on the moorside like a knot on a log.

"That is a shepherd's cottage. In season, if the flock is staying out, the shepherd needs shelter betimes. I, uh . . . his . . . his l-lordship provides for his men well. Keeps the cots in good shape. Some owners provide little more than tumbledown sheds."

"Is he a good master then?" Jenny asked, idly, wondering why Gerry stumbled over the viscount's name always.

"He is accounted to be," Gerry said, with a smile that was somehow secretive.

It said to Jenny that he would not criticize the man even if he had cause, and she honored him for it. She would not question him farther, for loyalty ran deep in such a man, she suspected. "May we . . ." She hesitated and gazed at him. A wicked little grin turned her lips up at the corners. "May we run?"

"Run?"

"Yes, run!" She hesitated only a moment more, but then gathered up her skirts and raced down the last slope toward the Lesley.

Gerry caught his breath, enchanted at once by the fey expression that had crossed Jenny's face in the moment she decided to run, and by the vision of her, skirts flying, hair streaming. He raced after her, catching up with her just as she tripped on a hummock of thick grass near the riverbank and tumbled down. His heart pounding he threw himself down at her side. "Miss Jenny, are you all right?"

She was laughing and panting, her skirts splayed out around her and her hair tumbled over the grassy ground. He was seized with a strong urge to kiss her, to gather her to him and make love to her, and it must have showed on his face, for her expression changed to one bordering on alarm and she sat up suddenly, then bolted to her feet, moving away from his side. Damn his expressive face! Mary had always said she could read him as if the words were in his eyes. If Jenny had read the desire in his expression it was no wonder she was nervous. For all the connection he felt between them, she still barely knew him.

He stood, leaving the space between them. He forced a smile and said, "Now that you have that urge out of you, how about that walk by the Lesley?"

Jenny acquiesced but her mind was racing. The intent look in his eyes; what had it portended? For one brief second she had thought he was going to kiss her and that would never do. She was not afraid of him; she did not think he would . . . her mind shied away from that which she was not afraid of with him. But still, it alarmed her to think of his well-molded lips pressed against her own, his heavy body touching hers, his strong arms pinning her to the heath—alarmed her because it sounded enticing and inviting. How far would she allow such transgressions? As a young lady of the *ton* she had never been so alone with a man, never been so free, so able, if she desired, to indulge in behavior that would "ruin" her in society's eyes. But what of other classes; did they indulge their whims? Were they freer with their affections?

She tidied her tumbled hair as best she could and demurely took his arm again, walking with him like the lady she was. Her heartbeat returned to normal and the odd light in his eyes died, she noted when she stole a glance at him. He spoke of the area, giving her more information than she would ever need to know about sheep farming, telling her that he had hoped she would see an example of sheepherding that afternoon, as it was a fascinating art. She couldn't have cared less about sheepherding. And yet it was pleasant listening to his voice, a rumble of deep sound that she could feel in her arm as he held it close to his body. He could have recited the biblical "begats" and she would not have minded.

The more she experienced of this life the more she liked it. This day, taking care of Molly, learning from Mary how to bake biscuits, and now walking with Gerry Neville, gentleman farmer, was like a dream of the life that could have been hers if only she had been born someone else. But she was Miss Jane Dresden, niece of the baroness Lady Mortimer, granddaughter to the third Earl of Kantby, and cousin to the current earl, with a portion of her own that would be adequate for her whole life if she was careful. She lived a life of ease, free from want, the dream, she was sure, of many a poor maiden without a portion, nor any hope of living without labor.

And so why had she turned tail and flown like a flushed partridge? She was an intelligent, well-provided-for young lady. Why could she not just seize the life she wanted and damn the consequences? It would take courage to defy her family, and that, perhaps, was what she had always lacked.

They entered a grove of trees just then burgeoning with a brilliant green unseen in any London park; their trunks were gnarled and twisted, probably from the persistent Yorkshire wind that swept down from the fells. The leafy glade was a verdant bower, a place where time and trouble did not exist. The turf underfoot was soft and springy, the new grass lush.

Gerry loosened his hold on her arm and she turned, gazing up at the ceiling of green overhead. "Why would anyone prefer the confines of a great house when there is such glory in nature?"

"You would not think nature so glorious if you saw this same grove in winter, with the wind howling between the trees and the snow burying the trunks up to the lowest branches, ofttimes." His tone was wry, but he was smiling. "It is treacherous in January, but I have been here then, rescuing a sheep that had escaped the flock."

She could hear the soft burble and gurgle of water ahead and the trees thinned, then parted ahead of her. A stream of crystalline water tumbled over smooth rocks, frothing and dancing, silver in the sunlight. She took a deep breath, inhaling the fragrance of clean water and sun-warmed grass. "I shall always remember this place in spring," she said, sadness overwhelming her for a brief moment, tainting her voice with its melancholy tones.

"Can't you . . . won't you stay, Jenny?"

She shook her head, touched by the deep emotion held within his simple words. There was something between them, she thought, but they would never know what it was, would never have the time to explore their attraction to each other. Refusing to be gloomy on such a day, she tripped lightly to the stream edge. He raced to join her and grabbed her hand. "Be careful, Miss Jenny. These rocks can be treacherous."

His hand was warm around hers, folding it securely in his square palm. It felt natural, sweet, perfectly right. "You do not sound like a farmer," she said, gazing at him curiously. "I heard some of the men at the inn when I arrived in Lesleydale and their accents were thick, but yours is not. Why is that?"

He colored, his cheeks turning ruddy as if she had asked him something extremely personal, and she did not think he was going to answer for a moment. "I was given a rather good education by the vicar in the village."

Perhaps he was the son of the estate steward, or some such almost-gentleman. Or . . . or a nobleman's by-blow. There was that Neville name, after all. But she could not think of a reason to pry further and did not want to ruin the perfect comfort into which they had fallen. They stood by the edge of the stream, their hands still entwined.

"Why have you never married?" he asked, suddenly.

"I . . . I h—have never found anyone to my t—taste in my own . . . in my own c—class," she stammered with perfect honesty, pulling her hand out of his. Abruptly, with his question, she realized how illusory their perfect harmony was, based as it was on his misimpression that she was of his same rank. If she asked him the same question the answer would likely be that he could not afford to marry. Most men of his situation could not until they were past middle age.

"Oh."

"I . . . I suppose we had better be getting back," she said.

He cast a practiced eye at the sky. "Clouds gathering. We'll have rain before nightfall. And I have work to do before then."

She realized with shame that this walk had probably taken him away from work that he would be in trouble for neglecting. "Will . . . will Lord Haven be angry with you for taking time away from your duties?" she asked, as they moved back among the trees and to the hill beyond it. "I hope you will not suffer for this."

"What an ogre you must think him," Gerry said, chuckling. "No, he is the most lenient of masters."

"I heard him spoken of as dour and uncommunicative," Jenny said. "I rather thought that would denote a sour and harsh cast of character."

Gerry looked startled. "Dour? I have never—where did you hear that?" When she did not answer, he answered himself. "At the inn, I suppose, or in the village. He is . . . he is not much understood in the village, although I think he is well respected. I suppose he could be called dour, but he just is not a chatterer. In Yorkshire that is considered a good thing, though some in London might think it connotes a bitter twist of mind, I suppose."

She had not said London, Jenny thought. But it was best they left that subject behind anyway. It came too close to revealing what she had truly heard and where, and a maid, though she might have heard downstairs gossip, would likely not have heard about Lord Haven unless he was a guest of the household.

They walked back up the long fell and through the new green grass mixed with brown from the year before. Rocky outcroppings burst through the soil here and there, and Jenny followed with her eyes the long, gray, stone fences that curved and marked off squares of grassy ground. It was a long way back and Jenny was thoroughly winded by the time they walked in silence up the last slope toward Mary's cottage, then through the gate, where Gerry stopped.

"If you'll say my goodbyes to Mary and Molly, I'll leave you here," he said.

Jenny, feeling suddenly shy, cast her eyes down at the mud-splattered toe of her walking shoes. She rubbed at the mud with the toe of her other shoe.

"Miss Jenny, may I walk with you another day?" he asked, in his voice the proof that it was the impulse of the moment that made him ask.

She looked up to find his steady and hopeful gaze upon her. "You may," she said, unable to conceal the joy in her voice. She wondered whether he would actually be back before she found it necessary to leave. At least he would not find out what a fraud she was that very day. She was safe for the time being, though that was a ludicrous way to think of it. If she was who she said she was, she would be hoping that this handsome farmer was bent on courtship. Her heart would be thumping as it was now, but with hope, not sadness.

"I'll be back, then, as soon as work permits, Lord Haven being an ogre and a slave driver," he said, with a smile.

She felt her own lips curve up in response. His smile lightened his broad face until it was not just handsome, but breathtaking. He was not a man the girls of her acquaintance would think handsome; he was too bluff and square and strongly built. He was not elegant in any way, but he satisfied her notion of manly good looks. He took her hand in one of his callused palms and turned it over wonderingly. "So soft," he murmured, and brought it up to his lips. She gasped at the feel of his lips and he turned her hand over and in a courtly gesture touched the pulse at her wrist with his lips. "Good day, Miss Jenny. I'll be back, never fear."

With that he turned and sauntered down the path, his hands in his trouser pockets, a jaunty whistle trailing behind him.

Six

"Have you found anything out?"

Gerry had no sooner walked through the front door of the Court than Lady Mortimer pounced on him.

"Have you found anything out?" she repeated, her dark eyes fixed on his face and her hand clutching at his arm, wrapping around his wrist, vicelike. "Have you found what happened to her yet? Where she is?"

"No, Lady Mortimer, I have not," he said, feeling terribly guilty. He could still feel the imprint of Jenny's small warm hand in his palm; for a few hours he had completely forgotten about the poor girl who had disappeared. The weight settled back on his shoulders and he gently said, "I will just be having my tea and then I will go out again. A neighbor heard something from one of his men and I am going over to his estate to talk to the fellow myself."

"If I was a man, I would beat him until he told me."

"Until he told you what?" Haven snapped, jerking his arm out of her grasp and slipping effortlessly back into his role as Lord Haven, viscount and landowner. "Until he told you what you wanted to hear? That is a brilliant way of conducting yourself, madam, if you only want to hear lies! I happen to want the truth about Miss Dresden's whereabouts and I was under the assumption that you did too!"

His voice had thundered through the great hall, and his

grandmother limped out of her chamber, her cane tap-tap-tapping on the flagstone floor.

"What are you roaring about, Haven?" she said, but there was an appreciative glint in her eyes.

"I am attempting to reassure Lady Mortimer that I am doing my utmost to find out what has happened to her niece."

"Well of course you are! Only an imbecile would think otherwise."

The baroness's face had frozen into an icy glare and with a muttered imprecation she swooped out of the hall and strode up the carpeted staircase that curved upward to the gallery overhead.

The dowager Lady Haven chuckled. "Fubsy-faced old turnip," she said, making a face after the retreating baroness. "Come have tea with me, Haven. Tell me what you have been up to today, for I'll warrant it was not completely taken up with searching for poor Miss Dresden. I saw you coming up the walk just now, and you had a look of moon-dreams on your face." She turned, assuming he would follow, and he did.

The dowager, though her home was nominally at Haven Wood, the dower house behind the manor house, had a room on the main floor of the Court, carved out of a section of the great hall. It was decorated in the heavy, ornate style of her youth, with large, carved furniture and brocade-covered walls. An enormous screen portioned off an area near the fire for her bedchamber, but she had a sitting area near the window and it was there that she retreated, pulling a bell-cord and ordering tea from the footman who answered the summons.

"So, who is she?" the dowager said, the moment the door closed behind the footman.

"She who?" Haven said, irritably. He paced to the window and scrubbed his face with one hand, suddenly weary.

He stared out at the leaden sky, but remembered the celestial blue overhead while he walked with Jenny.

" 'She who'! Do not try to cozen me, Haven. Is she a new barmaid at the Swan? You had the same look on your face as the first time you came home from a tomcat expedition to town. Tupping a lightskirt behind the inn? Eh?"

Haven flushed as he always did at his grandmother's earthy wit. "No, I was *not*. I wish you would not speak that way, Grand. It is crude and language not befitting a lady."

The dowager made a rude noise. "Not befitting a lady! Humph. So, not a lightskirt, and not one of our maids. You never were one to break in the girls. You leave that up to the footmen. No little by-blows of yours running around that we know of, eh?"

Haven flushed deeper and gave his grandmother a quelling look. She laughed, sputtering and gurgling as a footman brought in a tray, setting it on the table in front of her. She dismissed him and poured herself a cup, dumping some in her saucer to cool it and drinking directly from the saucer.

"I'll not embarrass you more, lad," she said, kindly, sitting ramrod straight in her chair, her white hair dressed in the elaborate style she favored, even though in the country there were few to see it. "Your wenching shall remain a secret." Her smile died. "I was glad to see you put that horrible Lady Mortimer in her place, Haven, but she has a right to be worried about her niece, for all she is a fussy old cod. The aunt, not the niece. What *have* you learned?"

Haven sat down across the ornate gilt and enamel table from his grandmother. She poured tea for him with a barely quavering hand and he sipped it, finding solace in the smoky depths of the cup. He could wish it were stiffened with a good shot of brandy but would not quibble, especially since her tea was many times stronger and better than the anemic brew his mother served.

"I have found a puzzling *lack* of information, Grand.

Miss Dresden seems to have started down the stairs toward the kitchen of the Swan and never arrived at the other end. I have heard not a single scrap of information to suggest that anyone saw a well-dressed young lady being seized or assaulted anywhere near the Swan. And I cannot believe that she would have been seized and hauled away without a soul seeing anything!"

The dowager frowned. "Almost as if she wanted to disappear," she murmured.

He nodded. "I must say I have considered that, but still, Grand, even if that were true, where would she have gone? A well-dressed young lady just walks out of the inn? Someone would have noticed her. I would like to think she left of her own volition but I do not think that is possible. And we cannot discount the note that was found in the stable."

"I suppose not," the old woman said. "D'you have the note?"

Haven took it out of the pocket of the disreputable jacket he always wore when out walking his own land and smoothed it out on the tabletop, sliding it across the table to his grandmother.

A more incongruous setting for the dirty, stained, almost illegible note there could not be, for the tabletop was an enameled painting of a lady with panniered skirts, sitting on a bench with an amorous swain at her feet, gazing up at her adoringly. Around the edge of the table was a series of smaller vignettes featuring ladies and gentlemen in much the same attitudes of pastoral love.

The dowager read the note and then pushed it back to her grandson. "Something odd about that," she said, frowning and chewing on her lip. "For one thing, the handwriting is far too good."

"That was what I thought," Haven said, glaring down at it as if it could offer new answers if only it would, though he had stared at it so much it was virtually imprinted on his mind.

"And I do not think," the dowager said, slowly, "that the same fellow who would misspell so many simple words, like 'to' or 'you,' would be able to spell perfectly when it came to the words 'we'll' and 'contact' "

Haven stared at the note. "You are right, Grand. But . . ." He stopped and thought. "What that means is that this was meant to look like the work of an uneducated worker, but was more likely the work of someone of a much higher class."

The old woman nodded. "So, not one of the local laborers. Perhaps not someone from around here at all. But that gets us not a single step closer," she said.

He refolded the paper and put it back in his pocket, moving awkwardly on the dainty chair. "I am not so sure of that; it at least gives me something to look for. I will go out to Varens' place. He has heard a story from his stable manager that I think I ought to investigate, even though it would seem to have no bearing on this case, merely the attack of a barmaid from the Swan. From what I understand he saw this girl being attacked and then the girl ran off. But if the girl was unwilling, and the men were at her *anyway,* it might indicate men who were willing to do that sort of thing to a female. I will go and see."

The dowager nodded. She glanced at her grandson and then away, choosing her words with great care. "If you find the poor girl—Miss Dresden I mean, not the barmaid—her reputation may well be in ruins, you know," she said, slowly, moving things about on the table as she expressed her concerns. "I feel we owe her something, for after all, she would not have been at the inn if she was not coming to meet you, Haven."

"I never wanted the damn match—it was Mother!" he protested. "I know I must marry some time, and I admit that I did not stop her from inviting this girl." He ran one hand over his thick, sandy brown hair and sighed deeply. "But I do see what you mean. I feel for the poor girl; who knows what she is going through right now. But does that mean I have to marry her?"

"Would that be so terrible?" the dowager asked. She frowned over at her grandson and continued, carefully, as if treading on ice. "She is of good birth, Haven, her dowry is excellent, the family females are said to be decent child-bearers, and from her miniature, she is tolerable."

"Tolerable?" he snorted. "Your eyesight is failing, Grand. She looks like butter would not melt in her mouth. She looks prim and ill-tempered and as though my lips would freeze if I dared kiss her."

"But she is handsome enough and has no visible defects."

"Is that all I should want?" he asked, standing and pacing to the end of the room. It was a corner suite, so there were windows overlooking both the south terrace and the west gardens. "No visible defects? Sounds like I am testing a horse's teeth or wind, not a young lady's qualifications for marriage. I could stand any defects at all. I wouldn't care if she was lame, or without hearing, or plain, or even ugly, if I saw a trace of warmth in her eyes, or—"

"What *do* you want?" the dowager asked, an acerbic edge to her voice.

"Damn it, Grand, I want a girl I can . . . can care for at least, if not love. I *don't* want some frivolous belle of the ball who will demand a new wardrobe every Season and will hate Yorkshire." He swore and slammed his hand against the window frame.

"Haven," his grandmother said, sternly. "Look at me." He turned toward her. "You are thirty-one. It is time for you to marry and *past* time that you got over this ridiculous prejudice against girls of your own class. Just because you were an awkward country gent in a sea of town tulips does not mean every girl who has had a London Season will look at you with scorn."

He turned back to the window, folded his arms over his

broad chest, and stared out bleakly over his land, his eyes traveling the well-known hills. "You have no idea the depths of their scorn, nor the vitriol of their sneering, Grand. You were not there. There is not a one of them I would be able to stand to bed, if you want the bare truth. Prim, prudish little 'prunes and prisms' misses, all of 'em." He spat out the last words.

"Then marry one of them anyway," his grandmother, exasperated, cried. "And spread her legs in the dark where you can pretend she is a bar wench!"

"Damn it, Grand, I want more!" Haven thundered, whirling and planting his hands on the table. "I—want—*more!*"

The dowager looked somehow satisfied. "What *do* you want?" she shrieked back in his face, thoroughly enjoying the turbulent confrontation.

"I want *Jenny!*" He could not believe he had said it. His words echoed in the high-ceilinged room, seeming to take on a mocking life of their own. *Jenny.* The name whispered back at him from the windows and paneled walls.

The dowager sat back, looking like a cream-filled cat. "Who is Jenny?"

Haven slumped down into a chair. "Mary Cooper's cousin. She's visiting."

"What's she like?"

"She is lovely." He closed his eyes and smiled. "Skin like Devon cream and lips like rose petals. Lovely voice. Laugh like a bell; sweet, though, not clanging. Unaffected. Intelligent. Good-natured."

"And clearly not of our class. Not if she is Mary's cousin."

He shrugged. "Does that matter?"

"Of course it does! Not to me." The dowager snorted. "Good Lord, Haven, I only have another two or three years on this earth if I am lucky. I will not waste any of it bemoaning your wife's lack of birth."

When the viscount stole a glance at his grandmother's

face, he saw only compassion. As always, there was an empathy between them. She understood him in ways no other person on earth did.

"But to her, it will," she said, gently. "I will not say that an unequal marriage cannot work; when there are only the two involved, it can. But you have a mother, two sisters who will marry in time, and a position to uphold. Is it fair to ask her to join you in a marriage in which—"

"God, Grand, I did not say I wanted to marry her!" He could not bear to hear all of her reasons why Jenny would not suit.

"Ah. You only want a poke at her?"

"No!" he shouted. "Well, yes, but not *just* that!" He was revolted, for once, by his grandmother's forthright, old-fashioned crudeness. In the normal course of things he might rail at her unseemly language but he would laugh as well, but there was no laughter in his heart just then.

He sat down across from her and looked her in the eye. She was getting old, was his Grand, and there was no disputing that. The once taut and smooth skin was a fine net of wrinkles and her eyes, though still blue, were rheumy and watering. Grand was always the one he could talk to over his own mother or even his father. She *had* to understand, he had to *make* her understand this one thing. He had caught a glimpse that afternoon of all that he had ever wanted, all that would make his life bearable—more than bearable, complete. It would make his life complete to have someone like Jenny to love. "I want to just talk to her. I want to sit by the fire with her while she sews. I . . . I want to watch our b-baby grow in her, and be there when she—or he—is born. I—" He put his head down, feeling the enameled panels cool under his over-heated skin. He felt his grandmother's hand on his head smoothing back his ruffled hair, and he smelled her rose perfume, as familiar as his own scent.

"You want someone to love." There was a deep sympathy

and understanding in her voice. "That is no mystery. And you have this fairy-tale romance in your mind of a cottage in the woods and you and some plump little wench filling it with children." She sighed. "But you are Geraint Walcott Haven . . . *Viscount* Haven," she continued, her voice taking on a bracing, stirring tone. "Lord and master of a grand inheritance. Your wife must be someone who can fill the position required of her with grace and elegance. That is for her *own* comfort, Haven, not for yours. Does this girl even know that you are Viscount Haven, holder of an old and illustrious title in your own right and noble descendant of the Earl of Warwick—Warwick the kingmaker—and the largest landholder in the North Riding?"

He sat up and gave her a rueful smile and shook his head.

"I thought not," she said, dryly. "Do not think she would be impressed, Haven. She would likely think you were just another nobleman looking to jump into her bed for a cuddle and a poke."

"Grandmother!"

"Grandson!" Her tone was mocking.

He could not stay angry at her. She only told him what she knew to be right, after all. Or what she believed to be right. "You, old dear, are incorrigible." He grinned at her and caught her hand in his own and kissed the palm, feeling the silk-soft skin under his lips.

"When you smile like that you are almost as charming as your grandfather," she said with a twinkle that changed to a rueful look. "He liked maids too, and bar wenches, and being married to me did not always stop him from indulging his tastes." Her expression grew more serious. "Do nothing until we find this poor girl. I feel we are committed to helping her and making what reparation we can for her terrible kidnapping. And do not put so much store in Miss Dresden's painting. After all, perhaps the day the portrait was made she had just eaten a rotten quince and had an upset stomach."

Haven nodded and chuckled. "Thank you, Grand," he said, cupping her cheek. "Thank you for listening. If I had told Mother about Jenny she would have thrown one of her more memorable fits, I am sure." He stood and walked toward the door. "I'll find Miss Dresden. If she has been kidnapped and is out there somewhere, I will find her. I promise I will not let myself become distracted again."

"I know you will find her, Haven," the dowager said. "I have faith in you."

Haven left, closing the door behind him, but the dowager sat where she was for at least half an hour, staring blankly at the teapot.

Seven

Miss Pamela Neville slunk out the door and raced to the stable, intent on not letting her mother see her in her disreputable riding clothes, a remnant of her childhood days. They were old—*very* old—breeches of her brother's. Not a soul in the household even knew she still had them, secreted in her hidden stash in a trunk in the attic along with reminders of her father and a precious gift of cherry-colored ribbons Colin Varens had given her when she was just eight. She saddled her mare with a groom's saddle instead of her hated sidesaddle and flew out of the stable yard, before the groom had a chance to even see her.

Free. She was free for at least the afternoon.

Haven Court, always the site of petty squabbles, quarrels and disagreements, had become even more unwelcoming of late with the addition of Lady Mortimer, whom Pamela detested, and the disappearance of the silly wench her brother was pledged to marry.

Quickening her mount—a bay mare named Tassie—to a gallop, Pamela flew over the familiar ground and instead of opening the gate and walking her mount out, she urged Tassie to jump one of the stone fences, the last barrier between her and the freedom of the high, barren moors. They soared together over the obstruction, the mare as eager as her rider to flee to freedom. The high moors beckoned and the gloomy gray of the sky could not dampen Pamela's delight.

Marriage. Haven was finally seriously considering it. She knew he was and she hated the thought of the changes that would bring to the easy relationship she and her brother enjoyed. She spurred Tassie, trying to outrun, over the high fells, the awful knowledge of change coming, change chasing her, years going by and the inevitable alteration of people and places.

Even her own wretched body. She was different now and she felt it, could see it in the mirror. Grand said she ought to be married by now and have babies. But even though she was easily old enough—she was all of nineteen, and some of her friends had been married for a couple of years now—she was just not sure whether she even wanted a husband. After all, it would mean an end to these glorious rides. She trotted to a prominence and stopped, looking out over the brilliant green landscape, shadowed by the darkening, thickening clouds. As always she felt a thrill of joy at the sensation of Tassie, heaving and huffing beneath her, and the brisk wind that swept up the moor.

It was all so different from London.

She had been to London the previous year for the Season and a sillier waste of time she could not imagine. She didn't mind so much the dresses. A lot of the clothes were so pretty and sometimes she had even felt like a princess, adorned in white and wearing Grand's lovely old pearls. She got impatient standing while clothes were fitted to her, but she would just lose herself for that hour that she stood being poked and prodded by her mother and the seamstresses in thoughts of the moor and riding Tassie. She started her mare down the descent into one of the valleys that snaked through the moorlands, going from a walk to a trot as she thought back to her "Season" the previous spring.

In the brief months she had been in London she had constantly been in hot water, for any free time she had was spent in the stable of their London house and she had picked up the colorful language she still peppered her talk with, to her mother's mortification. She had slipped out of the house alone on one memorable occasion, and had been seen once *galloping* in Hyde Park—oh horrors!

And that was all before the official Season had begun. Their London Season had been cut short by the death of their father's sister, an elderly tyrant whom nobody liked, but whose death could not be ignored. Rachel had sulked for at least one full month out of the three required for mourning an aunt, but Pamela had been rather glad. Not glad that old Aunt Viola was dead, just glad to escape London before having to attend too many of the stultifying balls, routs, card parties, and Venetian breakfasts that were the meat of the London social Season.

Not that she had not been enjoying herself; she had, but in all the wrong ways, according to her mother. She had met some jolly lads and had slipped away with them once to see a prizefight. She had caught no end of breeze about that particular escapade! Even Grand, when she heard about it, had told her she had gone too far.

This year, to Rachel's chagrin, it had been decided that the needs of the master of Haven Court must supersede his sisters' Seasons, so they would welcome his supposed bride to his home for a protracted visit rather than making the arduous journey to London. There had been no end of dustup over that, and Rachel was still not back to any kind of equable state.

Pamela trotted up to another rise, the loftiest hilltop immediately near Haven Court, and gazed across the land, letting her beast walk for a moment and finally halt so they could both catch their breath. London was all well and good and there had been any number of opportunities to kick up a lark or two or three, but really, when all was said and done, this was where she belonged. She gave a happy sigh. Yorkshire, where the air was clean and free and where a girl such as she was not looked at as if she was a caper-witted little gapeseed.

Marriage to one of those London dandies her mother had been pushing at her would mean leaving Yorkshire, likely, and she couldn't imagine never riding these hills again. Of course, she wouldn't have to leave if she married someone local, someone like—

She sighed once more, only this time it was a sigh of utter defeat. Tassie danced impatiently, sidling and throwing a glance over her shoulder at her rider, so Pamela raised her to a walk again and started down the hill. She would not have to leave Yorkshire if only she could marry someone like Sir Colin, who was desperately in love with Rachel, who didn't give a fig about the poor sot. Rash, wild plots pelted recklessly through Pamela's brain, audacious schemes to entrap the hapless Sir Colin into marriage with her, only to collide headlong with reality. In the end, she would be married to a man who didn't care for her and would likely despise her if she entrapped him. At least now he treated her with a careless, brotherly affection. If she trapped him into marriage, he wouldn't be able to stand the sight of her. That would kill her, she was sure. He was her friend as well as her perfect fantasy husband.

Pamela urged Tassie on to a canter, and then a gallop. She rode neck-or-nothing down the long slope into the valley, hoping to work out the fidgets both of them were experiencing. When girl and beast were both thoroughly exhausted, Mary's cottage was in view, so Pamela trotted up to the small barn, threw herself off the horse and tied her up, letting the poor animal rest and crop grass around the base of the ancient building that housed Esther and the chickens, and Lally, the very pregnant barn cat.

"Mary!" she called, striding toward the cottage, then realizing she really shouldn't shout so. The baby might be asleep.

The baby! Skeptical about children in all their grubby glory, Pamela had nonetheless been enchanted by Molly, by small pink fists and soft dark hair, by wide eyes and a tiny perfect mouth. She would likely never have children of her own—she could not see herself birthing and then caring for one of the little humans—but she hoped Rachel had lots and lots so she could spoil them completely, teach them to ride, and give them treats till they were sick! She strode to the cottage just as the door opened, but it was not Mary who stepped out. Pamela stopped and frowned. "Who're you?" she grunted, surprised into discourtesy.

The young woman's eyes widened, and she stuttered, "I—I'm M—Mary's cousin."

"Who is it, Jenny? Is it . . . oh, Pammy!" Mary came out from behind the younger woman. She looked Pamela up and down and glanced over at Tassie, heaving and snorting still, and laughed. "Escapin' the confines o' home, are you?" She cast one worried glance at Jenny and bit her lip. "Well, come on in. I've just finished feedin' Molly and she is nigh asleep, lookin' like a wee angel."

Gladly, Pamela followed the two women back into the cottage. "I . . . I can only stay a moment," she said, awkwardly. "Tassie's lathered and I mustn't let her stand too long." She moved toward the cradle and cooed over the baby. There was nothing so beautiful, she was now convinced, as a child, at least before they got to that grubby age where they could not stay clean and insisted on mucking about in mud puddles as *she* had as a child. She reached out one finger and touched the soft cheek, falling in love all over again as Molly gurgled and blew a bubble.

"Angel face," Pamela whispered. "You are going to be quite the belle of Yorkshire, I'll warrant." She straightened and turned. Mary seemed agitated and Pamela, frowning, wondered what was wrong that the normally placid Mary should be so edgy. She said, indicating Jenny, who stood near the table wringing her hands in a white apron, "So this is your cousin? M'brother said you had a cousin, but I don't think she's ever visited before." Pamela moved toward the woman and stuck out her hand. "I am Lord Haven's sister. Mary kindly lets me come here when things get too crazed at the Court."

Jenny's lovely gray eyes widened and she curtsied, then extended her hand. The two young women shook. "Pleased to meet you Miss—"

"Miss Pamela—P—Pammy," Mary stuttered into speech. "We are old friends and call each other by our first names."

Again Pamela frowned as she released the other woman's cool, soft hand. She hadn't missed that it was trembling in her grasp. What was the woman afraid of? And why was Mary so uneasy? It was as if she was uncomfortable with Pamela there, when normally she treated her with a sisterly affection and openness. Did she think that Pamela would make her cousin nervous? Perhaps that was it, for Jenny, too, was alarmed, as restless as a vixen in a pen of hunters. Glumly, she thought that even here she could not find the peace she sought. "I won't take up too much of your time," she said, slowly, hoping Mary would demand that she sit down to tea, at least. But she could not mistake the look of relief on her friend's face and sadly turned to the door. Was there no place left where she was not a nuisance?

At the last second Mary said, her words a little forced but with a more natural tone, "At least stay to tea, Pammy. You . . . you *know* you are always welcome here." Her smile was as kind as ever and her expression sincere.

Pamela glanced back and grinned. Inside, relief was flooding her heart. Reluctantly, she shook her head. "No, I suppose I must be going. Things are so upset at the house right now. Haven is in such a dither with that girl mi—"

"I will walk out with you, Miss Pamela, if I might!" Jenny swiftly crossed the floor, following Pamela to the door.

"All right," Pamela said, brightening. Jenny looked like a jolly sort and one could never have too many friends. Maybe she could tell her why Mary seemed so upset and nervy.

Mentally, Jenny breathed a sigh of relief as she threw a smile over her shoulder at Mary and then followed Pamela

out the door. It was a wind-tossed day and she drew her
shawl around her shoulders as they walked over to Tassie.

"What a lovely girl," Jenny said, moving to the bay mare,
who tossed her head as if in appreciation of the compliment.

"Isn't she though," Pamela said, scratching Tassie behind
the ears. She pulled the reins from around the post as Lally,
the heavily gravid gray tabby, wound ponderously around
her legs.

They silently contemplated the horse for a moment while
Jenny tried to order her thoughts. She reached down and
scratched the tabby's ears, and it mewed softly, then headed
back to the safety of the barn. Miss Pamela had almost
revealed the missing Miss Jane Dresden to Mary, and that
would have been an immediate betrayal of Jenny's identity.
Should she trust Mary and throw herself on her mercy? But
how could she? That would be dragging her newfound
friend into the complicated and wretched mess she had
made of things. Right now Mary was not implicated in any
way because she did not know who Jenny was and had
been kind enough not to press for an explanation.

But this could not go on forever. In fact it could not go
on much longer. She must leave before things became awkward for Mary.

"You were saying that your home life is not too pleasant
lately," Jenny said, carefully. Pamela started walking down
the path away from the cottage, leading Tassie, and Jenny
walked beside her. "Why is that?"

Pamela shook her head. With an unladylike snort she
tossed her curly cropped head and said, "Haven is in a
pother, as are Mama and Rachel and even Grand. And that
awful Lady Mortimer!"

Ruefully Jane realized that the fate of an eavesdropper was
likely to be hers. This forthright girl would hold back nothing
in her evaluation of those she disparaged. "Why are they beside themselves? And w—who is L—Lady Mortimer?"

"Haven't you heard? No, I guess you wouldn't. Mary is

rather isolated up here. My brother, Lord Haven, is as good as betrothed to this girl, Miss Jane Dresden, but on the way here she was abducted."

"Oh, my!" Jenny said, with what surprise she could muster. "Is . . . is there any sign of the girl?"

"Not a one! Except there was a ransom note." Pamela kicked at a tuft of grass and gazed up the moor. Together they watched a hawk climb an air current, circling and wheeling, only to swoop down into the thick grass and dart up again with something squirming in its talons. "Lady Mortimer is Miss Dresden's aunt. And a more pestilential old beldam I have never in all my life met! She natters and plagues poor Haven and flits about the Court like a bat."

Jenny stifled a chuckle at the apt description of the black-gowned Lady Mortimer. It was odd that she felt no compunction about her aunt's worry, but she didn't. Perhaps because she didn't believe it genuine. The woman had never gone out of her way to be a friend to Jane, much less a proper aunt. This mockery of a betrothal was just a way to enhance the family image and to recover from the shame of an aging, unwed niece. "Y—your brother is upset? He must . . . must love this girl very much."

"Lord, no! He's never even met the wretched, frosty-faced ninny! She sounds like a perfect fright to me, the way Lady Mortimer speaks of her. 'Jane this and Jane that,' " she fluted, in a dreadful imitation of Lady Mortimer's voice. "Enough to make me want to cast up my accounts."

Jenny glanced over at Pamela, thinking that if she had gone ahead with the visit this might be her sister-to-be, even now. She rather liked Pamela's plain-speaking and vigorous use of cant, but thought that it must be driving her aunt to distraction. "What is your brother like? He . . . he sounds rather fearsome."

"Haven?" Pamela laughed. Tassie tossed her head as if to join in the laughter. "Haven is a perfect lamb most of the time. He seems gruff and bearlike to others, but that is just because they do not know him. He is the kindest of brothers, and I should know, because he often must go to battle with Mama over me. I . . . I rather send my mother to Bedlam at times." She gave a rueful sideways glance at Jenny and said, "I am not at all what she would want in a daughter, you see. I leave that up to my prissy, perfect sister Rachel. I like to ride, and scandalously, to gallop. I never watch my tongue and invariably say the wrong thing at the perfect moment when everyone can hear me. I even got bosky on champagne at my first ball in London and started betting with the bloods over who would be the first diamond of the Season to get leg-shackled. If my ancient and detestable Aunt Viola had not died, sending us back to Yorkshire for mourning, I think m'mother would have had to gag me and bind me ankle and wrist to find a man willing to marry me."

Jenny could not help it, she laughed out loud at that, picturing all the old cats and dragons at the tonnish balls faced with this brass-faced little country greenhorn. The stiff breeze up the moor lifted the girl's curls and she tossed them out of her eyes in an appealingly free movement.

"Well you may laugh, but the lectures I was read!" She rolled her greenish gray eyes, and then fastened them on her companion. "You have no notion of how boring London is . . . I mean, when one is coming out! I must not do this, I must not do that! And prissy white dresses and no one to be friends with, all of them odious, simpering little pudding hearts. Not a lark among them."

"But your brother did not come down on you for this?" Jenny, remembering what her friend had said about Lord Haven, could not imagine the stuffy, grim old sobersides of her description allowing his sister to act in such a reckless, feckless manner.

"No, he laughed himself hoarse. Said I was a right proper rip and that I should have been born a boy, for then he could have whipped me for my impudence and bought me a set of colors to march under. I would have liked that," she said dreamily. "Marching gallantly off to war, wearing those ripping uniforms!" She sighed and came back to reality. "As it is he says I will likely never marry, but that I may stay with him forever and keep his house, so it doesn't matter."

He sounded, Jenny thought, improbably kind. But maybe with his sister it was different; after all, her behavior did not really reflect on him in the same way a wife's would. He would certainly not tolerate that from a prospective wife. He would never stand for a lady of the *ton* who preferred country walks to city promenades and longed to leave off gloves and bonnet and roam freely in the countryside. He would not be like Gerry, who accepted her as she was and gave her looks that made her heart pound with wonder and secret delight.

"Have you seen anyone strange? I mean, like this missing girl, or a couple of men who might have abducted her?" Pamela asked.

"No, neither Mary nor I have seen *anyone*," Jenny said, firmly, her heart leaping up into her throat. "You may tell your brother that, that Mary has not seen anyone strange." This was why she had come out with Pamela, to establish that firmly so there was no need to bring up the topic again, should the girl drop in to the cottage another day. Not that that would happen. Jenny was realizing again that she really must leave; her time was running out. It was not fair to involve Mary in her deception, especially when Mary clearly depended on the generosity of those at the Court for her cottage.

"Well, I guess that's that then." Pamela stopped. An inviting slope lay ahead and she gazed down it with longing in her eyes. She gave Jenny a calculating look. "I don't suppose you could give me a hand up so I can ride from here?"

"Certainly," Jenny said, swishing her skirts out of the way and cupping her hands. Pamela was as light as a cloud and soon sat astride her Tassie.

"It was very nice meeting you," Pamela said, gazing down at Jenny. "I so seldom meet truly jolly people. I . . . I hope Mary is not angry with me for dropping in."

"I am sure she is not," Jenny said, knowing that Mary's agitation was because she must mislead her benefactor's family as to Jenny's identity. She must leave soon; that unhappy refrain hummed through her mind, for it was becoming increasingly clear that she was not being fair to the woman. That Mary would have to deal, even after Jenny was gone, with the fact that she had lied to her benefactors and friends now unhappily occurred to her. "Good-bye, Miss Pamela."

"Good-bye, Jenny. But not good-bye—more like farewell. Adieu. For I am sure I will be back before you must go home. Where is home anyway?"

"I . . . I don't know. I am between p—positions right now."

"Maybe you will be able to stay here forever," Pamela said. "I hope so. I—I like you." With that, she dug her heels in and clicked to Tassie, who responded by leaping forward and cantering down the long smooth slope. "Adieu, Jenny!" was left on the wind, trailing after the fey and unpredictable girl.

"Your watch, milord," Laidlow, Haven's valet said, handing him the gold pocket watch and fob.

Haven took it as Laidlow shook out the disreputable jacket his master had been wearing. Something clattered to the floor at the edge of the plush Turkish carpet, and Laidlow picked it up.

"Pearls, milord. What would you have me do with them?"

"Good God, I had forgotten!" Haven took the perfect double strand of creamy pearls that had been found at the inn and tucked them in the inside pocket of his jacket for safekeeping. He gazed at them, a hollow pit in his stomach growling. What did they mean? Miss Dresden had had such a string, according to her aunt, and they, as well as some money, had been missing from the inn along with their owner. But the pearls and money were supposed to be in cloth sacks; the potboy claimed to have found the pearls without such a covering. He shoved them in his pocket, saying, "I will take care of them, Laidlow. They belong to the missing young woman, I believe."

Clothed suitably in riding breeches and jacket, Haven was just coming down the winding staircase when Varens was shown in by the butler.

"Haven," Varens said, "I am glad you are home. I am on my way back to Corleigh," he said, naming his estate. "And I wondered if you wanted to come along to talk to Jones about that girl he saw."

"Brilliant idea. I was on my way out to your place, as a matter of fact."

"Lady Haven requests the presence of the two gentlemen for tea in the parlor," the butler, a recent addition who had replaced the ancient and venerable Collins, intoned.

Haven sighed. His mother must have seen Varens ride up. She was ever promoting a match between Rachel and the baronet, but it was no good. Rach was blind to Varens' excellent qualities, seeing only his rough looks and country manners.

"Excellent idea. I would be delighted," Varens said, avoiding Haven's eyes. He strode toward the parlor.

Reluctantly Haven followed, to find everyone but his grandmother and sister Pamela present; even the redoubt- able Lady Mortimer was there, sitting stiffly and sipping sherry. Varens, of course, though he did the pretty to all of the ladies, made straight for Rachel, who sat in pale love- liness by the window. She really was a beautiful young woman, much prettier than Pamela, but the disdainful tilt to her head spoiled her looks. Haven was fond of her, but the fondness was mixed with exasperation. He remembered too well the unaffected little girl of the past, and how she and Pamela, happy as grigs, would tumble and play over the grassy slopes of Haven Court. He would like her better if she had kept some of her unaffected good nature. Being beautiful had spoiled her.

"I thought you were going out to look for signs of my niece," Lady Mortimer said unpleasantly, from her position sitting in state on an ugly settee. She wore another of her infinite variety of black dresses and jet jewelry.

"I was just on my way when Varens came in. Since I am going to his estate first to question his stableman and he was invited in for tea, there is no point in leaving without him."

She "humphed," and he took the cup of tea offered him, grimaced at the weakness of the brew—only his grandmother made tea strong enough, in his estimation—but stayed by Lady Mortimer, taking a seat beside her. "My lady, was your niece agitated in any way before she disappeared? Had she said anything about her trip here to indicate it was not welcome?"

The woman looked at him sharply, her beady eyes narrowing. "What are you implying, Haven?"

"Nothing, my lady. I am just asking." He put one hand in his pocket and touched the pearls. He did not want to shock the woman and would bring them out only after preparing her.

"She was just as she always was," Lady Mortimer said, her gaze slipping away to Lady Haven, who stood nearby.

"She was looking forward to the trip?" he persisted. "To arriving here?"

"Of course!" She did not meet his questioning gaze.

"And she had . . . oh, no alarming news or upsetting meeting at any time?"

Lady Mortimer did not answer and Haven felt the beginning of a gnawing worry. There was something she was not telling them. Something about Miss Dresden.

"She . . . she may have had . . . she *did* have a letter. From her mother."

A letter from her mother. What did that signify? Haven frowned. "Have you seen the letter?"

"No," Lady Mortimer said, slowly, still not meeting Haven's gaze. She drained her sherry glass and handed it to a waiting footman.

Haven discarded his full teacup in the same manner, concentrating all of his energy on the baroness. "Do you know what was in it?"

"I have no . . . I do not . . ." She looked away but then fastened her gaze on the viscount. "I-I suppose I may," she said, with a huge sigh.

"Do you know what it said or not?" Haven said, exasperated with the woman's obfuscation.

"I received a letter from my sister, too. Jane's may have said much the same as mine did."

"And that was? Lady Mortimer, I am trying to help. Please do not make this any more difficult than it already is!"

"But this has nothing to do with anything!" Lady Mortimer said, wringing her hands together in front of her. Lady Haven, looking on, frowned in confusion. "All right, I will tell you! Miss Dresden's mother, my sister, foolish old gudgeon that she is, has remarried. She must have done it within a day or two of our leaving Bath. She has married a Mr. Jessup, a ridiculous little ferret of a man. She likely told Jane of it in a letter."

Eight

So, Miss Dresden had every reason in the world to be upset just before she disappeared. But it still did not explain the kidnapper's note, nor the pearls. Haven held back the pearls for the moment, not ready yet to divulge his possession of them. There would be time enough after he questioned Varens' stableman. The baronet, turned away once again by a pink-cheeked Rachel who haughtily stared out the window instead of at her importunate suitor, strode from the parlor after sketching a distracted bow to the other ladies. Haven lingered in the parlor for a moment to reassure his mother that he would get to the bottom of the whole case, though how he would he still did not know. When he strode out to the stable to collect his mount, it was to see Varens, already mounted, meeting up with Pamela, who had, it appeared, just come back from one of her solitary gallops.

"What-ho, little cat," Varens said, grabbing Pamela's reins as she trotted past him, riding astride in breeches on a groom's saddle, face flaming. "No word for your old friend, Colin?" The baronet's voice was sharp and cutting.

He was likely still smarting from his dismissal from Rachel's presence, embarrassed, Haven thought, that it was such a public refusal. What did he expect, approaching her yet again when she had already refused him? And in front of company, no less. Idiot. And just how blind could the looby be? Pamela was clearly over the trees in love with him, and yet Varens saw her only as a little hell-cat, still more child than woman. He persisted in treating her with the casual, familiar affection of a man for a little sister. Getting a good look at his sister's garb, he could really not blame Colin. She was dressed in disreputable old breeches, a shirt of his, and a coat he had cast off at the age of fifteen. She looked like a stablehand, not a young lady of impeccable birth, nor a future wife.

"Let go of my reins, you cow-handed sapskull!" Tassie reared as Pamela jerked her reins from the baronet's hands and smacked at him with her crop.

"Spitfire," Colin said, shaking his hand and laughing as he saw the red stripe she had left across it.

His cheeks were still flamed with crimson and there was a hectic light in his eyes. He felt it so deeply every time Rachel was rude to him, and yet he persisted. He was making a good recovery this time, though, Haven thought. Or was he?

"Have a good gallop, child?" he said, to Pamela.

On her dignity, drawing herself up to her full height, negligible as it was, she said, "I have been visiting."

"Not dressed like that, I hope," Colin said, real shock in his voice. "Do not tell me you let anyone see you looking like a groom!"

"I went to see Mary Cooper," she retorted.

"Oh, good." Colin sighed. "Just Mary. Rachel would not be able to hold her head up if her sister was seen in town looking like such a guy!"

Pamela, tears starting in her large, gray-green eyes, whirled Tassie and trotted off into the stable without another word. Colin, pulling on his riding gloves, stared after her, puzzled. "What is wrong with your sister, Haven?"

"What is wrong with *you*, you insensitive clod?" Haven strode into the stable, but Pamela had handed her horse off to a stablehand and tore past her brother up toward the house, a mixture of rage and mortification on her pretty, narrow face.

She had been to Mary's. Haven stared after her as she stormed up to the Court and was admitted through the enormous wood doors to the great hall by the new butler. Should he follow her and find out what, if anything, she said to Jenny about him? Was the game up? Had she let spill that Gerry Neville and Lord Haven were one and the same?

Well, even if that was the case there was not a thing he could do about it this moment anyway. Not with this disappearance of Miss Dresden on his mind and conscience. Of all the times for this to happen, it *would* be just when he met a woman who made his blood pump and his heart melt! He longed to fly up over the hills to Mary's cottage just to see Jenny again, but duty called and he must answer. He shrugged and accepted his saddled mount from the towheaded stableboy and joined Colin.

At Corleigh, Varens' estate, a tidy modern manse made of gray stone quarried nearby, Haven headed directly for the stable, which was made of the same uniform stone cut into square blocks. Varens had handed off his horse to a groom and left his guest to go up to the house. He had already explained to Haven that he would leave the questioning to the viscount; his worker might not respond if he felt he was being cornered. Haven found his way through the dim confines of the musty stable and approached the stable manager, a young man named Joshua Jones. He was working on some leather tack, oiling it and rubbing it with a cloth.

He nodded as Haven approached, respect in his eyes. No one especially warmed up to the viscount, but neither did they prevaricate with nor deprecate him. Another groom approached and Haven handed the reins of his mount to him.

"Your name is Jones, I believe," Haven said. He put out his hand and the other man shook it and ducked his head again. "Sir Colin has told me you saw an incident behind the Swan the night the young lady disappeared," he said, after reminding the fellow of the night and the fact that a Miss Jane Dresden had disappeared.

The man nodded smartly. "Stepped out ta take a piss an' saw it all, milord."

"And?" Haven prompted.

He shrugged. "T'were a plump girl, carn't say as I know which o' the barmaids it be, for t'were shadowy in th'yard, ya know. Dark hair, though, milord, an' plump, like I sed. Wearin' a dark dress wiv a white bodice, y'know the kind that lets their bubbies show just a little." His grin was lascivious.

Haven sternly brought him back to topic. "And what happened?"

Jones shrugged again. "T'were two fellas, one as I reckernize as on o' t'owd ones. They was a'graspin' her, an' the one, he were a'tryin' to give her a kiss, like. She were strugglin' an' I sed summat—don't hold wiv forcin' no wummin to anythin'—an' the wench, she tore away and off she goes, hared off out o' the yard."

Frowning down at the dirt floor, Haven kicked at a pebble with the toe of his dusty riding boots. "Not Miss Dresden, certainly," he said, finally. "Or at least it does not sound like her. The clothing alone . . . it is the common outfit of all the barmaids, you say. What did the men do?"

"Went back inta the Swan, they did, an' me too, after my piss."

"You didn't try to find the girl?" Haven shoved his hand in his pocket and fingered the pearls, a talisman, he almost felt, of the missing Miss Dresden.

"Na, she were foine," the man said, tossing aside the bridle he had been working on and picking up a bit. He inspected it for rust, then started rubbing it until it shone. "Not e'en roughed up, I'd say."

Haven put one foot up on the boarded wall of an empty

stable and leaned on his knee. He picked up another bit and turned it over and over his in gloved hands. He had noticed one thing the fellow had glossed over. "You say you recognized one of the men. Who was it?"

Jones looked uneasy. He stared down at the bit in his hand, scraping at a minute blemish with his filthy fingernail. "T'weren't no harm meant, milord. Ol' Billy just thought o' his pecker an' saw a likely wench."

Anger boiling up within him, Haven threw down the bit. Jones jumped back a bit, but resumed his work with a determinedly unconcerned demeanor. The viscount straightened and ground out, his teeth clenched, "You said yourself that the girl was struggling and that you don't hold with forcing women. Was that not enough to make you confront old Bill, or follow the girl to see if she was all right?"

Jones muttered, "But some wenches need a bit o' persuadin'. I'm sure ol' Billy just thought o' persuadin' the mort to a little slap an' tickle, loike."

"*Persuading* is not holding down and taking your pleasure," Haven said. Still worried for Miss Dresden, he was beginning to feel concerned for the barmaid. He would go back to the Swan, track her down among the three or four Joseph Barker employed, and make sure nothing had happened to her and that she knew she need not be afraid of the customers. Lesleydale was his jurisdiction and he would have no woman mistreated, nor even "persuaded" if that was how the local men thought of it. "You did not get a look at the other man?"

"Na." Jones spat into the dust and wiped his mouth. His uneasy glance touched on the viscount but slid away again. "T'were darkish, milord, wiv the shadows in th'yard, an' t'were gettin' cloudy besides; I didna see naught. 'E follered Billy back in, anyways."

Making one last effort, Haven said, "So you are sure this girl was a barmaid? She could not have been the young lady we are looking for, the one who disappeared?"

"Na! Th'mort were a barmaid, right enough. Had that look about her, y'know. Would ha fancied 'er meself if she hadna run off."

Haven thanked the man—Jones had been helpful to the extent he could be—and slipped him a coin. Reluctantly he realized that he had to go up to Varens' house, for the baronet had invited him to come up for a brandy after questioning Joshua Jones.

It was not that he did not appreciate the hospitality; Sir Colin was a fine man and a good neighbor. Younger than Haven by several years, the two men still shared many of the same values and a dedicated love of the land, and of Yorkshire in particular. However, visiting Varens meant dealing with Miss Andromeda Varens, his elder sister. She was Haven's contemporary, and so she should have stood in the same light as a sister, but Miss Varens most emphatically did not view him in a brotherly manner. He slogged up to the house, stood staring up at the tidy facade for a moment, then sighed and surrendered to the inevitable.

Barley, the ancient and crabby butler, announced him at the parlor door and shuffled off with muttered expletives, the severity of which grew steadily more vinegary as the years passed and the ancient retainer aged. Just as Gerry had feared, there was Andromeda, on her dignity, sitting straight-backed and resplendent in her faded purple silk. She had refurbished the dress and now wore a matching turban, but Gerry remembered it from a ghastly local assembly many years before when Andromeda had led everyone there to believe that that was the night he was finally going to ask for her hand. The air of expectancy in the room that evening had been palpable even to him. All of the local gentry was there and there were hints and gentle jests at his expense that he did not understand until Andromeda cornered him in the card room of the assembly hall and attempted to squeeze out of him an offer for her hand.

It had been a close call and it still gave him the shivers. The thought of a lifetime of staring at Andromeda across the breakfast table gave him the cold shudders. He advanced across the room grimly and bowed over her hand. Since their mother had died three years before, she had steadily increased her "lady of the manor" behavior until now she was somewhat of a joke among the local gentry as being more queenly than even Queen Charlotte. And she still, quite clearly, had hopes for him.

"Lord Haven, how pleasant," she pronounced, her enunciation resembling faintly the strangled, unintelligible accent she had copied years before in her first and only London Season. She had not taken and her father had vowed not to throw good money after bad, stating baldly in his Yorkshire-broad accent, "Th'lass is a moite tooched, it seems, an' no lad wants a addle-brained mort t'wife." Andromeda continued. "We have not seen you for some time, my lord. We had begun to think you did not like us anymore."

Startled, Gerry at first thought she had finally *truly* descended into madness, using the royal "we," but then he realized, at a shrug and rolled eyes from Colin, that the baronet never told his sister when he visited Haven Court.

"Haven is a busy man. Runs a larger concern than ours, Andy." Varens poured two glasses of brandy and offered one to Haven, who took it gratefully, tossed it off in one long, fiery draft, and held his glass out for another. Colin, a humorous look on his plain face, continued. "Between the sheep and the crops, well, what's a man to do?"

"Leave it to his farm manager," Andromeda Varens said, haughtily, giving her brother a look. "Do not call me 'Andy,' " she hissed, *sotto voce*. "It is common and vulgar." She stood and glided across the room toward Haven.

He was trapped, he realized, for the time being anyway. As long as Colin did not desert him, he would be fine. Andromeda was a good-looking woman—tall, good hair, a long handsome face—but her coy attempts at flirtation with

Haven and her possessive manners toward him *more* than put him off, they gave him nightmares. He truly did not want to offend her—as children they had been very good friends and had shared many famous larks—but he had no intention of ever putting himself in a position with her where she might endanger his bachelorhood.

She put her hand on his arm and steered him over to the wall, where she indicated a large painting. "Do you think this a good likeness, my lord?" She thrust her arm through his and settled her angular body close to his sturdy, powerful frame. She simpered coyly, and batted her lashes. On a younger, prettier woman the attempt at flirtation might have been charming, but it was absurd coming from her. He liked her far better when she was just being herself, but that was seldom anymore.

He stared up at the painting, hardly seeing it at first in his panic. Why did women do this? It was exactly what he disliked most, the predatory demeanor and calculating coyness that made of every conversation a tribulation to him. His gaze cleared gradually, and he looked up at the painting. It was rather large, especially for the space it inhabited, but it was good as far as style went. It was of a lovely young woman with dark eyes, gorgeous skin, and a beautiful, regal, ineffably sad expression. Her lips were dewy and slightly parted and she gazed off into the distance, toward a folly on a distant hill in what appeared to be the countryside near Richmond or Surrey. She was dressed in a fine gown of purple silk—

He glanced over at the woman beside him. She was tall enough that her eyes were almost even with his. "Who is it?" he blurted, absolutely puzzled as to whom it could resemble. He felt her stiffen and recoil.

"It is me!" Her voice was a reedy wail.

Panicked, Haven turned to see Colin convulsed with laughter.

Holding his stomach and barely keeping from spilling

his brandy, he choked out, "Told you it didn't look a bit like you, Andy! Too beautiful by half!"

Haven shot him a minatory look, but the man was now positively doubled over with gales of laughter. Andromeda, mortified and offended, had jerked her arm out of Haven's and stood trembling, staring up at the painting and then glaring at Haven. "Could you not tell it is me?"

Caught, Haven knew he ought to lie. Some social mendacity was clearly called for, but all he could think to mutter was, "Painter fellow didn't catch your, uh, your expression. Your, uh, your commanding presence, Miss Varens."

It was the best he could do and it was not enough. An expression of pained fury crossed her face and her cheeks reddened, two ugly blotches coloring her high, sharp cheekbones. "I think it a remarkable likeness," she said, her accent clipped and her words dropped like individual pebbles into a lake.

"Then you ought to get a new mirror," Colin said, ruthlessly.

Andromeda turned on her brother and said, "You would not know a decent likeness from a . . . from a pig trough!" With that odd statement, she whirled and left the room, taking with her all the tension, the very air behind her drained of all unease.

Haven dropped into a chair, wiping the cold sweat from his brow and downing his second brandy. "Colin, that was cruel and indescribably unkind." He would never say such a thing to his own sisters, not even Rachel, whom he did not understand and often could not abide.

"As if you were better! 'Didn't catch your commanding presence'! No lady wants to be thought commanding! She sees herself as another Lady Frances Webster," he said, naming an infamous tonnish beauty, reputed to be mistress to Byron at one point, and the Duke of Wellington himself at another.

"Why would she want to see herself as *that* woman?"

Haven said, shaking his head. "Lady Webster is a byword for her affairs! I swear, Colin, there is no understanding women, I am convinced . . . at least, women of our own class."

Colin gazed at him curiously. "Why the exception, old man? Found a wench to your liking?"

Flushing with irritation, Haven could not help thinking of Jenny, contrasting her gentle, sweet voice, luscious, plump form, and shy manners with Miss Varens' self-conscious gentility, angular looks, and rapacious pursuit of him. What a life, when he could not have what he wanted! And why, because she was a lady's maid? She was more lady than many of the women he had met in his disastrous Seasons cruising the London marriage mart.

"You have, you old dog," Colin said, sitting down in a chair and leaning forward. He grabbed the decanter from the table and poured them both another glass of brandy, the color in his face suggesting the liquor was starting to have its expected affect. "Tell me who she is. Have you sampled her wares yet? Is she good?"

"It's not that kind of . . . she is not that kind of girl," Haven said, angrily, setting his newly filled glass aside. Even Varens sometimes was intolerable, it seemed. He stood and said, "I have to go. I am going to go back down to the Swan and try to find out what really happened. I have not yet talked to the chambermaids who served Miss Dresden and Lady Mortimer. So long, Colin. My best to your sister. Tell her I am . . . am sorry . . . or . . . or *something*. Anything."

Nine

At least the great hall was empty this once, Pamela thought, as she stormed in from her encounter in the stable with Sir Colin, when she needed its hollow solitude most. Hot tears streamed down her face; she was appalled at the casual cruelty of his words. All Pamela could think was to get up the stairs to her room as quickly as possible, for if her mother caught her she would be read the riot act and she was most definitely *not* in an appropriate frame of mind. Just as she thought she had made it to the bottom of the staircase safely she heard a voice—not *the* voice, but one she would as lief not hear.

"Miss Pamela Neville, come here, this instant!"

She paused on the step. "Grand," she said, controlling with an effort the quavering of her voice. "Let me change out of my riding togs first."

The echoing tap-tap-tap of a cane on the marble floor of the great hall announced that the old lady was moving toward the bottom of the sweeping oak staircase where Pamela stood on the lowest step, her hand on the railing, one foot up, poised to race up the stairs. Staring straight ahead of her, up the gloomy depths of the steep staircase, Pamela waited.

"I know you are crying," the old woman said, her voice kind. "Did you, by chance, meet with that dreadful Sir Colin on your way in?"

"He is *not* dreadful," Pamela said, her voice muffled as she surreptitiously tried to wipe her streaming eyes and nose on the sleeve of her shirt.

"Dreadful enough to make you cry, child. Come have tea with me. There is nothing for you to hide, my dear; I know you are wearing men's clothes and I know you are weeping. Come. I want to talk to you."

Reluctantly, realizing there was no escaping her grandmother's summons and with an odd desire to unburden herself, Pamela turned and followed the elderly woman into her room. The household was like a web, in many ways, and Grand was the great, fat spider that sat in the middle reaching out to snatch all of her "victims," bundling them into her room to extricate, like juicy insides, all of the gossip and information about the outside world that the old lady could no longer get herself. It was no wonder that she would not stay at Haven Wood, the dower house that was supposed to be her home. No one ever visited there, and without information the old woman would wither and dry up.

She entered the old grand dame's lair and threw herself into a settee, petulantly reliving all of Colin's casual cruelty. He saw her as nothing more than a brat, an unformed child, a hoydenish little terror. And all the while he idolized Rachel. *Rachel!* Rachel, who didn't give one fat fig for him. Rachel, who ridiculed him behind his back for his plain face and hooked nose and plain country clothes. It was beyond humiliating. She hate, hate, *hated* him!

But no, she didn't. Not really. She loved him. Loved his country ways and his plain speaking and his talent with horses. She adored his estate and his funny old sister, Andromeda, who was kind at heart, even if she was a bit strange. And she craved the absolute peace of Corleigh, his beautiful little house. She could imagine it; no mother condemning her every hoydenish move and no lovely sister to forever compare herself to, only to be found lacking. Just easy, friendly Colin and sweet, addled Andromeda.

Grand tapped over to the tea table. Her elderly maid moved stiffly in the background, ignoring as she always did Grand's company. She was the only servant in the entire house that did not indulge in below-stairs gossip. One never needed to care what one said in front of her.

Dropping a lump of sugar into a cup and filling it with steaming dark brew, the color of brackish peat water, Grand handed the cup to her youngest grandchild and stood looking down at her. With one crabbed hand she gently stroked Pamela's curly, close-cropped locks. "My little darling," she murmured to her favorite, her voice a crooning, comforting lullaby. "My sweet child. Why you like that long-nosed supercilious baby baronet I do not know." She paused and continued gazing down at her youngest grandchild. "But if you really want him you can have him, you know."

Pamela had just taken a swallow of burning tea and she yelped, put the cup down, and stared up at her grandmother. "What do you mean?"

"I mean just what I say, as always; you can have him. You have the wherewithal," the woman said, holding out one hand, "in your little hands to attract him, elicit a proposal, and decide whether or not you wish to marry him."

"But he's mad for Rach! He would never look at me like he looks at her. He absolutely *adores* her."

"You're worth two of her," Grand said, fiercely. "And that country turnip would know it if you would follow my plan. But you must decide if you really want him."

Pamela, thoughts racing pell-mell through her mind, stared blindly at the figured carpet, tapping her fingers against her breeches-clad leg. Grand knew everything there was to know in the world, she had always thought. Once upon a time she had been a great London beauty, with scores of men at her feet. But times had changed. Life was different. She looked up at her grandmother.

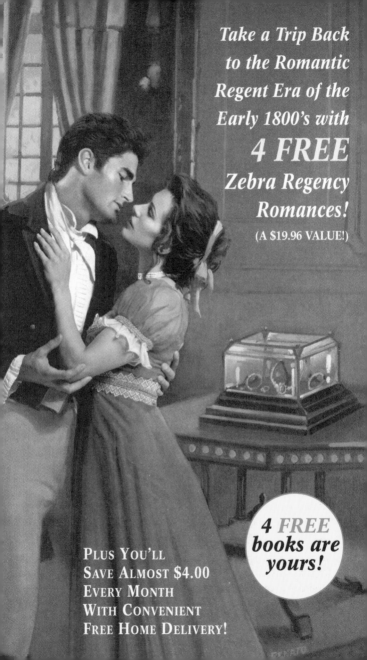

Take a Trip Back to the Romantic Regent Era of the Early 1800's with **4 FREE** Zebra Regency Romances! (A $19.96 VALUE!)

4 FREE books are yours!

PLUS YOU'LL SAVE ALMOST $4.00 EVERY MONTH WITH CONVENIENT FREE HOME DELIVERY!

We'd Like to Invite You to Subscribe to Zebra's Regency Romance Book Club and Give You a Gift of 4 Free Books as Your Introduction! (Worth $19.96!)

If you're a Regency lover, imagine the joy of getting 4 FREE Zebra Regency Romances and then the chance to have these lovely stories delivered to your home each month at the lowest price available! Well, that's our offer to you and here's how you benefit by becoming a Regency Romance subscriber:

- **4 FREE** Introductory Regency Romances are delivered to your doorstep

- 4 BRAND NEW Regencies are then delivered each month (usually before they're available in bookstores)

- Subscribers save almost $4.00 every month

- You also receive a **FREE** monthly newsletter, which features author profiles, discounts, subscriber benefits, book previews and more

- No risks or obligations...in other words, you can cancel whenever you wish with no questions asked

Join the thousands of readers who enjoy the savings and convenience offered to Regency Romance subscribers. After your initial introductory shipment, you receive 4 brand-new Zebra Regency Romances each month to examine for 10 days. Then, if you decide to keep the books, you'll pay the preferred subscriber's price.

It's a no-lose proposition, so return the FREE BOOK CERTIFICATE today!

Say Yes to 4 Free Books!

Complete and return the order card to receive this
$19.96 value, ABSOLUTELY FREE!

If the certificate is missing below, write to:
Regency Romance Book Club
P.O. Box 5214, Clifton, New Jersey 07015-5214
or call TOLL-FREE 1-800-770-1963
Visit our website at www.kensingtonbooks.com.

FREE BOOK CERTIFICATE

YES! Please rush me 4 Zebra Regency Romances without cost or obligation. I understand that each month thereafter I will be able to preview 4 brand-new Regency Romances FREE for 10 days. Then, if I should decide to keep them, I will pay the money-saving preferred subscriber's price for all 4...that's a savings of 20% off the publisher's price. I may return any shipment within 10 days and owe nothing, and I may cancel this subscription at any time. My 4 FREE books will be mine to keep in any case.

Name _____

Address _____ Apt. _____

City _____ State _____ Zip _____

Telephone (   ) _____

Signature _____ RN062A
(If under 18, parent or guardian must sign.)

Terms and prices subject to change. Orders subject to acceptance by Regency Romance Book Club.
Offer valid in U.S. only.

Treat yourself to 4 FREE Regency Romances!

A
$19.96
VALUE...
FREE!

No
obligation
to buy
anything,
ever!

PLACE
STAMP
HERE

lll..l..lll....llll.l.l.l.l.l.l.l.l.l.l.l.l.ll.l.l.l.l.ll.l..l

REGENCY ROMANCE BOOK CLUB
Zebra Home Subscription Service, Inc.
P.O. Box 5214
Clifton NJ 07015-5214

With that uncanny mind reading she often seemed to engage in, the old woman said, "Do not think just because I am old I do not know how to capture a man's attention. Life has not changed so very much, and men not at all. Men are still the same, my darling. Men are hunters by nature, but with a strange sentimental streak running through them. They seek to idolize a lady, put her on a pedestal, and worship her. Sir Colin adores your sister because she treats him as if he is not fit to lick her dainty shoes and he believes it, the idiotic country toad. So every time she deigns to speak to him or look at him it is a great boon. A favor, bestowed in kindness by the lovely lady of the manor."

Her voice hardened. "But you! You chase him, throw yourself at him, act like a little boy worshipping a great gentleman. Of course he cannot see you as a lady, as a woman. No more than he would see a stable lad that way!"

Pamela thought for only a moment. Then she nodded and looked up at her grandmother. "All right. Say for one minute you are right and that I can get Colin to look at me. Tell me what I need to know."

She shook her head. "Slowly my dear. First let us talk of other things."

"But"—she flounced in her chair, straightening—"but I—"

"No," Grand said, steel in her voice. She sat down opposite Pamela and stared into her green-gray eyes. "We will get to you and your problems, my little miss, but first we will talk about *my* concerns. Did you happen, in your ride, to stop at Mary Cooper's cottage?" When Pamela nodded, she continued. "And did you happen to meet the widow Cooper's cousin, a 'Miss Jenny'?"

Pamela's expression lit up. "I did! She is the jolliest girl you could imagine! I liked her very much."

"What does she look like?"

Pamela frowned and stared off toward the window. She

picked up her cooling tea and took a long draft, then put her cup down. "She is pretty, I suppose."

The elderly woman sighed deeply and snapped her fingers. Pamela looked over at her, a quizzical expression on her pixie face. "I mean, what does she *look* like! *Describe* her to me! Color of hair, face shape, eyes."

"Oh. Well—" Pamela paused and collected her thoughts. "Well, she has dark hair, lovely and long, and curling." She rubbed her hand over her own hair and sighed. It was a frizzy mop when it was long. Keeping it close-cropped was the only thing that had ever tamed it. "Her face is kind of round, with a small chin—kind of like Rachel's only with a bit of a dimple in the middle—and her eyes are . . . well, gray; you know the gray the sky gets just before a storm? That is the very color. She is plump, I suppose. Certainly deeper bosomed than I," Pamela said, with a rueful look down at the flat stretch of cambric shirt under her disreputable jacket.

"And her manners?"

"What d'you mean, Grand?" Pamela searched her grandmother's blue eyes, looking deep into the bloodshot depths.

The old woman put both hands on the head of her cane. "Are her manners what you would expect from a maid? I understand that is what this girl was before visiting Mary."

"Really? I would not have thought her a maid. She talks . . . oh, scads better than me . . . I, I mean. Better than I. Lovely voice, I suppose. Soothing. I'd wager my best hunter that she can sing, likely better than Rachel's dreadful caterwauling."

The dowager stood and tapped over to the window, staring off into the distance. She had chosen her suite with care. She had a corner room that overlooked both the front drive and walkway and the side lawn, that rolled off behind the house to the stables and beyond that to the green and tawny moor. Jenny. A lady's maid?

If only she had thought to tell Haven to leave that ransom

note with her. She would give much to be able to look at the handwriting again. But why—?

The dowager considered the current state of affairs. Lady Mortimer and Haven's mother had arranged this match between them, their dead husbands being some kind of cronies in London in years gone by. But girls now did not want matches made for them. They wanted to pick their own husbands and the old customs were dwindling. What pressure had been brought to bear on Miss Jane Dresden to force her to travel up to this northern wasteland? The dowager had never yielded to any kind of liking for Yorkshire and still remembered the trepidation she had experienced as a very young girl on learning her own fate was to marry Lord Haven of that fearsome, dark, wild county. Granted, in those long-ago days travel this far north was not at all the usual thing. The roads were so dreadful. In this modern day with the mail carriages whizzing by at unheard-of speeds, every soul with two pennies to rub together could visit the great northern wasteland of Yorkshire.

But still, Miss Dresden could very well have been suffering the same feelings of dread she had experienced so long ago. And then while at the Lesleydale inn, the girl learned her mother had married. Had she suffered some sort of breakdown on hearing the news? Was the child mentally unstable?

What, among all of these reasons, could be the cause of her running away, if in fact she had?

She stared off to the distant moor, the long rolling hill beyond which the Haven home farm cottage nestled. It had occurred to her that it could be . . . it just *might* be, that this ladylike Miss Jenny, supposed cousin of Mary Cooper—that coincidence seemed just too great for the woman to swallow, that the girl had turned up so soon after Miss Dresden disappeared—was, in truth, Miss Jane Dresden. Had she suffered a mental breakdown? Had she forgotten who she really was? Was she the supposed barmaid who had been attacked outside of the Swan? She would have to ask Haven, when he came in, what he had found out.

But then why would Mary Cooper claim her as her cousin? Mrs. Cooper had reason to be loyal and grateful to the Haven family. Surely she would not mislead them if she knew that this girl was the one Haven was so frantically searching for, and Haven must have asked her if she had seen anyone fitting Miss Dresden's description. Another thing to ask him; had he checked with his childhood friend?

No, she could not be sure. And until she was sure, she would say nothing about this to anyone. Two words to Haven would settle the whole affair, but he was taken with this girl, this Jenny. If she was Miss Dresden, perhaps this was the kind of time they needed to get to know each other. He had always shrunk from contact with aristocratic ladies, and of course the very girls who would confirm his worst opinions of ladies of his class—that they were all snobbish, selfish, prim, and humorless shrews—were the very ones his mother inevitably found most suitable to introduce him to.

Her grandson was, in her mind, the most handsome Haven to ever hold the title. His father had been good enough, in his way, but this generation held all the sturdy, healthy looks that the father had not had. To those good looks he added a fine mind and a tender heart, which he hid behind a brusque manner. But when his guard was down he could be charming. If the girl had eyes in her head and a heart to be captured, she would fall in love with Haven.

And so she would hold her tongue and wait. And ask questions. If this girl was just a maid, she did not believe Haven would ever disgrace his family by marrying so far beneath him. And if she was Miss Jane Dresden, then he was on his way to falling in love with and wooing his future wife. How interesting a turn of events. She chuckled. Oh, what she would give if she could convince her daughter-in-law for just one moment even, that Haven was going to elope with a maid!

She turned to her granddaughter, who was drowsily yawning. "We shall talk more, Pamela. But it is high time you dressed for dinner, I think. We will talk about Sir Colin later—" Pamela was about to protest, but the dowager held up her hand. "Later. I promise. Go and change into that yellow dress, the sarcenet."

Pamela reluctantly obeyed. There was no real choice. When Grand said something, she meant it, not like Mother. Their mother was all bluster, but very little real power. She could make life miserable, but if one held out she eventually crumbled. Her older brother had yet to learn that, Pamela knew. He valued peace in his household above all else, and so their mother got her way far more often than she should.

When Pamela came down two hours later, feeling a little stiff and ridiculous—she had told her mother's abigail to "do something" to her, and now she was primped and prodded and fluffed into a creature hardly resembling herself, even more so than in London—it was to find her brother on his way into Grand's suite.

"Haven," she called out and flew down the rest of the stairs, forgetting her fresh determination to act like a lady.

"Hey, Pammy—" He stopped and stared. "My, you look like a princess, pixie! What a difference from last time I saw you."

She had stumbled to a stop in front of him. She made a face. "If only Millicent could do something about my manners while she primps my hair!"

He put his arm over his sister's shoulder, dropped a kiss on the top of her head, and said, squeezing, "There is nothing wrong with your insides, pixie. Any man would be lucky to call you his wife, and never forget it," he finished, referring obliquely to Sir Colin's behavior earlier. "You are gallant and pluck to the backbone and perfectly adorable."

He chucked her under the chin and she gazed up into his eyes adoringly.

"Are you going in to see Grand?" she said, laying her head on his shoulder.

"I am." He sighed deeply.

She looked up again and searched his eyes. "Are you that worried about that little nodcock, Miss Dresden?"

"I feel that she is my responsibility, chuck. If she has been abducted, it is in my jurisdiction, and she was coming here to stay with us. It is my duty to find her. I cannot imagine what the poor girl is going through. Just think about being seized by some basta . . . uh, wretches and held against your will." They started together toward the door of Grand's suite.

Pamela, subdued, said, "I guess I hadn't thought of it that way. Will you marry her?"

"No. I do not see myself marrying her."

"Who *will* you marry?"

"You ask entirely too many questions, pixie." He tapped on the door to Grand's suite and at her "Enter," pushed it open and swept his sister a deep bow. "I bring you the honorable Miss Pamela Neville, famous beauty of the *ton*, Lady Haven."

"Idiot," Pamela said, kicking him in the shins.

Lady Haven took in a deep breath. "Pamela, all of the window dressing in the world will not make you look like a lady if you persist in that kind of hoydenish behavior."

"But it is just Haven! And I am at home!"

"If you are to be a lady who attracts the gentlemen's attention, you must be one at all times!"

"Grand, don't make her over into one of your prim and proper fine ladies," Haven barked. "I like her the way she is!"

"*You,* sir, are not an eligible *parti,*" the dowager retorted. "No man will marry a chit who outrides him, uses stable cant, and strides around the house like a boy. Especially not the man she is interested in."

Pamela gave her grandmother a quelling look, but the dowager was not one to be cowed by a child. She gave her granddaughter a stern look and then turned to her grandson. "What did you learn, Haven?"

He moved over to the window and stared out at the hills beyond the stables. "I don't know, Grand. The girl who was attacked by the fellows at the inn, they all say she looked like a barmaid. Varens' stable manager says the girl was not harmed and that the fellows who accosted her just went back into the inn and continued drinking. That was verified, when I went back to the Swan, by the innkeeper. I even spoke to old Billy, one of the men who manhandled the girl, and he swears he just saw a likely lass, followed her out to the back of the inn, and tried to get a kiss."

"Repulsive," Pamela shuddered. "How do they think they have the right to kiss a girl, just because she is wandering past?"

The dowager gave her grandson a warning look. Pamela was not a sheltered little miss—any girl who spent the hours she did in the stable knew at least some of the facts of life—but there was still much she had either ignored about life among the human tribe, or did not know. She would not understand about the casual use of barmaids and serving girls as relief for a man's bodily needs, nor had she likely ever heard of the exchange of money that often took place after such a casual coupling.

"He was drunk, love," Haven said. He did not need his grandmother's warning to protect his little sister. "Men act brutally on occasion when they have been drinking."

"I would have kicked him."

Haven stifled a chuckle and said, "I doubt any man would have used you thus, pixie. But if he had, kicking him would be the appropriate way to handle it. I commend you for your sense."

Pamela gave him a look to see if she was being roasted, but nodded, satisfied that he was serious about that, at least. "What is this all about? What girl was this, and why is she important?"

Haven explained that it had to do with Miss Dresden.

"You don't suspect this barmaid was Miss Dresden!" Pamela said, aghast.

"No," Haven said. "I cannot imagine that it is. But the odd thing is, no one can seem to find out which girl who works there is the one who was accosted. I have asked them, but not one of them will admit to being the one. And too, the girl's dress was torn. I would think that would have been noticed."

"I asked Mary and Jenny if they had seen anyone and they said no," Pamela said.

Haven felt the color drain from his face. He had forgotten about his sister's trip to Mary's cottage. "They said that?"

Pamela nodded.

Haven swallowed and said a silent prayer of hope that Pamela had not said anything to Jenny that revealed him as Viscount Haven. She may have inadvertently unmasked him, and he would not know until his next visit. But at least he did not now have to ask Mary if she had seen the girl. He had been trying to figure out how he would do that and yet stay in the character of the farmer he was supposed to be.

His grandmother, during the conversation, had held her tongue, only nodding occasionally. She had a sly smile on her face but all she said was, "I am sure everything will be just fine, Haven. Do not worry unduly. Everything will come out all right in the end, I feel sure."

He shook his head. It was all well and good for her to be so sanguine; he only wished *he* could be so sure.

Ten

"No, no, Jenny, not that way! If'n you mix the dough for the dumplings too long or too hard they'll be like lead!" Mary took the wooden spoon out of Jenny's hand and gave one skilled swipe around the bowl, collecting every morsel of dry flour and mixing it into the batter. "There, now. Drop it by spoonsful into th'stew."

Jenny bent over the fire and spooned the mixture into the bubbling gravy of the stew.

"It'll work better if you dip the spoon into the gravy between—that way the dumplings'll scoop up better from the bowl," Mary said, glancing up from rolling pie dough.

Doing as she was advised, Jenny found that the mixture did, indeed, scoop onto the spoon easier when the spoon was hot and slicked with the stew gravy. There was so much to learn! Jenny realized that to Mary all of this was second nature, just as entertaining the vicar, tatting lace, and making small talk was to her. But at her age, to learn all of this? She would make a miserable farmer's wife, she thought, with a tug of regret. Not that she would be called upon to fill that role in the near future. The only thing so far that had come naturally to her was caring for Molly.

There, they were simmering nicely, she thought, standing back and admiring her work much as she would have a flower arrangement in the past, and in a few minutes she would put a cover over the pot so the dumplings could fluff up. It was twilight. On the horizon the purple hills loomed like great hump-backed beasts, lying along the moors, slumbering. The cottage had only the one window, so the interior was ever dim, but now the only light came from a tallow candle on the scarred table that served as workspace and dining table.

That was where Mary worked, sprinkling flour over her circlet of pastry, her dress sleeves rolled up over her forearms, flour clinging to the small hairs. So far that day she had milked the cow, collected eggs from her chickens, spun several bobbins of her fine wool—selling the wool would bring in much-needed money for necessities such as flour, tea, sugar, and the occasional treat—as well as feeding and caring for Molly, washing clothes, cleaning her tidy cottage, reading the Bible for half an hour and, making the meals in the meantime.

And all had been done with a cheery smile and a song, some of which Mary had taught her. Jenny had tried to help, but more often than not her "help" had hindered. She was best at simply playing with Molly while Mary went efficiently about her business.

But at that moment Mary's forehead was puckered in a frown, and she looked up at her guest with a doubtful expression. "Jenny, I'd not make you feel unwelcome . . ."

In the pale pool of light from the candle Jenny could see the worry on her hostess's face. Here it came, the polite request to move on. Well, she had known she could not stay there indefinitely. Trying to be casual, determined to seem unconcerned, she moved over to the table and took the clean cloth from a loaf pan, peeking to see if the bread dough she had just learned to make was rising. It was a little, but it still did not look like Mary's loaf, proudly filling the pan beside it. "What is it, Mary?" She braced herself for what was to come, feeling sure it must be the inevitable politely couched ejection from the idyllic cottage on the moors.

The woman dusted flour from her hands and folded the circle of dough into a triangle, then laid it gently in the deep pan. As she patted the dough into the pan, she took a deep breath and said, "I've always considered meself a good judge o' character. It was why I waited and married Jem rather than some o' the lads who had already asked me. Jem was older, but he had kind eyes an' a good heart. I never once regretted waiting, e'en though I be a widow now." Wiping her hands on her apron, she gazed at the younger woman, the firelight from the hearth, the only other light in the room, casting her features in sharp relief. "Jenny, what I'm trying' to say is . . ." She paused, pursed her lips, and gazed at her houseguest, but then continued in a rush of words. "Jenny, yer not a lady's maid, and you never have bin."

Jenny's heart thumped and she bit her lip. Well, what did she expect? Mary had asked her a few rudimentary questions, such as how to get bloodstains from undergarments, and she hadn't had the slightest idea how to answer. She did not even know if it was something that a lady's maid *should* know. Perhaps she should have declared haughtily that that was up to the laundry to take care of, and was no part of a lady's maid duties.

When she didn't speak, Mary continued. "If'n you don't want to talk about it, just tell me to shut me mouth." She spooned the chicken filling into the pie shell and picked up the other circlet of pastry. "When I said I was a good judge o' character, I meant I like you. Yer a good woman and so I'll not question you too close about what yer past is, nor why you happened to be in my barn late of a rainy evening with a torn dress." A faint shadow of anger crossed her face. She vigorously pinched the dough into a raised rim and said, "But if some man in Lesleydale has abused ya, I'll *get* the devil, I promise you that. Don't be afraid o' him. I'll get him and turn him over to Gerry, and Gerry'll beat the tar out o' him. I've seen 'im do it before."

"Really?" Impressed despite her long-held aversion to violence, Jenny sat down at the table, watching Mary's deft movements as she slashed gashes in the pastry-covered pie and set it aside. She was inevitably fascinated by any new view of Gerry Neville's character. She had not stopped thinking of him all day, a tiny trill of excitement racing down her back at the memory of their hours together. "He . . . he isn't violent is he?"

"No. Nobbut more gentle than Gerry." Mary looked deep into Jenny's eyes. "He's a good man. Doesn't hold with mishandlin' women, though. That's the only time I've seen him angry, and then he near killed the scum what abused one o' his maids . . . uh, a—a village maiden."

Abstracted by her own thoughts, Jenny hardly heard the last part of Mary's speech, nor did she notice the stuttered amendment. She put one cheek in her hand and stared off out the window at the twilit hill, lost in remembrance of Gerry and their long walk through the hills, the look in his sparkling blue eyes, the gentleness of his hands. Everything about him, from his voice to his physical being fascinated her. What a champion he would make, she thought, feeling again the strength of his hands and seeing the breadth of his shoulders. A woman could feel secure and loved being held by a man like that. A woman could . . .

"But I was askin' about *you,* lass." Mary's voice brought Jenny back to the dim interior of the little cottage. "Yer no lady's maid. If . . . if yer of th'gentry but down on yer luck, or . . . or if ya bin abandoned by yer man . . ." She let the subject drop as her cheeks turned a rosy red. Molly set up a thin wail just then and Mary bustled over to the cradle. "Time for yer dinner my little lady," she said. She sat down in the chair near the fire, unbuttoned the top of her gown, and shifted Molly.

"No, Mary," Jenny said, moving over to the low cot in the corner so she could still see Mary's face. She smiled, not offended at all by her new friend's surmises. It is what she might have thought, in the same circumstances. "I have not been seduced and abandoned without benefit of clergy."

Mary, even pinker, grimaced. "I didna mean to offend you."

"I'm not offended," she reassured Mary. "You have a right to your surmises. But I am not an abandoned woman, merely . . ." She took a deep breath, but then let it out without finishing her sentence. Should she tell Mary the whole story? But that would make her a partner to something that the woman should not be burdened with. Mary had an obligation to the lord of Haven Court. She had told Jenny that the viscount was good enough to let her live in the cottage even after Jem's death and even though she no longer had any right to the property. It was hers as long as she needed it, he had apparently told her, and until she married again. *If* she married again, for there were no conditions attached. How could Jenny make her a party to the deception? For the viscount would likely be at least angry that Mary, to whom he had granted a valuable boon, had hidden his supposed betrothed from him.

Sadly Jenny realized that it just emphasized that she must move on, that she was doing Mary a grave disservice, one that she must right eventually by telling Viscount Haven that Mary had no part in the deception, that she thought she was shielding a frightened, friendless woman, not Miss Jane Dresden, runaway bride-to-be. Guilt overtook Jenny but she didn't know how to correct, at that moment, the wrong she had done Mary Cooper. She could only hold her breath and know that within days she must move on; she could not keep delaying the inevitable in the hope of seeing Gerry one more time. She must leave. Then she would send a letter to Lord Haven explaining everything and stating outright that Mary Cooper was an innocent bystander.

But for the time being—"Mary, I . . . no, I am not a lady's maid. And I am . . . well, I am hiding." She caught the worry on the other woman's face and rushed to continue. "But I have done nothing illegal, nor do I feel I have done anything morally wrong, though I may have hurt some people inadvertently. I don't think I have. But there are things . . . my . . . my life is not simple. I . . . I'll not be here much longer. I promise." As much as she tried, she could not keep tears from choking her voice. In three days the cottage had become such an important part of her life, as had Mary and Molly and . . . and Gerry. In one meeting, just three short hours, she had learned what it was to see the future in another's eyes.

"I trust you, Jenny."

Simple words, but they held a wealth of meaning.

Silence fell in the little cottage, broken only by the faint crackling of the fire, the hissing of the bubbling pot on the stove, and the tock-tock of the mantle clock. Jenny stared into the fire and reflected on what had made her take such an extreme measure as running away.

The journey to Yorkshire had been excruciating, for the whole way was taken with her Aunt Mortimer's long lectures on how disgraceful it was to the family to have a girl, well-dowered and seven-and-twenty, and not yet wed. "People" she had said, "are beginning to talk, beginning to say there must be something wrong in the family that the girl was not yet wed."

Jenny began to see how she was going to be tormented and cajoled and threatened and wheedled into marrying the horrible Haven. He had become an ogre in her mind, the criticism she had heard of him growing into condemnation. Dour. Cold. Hard. Cruel, even. Bumbling and clumsy and doltish and brutal. Life would be one squalid scene after another. She had seen it happen, had seen childhood friends descend into fretful, neglected, or even abused wives. It would not happen to her, she vowed. If she could not have a marriage of her own choosing then she would have no marriage at all.

And as if Haven was not bad enough, there was his family, described by Lady Mortimer in excruciating detail as the jolting miles had mounted in number and Yorkshire drew ever closer. The grandmother was an ancient harridan, according to Lady Mortimer, and though her aunt extolled the viscount's mother's virtues, she sounded a perfect fright—high in the instep and as demanding, selfish and cold-natured as even her Aunt Mortimer. Her wholehearted endorsement of the woman was enough to earn Jenny's dislike. And the viscount had two sisters, one of whom was a wild hoyden and the other who sounded a perfect prig. For one second she wondered which one of those Miss Pamela was; probably the hoyden. She seemed a rather nice girl, but then maybe Jenny just did not know her well enough. The thought of living in that uncomfortable household brought back all the worst moments of her life in London, all the whispering, all the unkind jibes, all the feeling of not fitting in.

Whether in London, Bath, or Brighton—another social milieu to which her mother had dragged her, hoping to find her a husband—friendly faces were few, outnumbered hopelessly by the masks of those false friends one met within every one of those quagmires of insipidity. She had never, even from her first Season, fit in, and suspected it had to do with her inability to maintain a social mask of frigid gentility. Too often her true feelings and thoughts escaped, marking her as an outsider, little better than a parvenu. She was far too honest for the liar's den that was society.

And she despised the life she was forced to lead, the endless boring morning visits, the gossip, the enforced stillness. She hated the people she had been constrained to smile and chat with, the sycophants and sneerers of London, the pathetic royal hangers-on of Brighton, and the faux invalids and toadying bootlickers of Bath. She had never known whether there were other more worthy people in those cities because as an unmarried woman her circle of acquaintances was restricted and her behavior carefully monitored. When her mother's health became too poor for her to go about much, her Aunt Mortimer was enlisted, and that woman's rigid list of those she considered acceptable to socialize with was severely limited, restricted to only the most dull and lifeless of beaux.

All of that was bad enough in London or Bath, but how would it be to live with that day in and day out in the home one could never leave? And divorced, as she would be, from every familiar scene, every friendly face—

But still, Jenny would not have done such a wild and ridiculous thing as flee her aunt and the Tippling Swan Inn, if she hadn't gotten the letter.

The letter.

My dear, it read.

> *By the time you get this I will be Mrs. Jessup. I hope you understand why I encouraged you to go. Every girl should be married, and every woman. Mr. Jessup has promised to look after me most tenderly, but, dearest, he really wants only me. You are old enough, past old enough, really, to understand that your best chance at happiness lies in making an arrangement with the viscount and staying in Yorkshire. I will miss you terribly, but I send my regards to your new husband. He is a lucky man to marry you. Good-bye, and good luck, dearest.*
>
> > *Affectionately,*
> > *Your Mother*

And that was it. She wasn't expected back. She had nowhere to go. Her mother was consigning her to the tender mercies of a man she did not even know! At that moment, reading that despicable letter in the room she had been assigned at the inn, rebellion had surfaced for the very first time in all of her years. She had always been a dutiful daughter, a demure and respectful niece, but at that moment anything seemed preferable to allowing her aunt to lead her like a bridled horse to Haven Court and present her to his lordship for inspection, to marry if he found her worthy. She would not want to marry him—she already knew that—and there would be endless hideous scenes, harrying from her aunt, bullying from the odious Lady Haven. She could not do it, she just could not! She didn't know if she was strong enough to resist their demands in her emotionally drained state.

And so, on a mad impulse she had run. Then even her hasty plans fell about her in disarray and she had gotten lost in the darkness. She had wandered for hours, fear and shock making her mindless in her wandering. It had been a long and horrible night, worsened by the advent of a light rain that soaked her to the skin. Finally she had crawled into the first barn she found after what seemed like hours of walking, and that was where Mary had found her, cold, scared, and desperately tired. She now knew that she was many miles from both Lesleydale and Haven Court, but that had been merely luck.

"The bairn's asleep," Mary said, buttoning her nursing gown and standing. She laid Molly in her cradle.

Jenny, awoken from her reverie, gazed at Mary. "If . . . Mary, if my being here is a burden or troubles you in any way . . ."

"Don't be daft, Jenny," the woman said, kindly, as she straightened from the cradle. "Yer welcome to stay here as long as you like. I bin lonely these long months and ne'er really knew it till now. But enough o' that. Shall we eat yer dumplings, Jenny?"

As they took up the stew and the surprisingly light dumplings, Mary laid her hand over her new friend's and said, "Jenny, I can see yer still troubled in yer mind. I canna say it strongly enough. I want you to stay here as long as you need to. Yer welcome here, and I need not know yer story. Whatever time you need to think, take it, and be sure about yer life, for you only get the one. I refused many an offer that folk in the village thought I was out o' my mind for refusin', but I waited and then Jem asked me. It were the right thing and I was wise to wait." She glanced over at the cradle and put one hand over her heart. "It were the right thing to do. When it is right, *whatever* is right, you will know it deep in yer heart."

Morning was the best time for walking the moors, Haven had always thought. Or had he only begun thinking so when the morning ahead promised such a fine distraction? His heart thudding in his chest, the viscount strode down the long hill toward Mary's cottage, where it sat cozily tucked between two high fells, gentle puffs of smoke drifting up from the stone chimney. Perhaps he should not be taking this time for himself, but he had done nothing for the past days but worry and search for Miss Dresden. Surely a couple of hours out of his day would not hurt anyone.

What would he find this morning at the Haven home farm? Would he get a cold reception from Miss Jenny? Would she know that he had misled her as to his identity? The next few minutes would tell if Pammy had let slip anything that would connect, in her mind, the lord of Haven Court with the farmer, Gerry Neville.

He saw the door of the barn standing open and moved to investigate, remembering that he had noticed that the latch was beginning to work loose at the haft. But no, the latch was still intact. He poked his head in the door and looked around; there in the shadows, by Esther, sat Jenny on a stool, her hands on the cow's teats. Lally, the barn cat lay near her in contented sloth. He enjoyed the sight of Jenny's full hips swaying as she tried to get the necessary rhythm, and thought how he would like to see her from the front moving like that.

He fought back the lascivious direction his thoughts

would take and watched for a moment. She was getting more and more frustrated, he thought, gleefully, and so was Esther. Finally the cow let out a low bawl and kicked out, upsetting the pail, which luckily only had a small amount of milk in it.

"You'll starve at that rate," he said, dryly, leaning against the door frame with his arms folded over his chest.

She jumped and staggered off the stool. Her cheeks were flushed with exertion and her curls disheveled, and to Haven she looked utterly adorable.

"This is a ridiculous way to have to get milk," she said, huffily. Her mouth primmed in a straight line. Esther shifted her bulk and knocked Jenny off balance. Haven chuckled, pushed away from the door frame, and moved toward her, grabbing her arm and helping her stay upright.

"Let me show you how it's done, my girl," he said. He righted the pail, straddled the low stool, and grasped Esther's teats in his hands, starting the strong and steady movements that sent a stream of milk into the bucket.

"One can certainly tell that you have done that before," Jenny said, her eyes on his capable hands.

"You might say I am very experienced," he said, and watched her face color an even deeper red. "The female of *some* species is no mystery to me."

He suppressed a chuckle at her discomfiture, enjoying the flood of warm feeling he experienced watching her pretty face. Seeing her again, he knew that what he had felt on their walk was real. There was something between them, something true and fine and deep, and he wanted badly to explore the new feeling he was experiencing, new emotions that flooded his heart and his mind. To hell with Grand's assertion that naught but a lady born could ever be Viscountess Haven. Some things were more important than rank, and love was one of them.

Wasn't it?

Granted, he had known her for too short a time to know

if what was between them was love, but he was certain that there was a budding of something, something that waited only for a tiny push to grow into a deeper feeling than the blend of physical desire and blooming warmth. Should he give it that opportunity? Did she feel it too?

He filled the pail and carried it into the cottage for her. Pammy had evidently not unmasked him, for Jenny treated him just as she had the day before, and he would know the difference immediately if she knew him to be Viscount Haven. Mary was spinning and she looked up from her wheel and said, "That was quick, Jenn—ah, Gerry. I might o' known." A wry smile twisted her mouth when she saw the full pail that he plunked down on the table.

"Mary," Gerry said. "If you do not mind too much I would like to steal your cousin away for another walk." He turned to Jenny. "Would you walk with me, Jenny? It is a fine day, and early spring is often not so kind here in Yorkshire. One must seize the day, *carpe diem,* as the old vicar used to command his pupils."

Jenny nodded wordlessly and retrieved her shawl from a hook on the back of the door. Gerry held it open for her and together they stepped back out into the sunshine. He glanced back in to say good-bye to Mary but she was busy, a frown over some snag in her wool pulling her face into a grimace.

Eleven

Mary moved from her spinning wheel to the door and watched Jenny and Gerry stroll off together, not missing the way Gerry took her arm and tucked it possessively close to his own body. They were like magnets she had seen demonstrated once; their attraction was mutual and powerful. But how would it end?

She thought back to the conversation of the night before. Jenny was hiding something. Mary could not believe that it was anything terrible or sinful, but how did she know? When she found Jenny, scared and cold and shivering in her barn late that night, and with a torn dress, as well, her only thought had been pity and a desire to protect her, nurture her. The girl had been through some kind of ordeal, that was clear. Mary had first thought she might be a barmaid who had been attacked or raped, or a servant of some kind fleeing a lecherous master. But living with her for a few days now, Mary knew she was no maidservant of any sort, even one in the elevated position of lady's maid.

The girl was gentry, but if that was so, what was she doing out on the moors at night alone? And why was she content to bide at Mary's humble cottage, when it was clearly all so new to her? She did not know the first little thing about housekeeping, though she seemed eager to learn. Who *was* she?

When she had first seen Gerry's reaction to Jenny, that

instant attraction and flare of interest, Mary had to admit to herself that her only feeling had been one of relief. She would never *ever* let her old friend know the burden his silent adoration of her had been. It would have been bad enough if Mary had believed it genuine, but she had felt all along that Gerry, with a tender, loving heart too often hidden by an outwardly dour demeanor, had just been lacking a proper object for his affections. He was a man of strong passions, though he kept them subdued with a strength of will and stern morality that did him credit. He needed a woman to love, a feminine companion to adore and care for and look after, but it would never be her. Aside from their vast differences in station and wealth, she just did not love him in that special way and he deserved that, needed it.

But now things had come to a difficult pass and Mary quite frankly did not know what to do. Attraction was swiftly becoming something more between him and Jenny. She had seen it in his eyes, in the way he had looked at her as they exited the cottage. She did not know the young woman well enough to know what she felt for Gerry, but in his case he was smitten and could easily tumble into love, and yet Mary was lying to him, letting him think that Jenny was her cousin when really she had no idea who or what the girl was!

It was unconscionable and Mary was deeply ashamed to have lied. There were so many questions in her mind, questions that had no answer. Thinking that Jenny was Mary's cousin, was Gerry just transferring his affection for his old friend onto a more receptive female? Would he feel the same if he knew her to not be Mary's cousin?

And what was Jenny's motive in all of this? It could be that she, being in some sort of trouble, saw Gerry as a potential knight errant, to rescue her from her dilemma. Mary would not for the world have Gerry used that way.

And yet they were both adults. This attraction would likely exist no matter who they thought the other was.

In fact, once Jenny knew Gerry was in truth not a simple farmer, but a wealthy and powerful viscount, she would likely do all in her power to cultivate his attraction and growing affection for her. What girl would not?

She stared up the moor to where the two were now just small figures moving so close to one another they appeared to be one. She rubbed her arms and shivered. Ah, it was all a mess, and she would not hide from her own part in making it thus. Mary closed the door and went back to her spinning wheel. One thing was clear. The concealment must end; she must tell them both the truth and let things sort themselves out how they might. And her first duty was to her old and valued friend, Gerry. She must take him aside and tell him the truth, that not only was Jenny not her cousin, but she had never laid eyes on the girl before just a few short nights ago. He would be angry. He had a right to be, and hurt, too, but she hoped he would forgive her.

And then she would leave it up to him to tell Jenny the truth. It would be a much more pleasant surprise for her, no doubt, for she would find that her country swain was in reality a powerful and rich man. Whatever trouble she was in he could likely fix it.

Unless she was, after all, married and running away from an abusive husband. There was very little remedy in law or religion for that. Mary started the even foot movements of the treadle of her spinning wheel and concentrated on just the right positioning to get the even texture and thickness her wool was known for throughout Lesleydale and the entire North Riding. She would tell the truth and shame the devil.

Jenny glanced over at Gerry. His brow was furrowed and he was deep in thought. They had climbed the high moor again, standing for a few moments—mostly so she could catch her breath, as the walk was long and she was not accustomed to it as he was—at the top to survey the valley of the Lesley, but now they had descended and were walking among the burgeoning trees, the color of their new leaves an incredible, brilliant green, like the most lovely, translucent peridot.

She thought back to all the lonely evenings spent in London ballrooms and Bath parlors, all the hours of idle chatter and fatiguing gossip, and she knew that in all of her dreams of a man—a *real* man, not one of the posturing London bucks or beaux—she could never have conjured Gerry, the perfect blend of earthy country manners and compelling intelligence. They had talked the whole of the way, up and down moors, speaking of farming in Yorkshire, of all topics, for his knowledge of sheep farming was deep—not surprising since it was his life. But they had moved from there to other things. He was intelligent, well read, with an interest in the most amazing array of topics, including astronomy, history, science, and even politics.

He knew the arc of the stars in the earth's nightly travels, and had promised to show it to her one night. He had an opinion on the Poor Laws, could debate Mary Wollstonecraft and Jeremy Bentham, and had his own opinions of the Wars of the Roses and the true causes. He was amazing, a compendium of useful knowledge, esoteric information, and deeply held conviction. That he was delighted by her own erudition on these topics was a lovely surprise. She had expected him to be horrified, as many in London had been, by her wide-ranging knowledge of and interest in politics, but he seemed to truly appreciate an intelligent response. It was refreshing. How he thought a lady's maid came by such information as she displayed, she did not know. Nor care. She would never be anything but what she was with him, even if she *was* concealing her identity.

But now he was silent.

She sighed and let herself lean against him as they strolled among the swaying, whispering trees toward the banks of a silvery gill, one of the narrow, undulating streams that fed the Lesley. When he stopped in the unneeded shade of a twisted, gnarled old oak, she looked up at him questioningly. Her heart was at peace and she was ready to accept whatever her life should bring now.

"Jenny," he said, hesitantly. He released her arm and turned her to face him. She leaned back against the trunk of the tree and looked up into his honest blue gaze.

"Yes, Gerry?"

He reached up and touched her hair, stroking it back from her cheeks, and she felt a shiver rush through her at the gentleness of his touch. How could such broad, strong hands be rough in texture and yet so gentle at the same time? His fingers trailed down her cheek and cupped her chin. His sturdy, powerful body moved closer until she could feel his heat infusing her with warmth. She gazed up into his eyes still, reading there tenderness and affection and something else, something deeper and more elemental, more to do with the night secrets that were whispered between man and woman, lover to lover.

"Jenny," he whispered.

Pinned, trapped against the gnarled trunk of the tree, the first touch of his lips was almost frightening, the intensity startling, the raw twist of restrained passion that surged from him through his lips a bewildering shock. Her eyes closed, she was a prisoner of the delicious sensations that raced up her spine and down to her fingers. Without thought she put her hands on his strong shoulders and felt the flexing muscles beneath her fingers.

His lips, soft at first, moved over her chin and cheek and up to her hair and her ear; her whole body trembled as her fingers moved, as if of their own accord, up to thread through his thick, soft hair. He smelled of clean air and wool and wood smoke: delicious, enticing, beckoning.

He was muttering her name over and over, "Jenny, Jenny" like a chant against her skin, and when he took her lips again, his heavy body moved closer, pinning her until she could feel the rough texture of the bark at her back and the unyielding muscle of his legs and torso against her front. It was thrilling and frightening and astonishing. The world had shrunk to this one space, the two of them and the delectable desire that throbbed between them.

His hands moved down from her shoulders, down her back until he was holding her firmly against his body and she could feel him, feel his need for her and the power of his passion. A shudder shook his body and he broke the contact, releasing her from his arms. She opened her eyes and gazed at him, numb with shock at the sensation of his body stirring to life against her.

"Pardon me, Jenny. I . . . I did not mean to take advantage."

She couldn't say a word. She just stared at his face, tracing his lips, letting her gaze lock, finally, with his. So this was it, this was what falling in love felt like. Or was this merely the physical manifestation of the dangerous attraction between man and woman? Perhaps this was what young ladies were so protected for, this urgent siren call that beckoned the unwary to wander near the lip of the abyss, the deep chasm of temptation.

But no, though the attraction between them was powerful she could not believe it was only physical, for she felt a connection with Gerry. Where the touch of other men's hands and lips had inspired distaste, this felt right and good and meaningful. And for him too, she thought. She searched his eyes, finding tenderness and honesty there; she concluded that his desire for her was a clean, sweet thing, nothing to be ashamed of.

For the first time in her life she had met a man with whom marriage would not be a distasteful duty, but a thrilling adventure. Loving him, caring for him, taking care of him—she reached out and touched his face, feeling the rough texture of his beard stubble against her sensitive fingers. He turned his face into her palm and kissed it, nipping at the fleshy part near her thumb. A wild, tumultuous thrill of sheer joy raced through her. Life was good, the world was beautiful!

For once in her long, constricted, restrained life she gave in to impulse and pushed past him. She dashed away from the tree, looking back at him and saying, "If you want another kiss, sir, you will have to catch me!" She laughed out loud at the look of astonishment on his handsome face and turned, picking up the skirts of her maidservant dress and racing off along the soft-turf bank of the gill. She felt young and free, lighthearted and happy for the very first time in her life, and it was magical!

Gerry, in the powerful clutches of restrained passion, took a moment to respond, but a surge of desire raced through him as he watched her fly along the bank. The thrum of primitive instinct, the urge to capture her and make her his own, raced through his blood, and he ran, chasing her. But she was quick and light on her feet for such a city-bred lass.

Her laughter floated back to him as he thudded along the bank. And then, to his horror, he saw her tumble, and she fell to the ground.

"Jenny!" He raced to her and fell at her side only to see her grinning up at him, panting, but unhurt. He covered her mouth with his own and their gasping breaths were exchanged and mingled as they kissed and breathed and kissed some more. The soft turf beneath them felt remarkably like a bed, and the lust that had throbbed through his body pulsed back, more powerful and more frantic. It knifed through his groin, almost doubling him over with its power.

Lord, but he wanted her! Tamping down his animal urges, anxious not to frighten her with his passion, he clenched his fists and pulled back, gazing down at her lovely face, pink-cheeked from exertion, her gray eyes sparkling. Was she inviting him to make love to her? What would she do if he—

He let his fingers trail the skin of her heaving bosom, above her neckline. She shivered and looked up at him, the delight in her eyes replaced by a question. He flattened his hand over the swell of her ample breast and felt her jump. Her eyes widened and she moved away from him in one swift movement. Ashamed, he swallowed back his desire and let her go.

"I'm sorry, Jenny. I . . . I'll not take advantage of you. Slap me if you must, I will understand."

She shook her head, shyly. "I'll not slap you, Gerry. Just behave and there will be no need."

He rolled onto his back and stared up at the sky, relieved in an odd way. There would be no heady lovemaking on the banks of the gill; he could not say that it would not have been a pleasure and a blessed relief for his body, but what it meant was that she valued herself above that, beyond a quick and furtive tumble on the riverbank, and he respected her for it. Loved her for it?

He lumbered to his feet and offered her his hand. "Now, Miss Jenny, will you walk quietly with me or must we race along the bank like ewe lambs again?" He deliberately chose a light and teasing tone for his words.

She smiled and sighed. "We shall walk, sir," she said, primly.

He took her arm and they strolled. How different this country courtship was from any other association with a female he had ever had. There had been, in his life, the inevitable barmaids and serving wenches. They offered themselves to him as the lord of the manor, asking in return only lovemaking and maybe an occasional gift. He had stopped that years before, though, realizing he was merely lucky that there were no by-blows born from those fleeting physical unions. For some time now he had been celibate, unwilling to make any woman a mother to his child unless she was also his wife. He was not one to take mistresses and he could not see a casual relationship with any of the local widows, though there were those who had cast their eyes and their suggestions his way.

But every relationship of that sort was tainted with conflicting hopes and desires. Inevitably differing assumptions would lead to hurt feelings and ultimately a painful separation when expectations were not met.

With Jenny there was an honesty—

No. There wasn't that. He would not mislead himself, no matter how much he might lie to *her*. There was no honesty as long as she thought he was Gerry Neville, local farmer. Would her feelings change when she found out he was Lord Haven? Would doubt of his intentions cloud her eyes and her heart turn away from him? He did not know. And he was afraid to ask. Perhaps he was even more afraid that finding out he was Viscount Haven would make him *more* desirable in her eyes.

Jenny felt Gerry's hand seek out hers and clasp it in the warm confines of his palm. Her heart was still pounding and she did not think she would soon forget the churning— it was almost stomach-turning, oddly enough—of desire that simple action, his hand on her breast, had inspired. She had not wanted to turn him away. She had wanted him to continue, wanted him to slide his fingers under the bodice of her dress and touch her in intimate ways.

But it would not have been right for so many, many reasons. And so she had found the strength for both of them and turned him away. What did she want from Gerry Neville? More, certainly, than an end to her maidenhood. If it was marriage he sought and not just a quick tumble on the turf, would she say yes?

The warbling of a lark drifted on the breeze and the little gill chuckled and burbled like Molly in a happy mood. She glanced at her companion, saw his brow furrowed again, and she wondered what he was thinking. If he asked her to marry him—and many proposals had been received by ladies after *less* time spent with a man—would she say yes? Why not? She had not been raised to think she would find love in marriage, but with Gerry she thought there was every chance it would seek her out and steal into her heart; perhaps the process had begun already with this country walk and stolen kisses.

She did not measure him as the kind of man to trifle with a lady's heart. And yet, she did not even know if he had the wherewithal to marry. Perhaps marriage would be many more years off for a farmer who must depend on the erratic market for his goods to make his fortune. Or on the goodwill of his master, the mighty Lord Haven.

Ah, a tiny, secret voice whispered, *but you have money!* It was not a fortune, but with careful husbandry it could last, especially living modestly as one would surely live as wife to a farmer.

She realized suddenly that she did not even know where or how he lived, her knowledge of him was that sparse. Did he live with parents? Did he have his own cottage, as manager of Lord Haven's vast holdings? Was that his position? She did not even know that; she had just assumed from his intimate knowledge of every inch of the viscount's property and every detail of his business.

But he was independent; that she was sure of. She did not think he was the kind of man who could live on his wife's dowry. A man in his position could possibly expect to marry a merchant's daughter, a young lady with a thousand pounds as her portion. But her dowry was many *many* times that. Would that offend him? And once she told him the truth, for she knew that it was inevitable that she must, would he think that marriage to the granddaughter of an earl would be beyond him? No man wanted to be less than his wife. She did not happen to think that position in life meant a thing, but most folks did.

And when the whole truth came out, would he risk marrying the lady his master had already offered to wed? He would surely not hazard offending the man who held his livelihood in the palm of his blue-blooded hand. That was the plain and simple truth of the matter. She was being dishonest and unfair to him in not telling him the truth about who she was.

Gerry had been talking for a while, telling her about the area, the valley of the Lesley, the town, something about the people. And she had asked a few questions just to show she was listening. But now they paused and he gestured to a log.

"Would you like to sit for a few minutes?" he said.

She gladly took a seat and he sat beside her, his thick muscled thigh pressed against her leg. The sun was warm on her face and she turned it up to the sky and closed her eyes. Gerry took her hand again, and they sat for a few minutes in silence.

"Do you think to find work around here, Jenny?"

Reality. He probably looked forward to a long courtship, if that was his aim at all, before he could afford to take a wife.

"I . . . I hadn't thought about it. But . . . but I cannot stay with Mary long." That, at least, was the truth. Her little house of cards was about to fall apart, she thought, sadly. She was as good as betrothed to the viscount, Lord Haven, and never had that prospect seemed more bleak than at that moment, sitting beside the one man in the world she could dream of marriage to without shuddering. Even willing as she was to abandon her family—her mother loved her, she knew, but she had never needed her, and now she had a husband to care for her—it did not change her relative position in life, nor Gerry's.

"I guess you can't," he said. "Stay at Mary's too long, I mean." He pulled a piece of new grass and chewed on the end. He squinted up at the sun. "Lunch soon. We should

be getting back." And with that he stood and offered her
his hand, pulling her to her feet.

They walked back slowly. Where the valley was warmed
by the sun, the high moor was still very chilly. It was finally
April and the wind whipped and scudded puffy clouds up
one hill and down the other while the spring sunshine tried
its best to provide some warmth. They stopped at the top
of the fell. Her companion pointed to the hills in the distance, purplish on the horizon. "That, in the distance, is
the Pennines. First road closed in the winter goes through
there."

"What is that patch of different color," Jenny asked,
pointing to a large swath of the fell that was a different
green from the grass around them.

"That there is the heather; by summer it will be in full
bloom. Lovely, it is, to walk among it in full bloom, a field
of lavender all around you, and to fall down in it and smell
the wonderful scent. It rises up on the breeze and perfumes
the air."

Jenny gazed up at him. "You have a poet within you
struggling to get out."

"Well he's not struggling very hard," he chuckled, a rich
warm sound. He put his arm over her shoulder when he
noticed her shivering and held her close to his warm, sturdy
frame. "I suppose," he said, reluctantly, "that we should get
back."

"I . . . I suppose we should. I am to help with churning
butter this afternoon and I wouldn't want to miss that." She
chuckled.

He turned her to face him. "Jenny," he said, a serious
look on his face, "I have not known you long and you have
not known *me* long, but . . . but I . . ." He faltered to a
halt, turned away, and stared off into the distance. "I must
get back. There are some things I have to do that cannot
wait."

Disappointed, Jenny agreed and they walked the rest of

the way back to the cottage—a fair piece in this countryside of long sloping moors—in silence. He left her at the gate, but then returned to her and bent over, brushing her lips with his own. "I'll be back, my sweet Jenny. I will be back, and shortly, too."

When she entered, singing one of the songs that Mary had taught her while they worked, she hoped he was coming back to ask her a question. Even though she knew deep in the farthest regions of her heart that she was courting disaster and heartache, she still couldn't help hoping, wishing, *praying*. Until the very last second she would squeeze every drop of joy out of this country courtship, if that was what it was. If it fell down about her in a tangled mess of pain and sorrow—

But she wouldn't think of that just then, not with the feel of his lips on hers and the scent of his warm body still in her nostrils. There was always time for heartbreak and pain later. For now there was love blooming.

Twelve

"My lady," Lady Mortimer said, her pinched face twisted in her perpetual frown. "I do not know what you are asking?"

"I just asked if the miniature you sent to us is considered a good likeness of Miss Dresden?" The dowager tapped her cane impatiently, wondering why this was such a difficult question for the pestilential old hen-wit. "Is that so hard to understand or answer?"

Lady Mortimer drew herself up and sniffed. "Why, of *course* it is a good likeness. It is her very *image!* Why do you ask such insulting and imbecilic questions? I am inclined to believe that age has touched your mind."

The old lady chuckled. The one thing she appreciated about the bilious baroness was her willingness to belittle anybody and her absolute lack of compassion for the dowager's infirm state. Sometimes the dowager Lady Haven—Lord how she hated that title!—got just a trifle weary of being deferred to by almost everyone when she was around, only to be dismissed as an ancient beldam with wandering wits in her absence. She knew how some of her household thought of her, but was powerless to change anything. It was frustrating. "I have lived long enough that I do not care who is insulted nor who thinks I am an imbecile. I care only for those close to me, and for them I would do anything."

"This is the most absurd household," Lady Mortimer fumed, standing and pacing the drab carpet of the elderly dame's sitting room. "Rachel and Lady Haven are, I think, the only two with any claim to gentility. Just look at that child, Pamela! She is mad! I saw her out riding in breeches . . . *breeches!* And your grandson; he is a great idiotish lummox. And you—" The baroness paused and turned back to stare at the dowager. Her beady eyes sharpened and focused, intelligence snapping in their dark depths. "Why does it matter if Jane's picture is accurate?"

The old lady shrugged. "It doesn't. I was just curious. Do you consider that she looks like your sister?"

The baroness snorted. "Jane takes after the Dresden side of the family! No gentility there at all; all the women plump, with sluttish serving girl looks. No nobility. No breeding."

"But Dresden was the younger son of an earl!" The dowager sat forward on her chair, fascinated by the description of her proposed granddaughter-in-law to be. Lady Mortimer was only so candid because she had the impression that talking to the elderly dowager viscountess was harmless, of no more consequence than speaking to a chair or armoire.

"A newer creation." Lady Mortimer sniffed. "There is the whiff of the trades there in the not-to-distant past."

The elderly lady sat back, satisfied in some respects. The tiny painting of Miss Dresden that had been sent on ahead of the girl was of a narrow-faced tight-lipped miss, but the baroness had just described her as favoring her father's side of the family, on which side the women were all 'plump with serving girl looks.' So to sum it up, the painting was as accurate as such works often were when done by an inferior artist, reflecting the prejudices of the painter and the prevailing notions of beauty of the age. It bore only a passing likeness to the girl, in all likelihood. Enough so that to meet the original in person one might not be struck by the resemblance at all.

A tap at the door made both women stop and look.

"Yes?" the dowager said, imperiously. She had more to ask of the embittered baroness and she did not especially want interruptions.

"Grand, have you seen—" It was Rachel, but as she poked her head into the room and scanned it, she saw Lady Mortimer. "Oh, my lady, you are just who we are looking for. You must come at once! Dreadful, *dreadful* news!"

Lady Mortimer paled. "What is it? Is it Jane . . . have they found . . . ?"

"I'd best let Mother tell you. Come to the parlor, my lady, if you please."

The entire family—except for Haven himself—was assembled, but waited politely while Grand hobbled in, following the baroness, and took a seat by the large windows that overlooked the terrace garden side of the old priory. Grand cast a look over at Pamela and saw the child wearing the gaudy pink dress her mother had recently ordered for her, a horrible confection of bows and lace that overwhelmed the girl's slim, boyish figure. She sat stiffly in a chair near Sir Colin Varens, who stood, brow furrowed, posed by the hearth.

"What is it? What is all this fuss about?" the dowager asked, irritation in her voice. It was likely some overreaction on her daughter-in-law's part, and she was already planning how to get Lady Mortimer alone again to question her for more details on Miss Jane Dresden. "Why must we all gather and wait the pronouncements of this self-important baby baronet?"

Rachel giggled but Pamela shot her grandmother a hurt look, and so the dowager clamped her mouth shut. Soon she would make Pamela see that Varens was not good enough for her, but it would take time. The child idolized him.

"Ma'am," Varens said politely, turning to the dowager. "I assure you I would not take your time for anything less than vital." He turned toward the younger Lady Haven, the viscount's mother. "Where is Haven, by the way, my lady? He should be here."

She shrugged helplessly. "I can only assume that he is off looking for Miss Dresden."

The dowager held her tongue, annoyed that Varens, like so many others, passed her over because of her age, seeing her as a venerable object to be polite to, but not to consider of any aid. *She* could tell him where Haven was likely to be, but she wouldn't. Nor would she tell them her own suspicions of the whereabouts of the girl. Let them all stew in their own juices, the pack of dolts!

"What do you want to say, Sir Colin," Rachel said, clearly bored by the wait. She played absently with a gold bracelet, letting the tiny bells attached tinkle and clank.

Varens cast her a worshipful glance and said, "I will get to the point, Miss Neville. I have some disturbing news from the village. I was at the inn this morning, and—" He paused and held out a paper package to Lady Mortimer. "Ma'am . . . my lady, please look at this reticule and jewel bag and tell me if you recognize them."

Lady Mortimer took the package, slipped the string out of it, and ripped it open; with a faint cry she let it drop from her hands. "It . . . it is Jane's!"

"I suspected as much," Varens said. He cast a look at Rachel and straightened, looking very much aware that all eyes were now on him.

Puffed-up little toad, the dowager thought. What did Miss Dresden's reticule prove?

"But there is nothing in them!" Lady Mortimer continued, picking the items up and looking them over. She opened the reticule and shook the soft chamois sack. "There should be a small embroidered purse with money in it in the reticule and . . . and Jane's pearls should be in the jewel bag!"

"There's more," Varens said. "A serving girl in the village has been seen wearing a brown carriage dress of good quality, a dress very much like the one purported to be Miss Dresden's, if I am not mistaken. My housekeeper, Mrs. Farrell, says that one of our maids, a friend of the other girl, told her the wench will not say where she got it."

Lady Mortimer leaped to her feet. "Take me to the girl. I will beat it out of her! It sounds like Jane's dress. How would she get Jane's dress if there was not—" Her face bleached and without another word she crumpled to the ground.

"Useless nodcock," the dowager said, her voice echoing in the shocked silence of the parlor.

Lady Haven rose from her seat and started gabbling, twisting her hands together uncertainly.

"Does that mean that Miss Dresden is dead?" Rachel asked, plaintively.

Varens knelt by Lady Mortimer and gently tapped her cheeks, trying to revive her, while Lady Haven regained her wits and shrieked out the door for the butler to get hartshorn. The baronet glanced up at Rachel and said, "No, Miss Neville, that does not necessarily follow, though I fear that is what Lady Mortimer has assumed. I would say the kidnappers have likely taken the young lady's clothes and jewels and money and gave the dress to one of their doxies." He colored at the information he had to impart.

But Rachel did not seem perturbed. "Then I do not see what the fuss is about," she said. "This tells us nothing new at all." She left the room without another word.

Lady Mortimer regained consciousness just as Haven strode into the room.

"Where have you been, you idiot?" Lady Haven howled.

The dowager snapped, "Shut up, Lydia. You should have more respect for your son. Let the boy speak."

Haven frowned at his grandmother. "Grand, it does not help for you to speak to Mother that way. What is all this fearful clatter about? I have never seen that man," he said, referring to the butler, "move at a pace faster than a tortoise, but just now he was tearing up the stairs bellowing for hartshorn."

Varens, helping Lady Mortimer up to a chair, repeated what he had just imparted. "It does not look good, Haven," he finished.

The viscount sighed and rubbed his eyes. "Colin, if you had waited—I have just been to the village myself. It seems that the servant in question . . ." He broke off and shook his head. "I spoke to the girl; she was terribly frightened by all of the commotion and your questioning, Varens. That explains her reticence before this; the truth of the matter is, she claims she 'found' the dress tied in a bundle and discarded in a hedge just outside the inn. I am not sure what that means, but I feel certain she was telling me the truth. It took a lot of courage for her to tell me that much."

"How does that make anything better?" Pamela said. "I still think Sir Colin did the right thing, to tell us what he had found out. We have to know what is going on. And there is the jewel bag and reticule—"

"Where were they found, Colin?" Haven asked, cutting his sister off. "Barker was not around when I was there and no one else could tell me."

The baronet, still stinging from Haven's rebuke, sullenly said, "Joseph Barker told me one of the maids found it in her room . . . that is, the room Miss Dresden was resting in before she was kidnapped. It was under the bed mattress. When the servants turned the mattress in their weekly cleaning, they found them."

"Well, then, it could not have been taken by the supposed kidnappers then, could it?" He frowned and glared down at the carpet. "There is no suggestion that she was taken from her room. All agree that she was last seen on the stairs leading to the kitchen. If these items were found in that room, then the only possible answer to that question is that Miss Dresden put them there herself, for whatever reason. I suppose by some stretch of the imagination one could argue that the kidnappers accosted Miss Dresden and forced her to take them back up to her room, where they proceeded to take the time to remove her money and jewels from their coverings, but it does not hang together, to me. And I . . . I have her pearls, you know." He drew them out of his pocket. "Or at least I believe them to be hers."

After the hubbub had died down and Haven had explained himself and his possession of the pearls, he turned to the baroness. "Tell me, Lady Mortimer, did Miss Dresden have any . . ." He paused and glanced away, squinting for a moment at the rococo carved hearth. "Any admirers, any beaux, any gentlemen who wished to marry her?"

"Lord, no! The girl is a cabbage-headed little . . ." The baroness stopped and clamped her mouth closed. When she spoke again it was with her usual cultured tones. "That is, my niece is of impeccable virtue. What are you suggesting, Haven?"

Calmly, he said, "I was wondering if the young lady might have preferred another gentleman, but had been convinced against her better judgment to come up here to meet me. If that was the case and she had an ardent suitor, he could have followed her and convinced her that the only thing to do was run away and get married."

"An elopement," Pamela said, eyes wide. She clapped her hands. "How romantic!"

"It is not romantic, bird-wit," Varens said, his voice hard with spite. "It is immoral and mutton-headed."

Lady Haven, looking faint, said, "Why would any girl want to marry some low fellow when she could have Viscount Haven?"

Haven raised his eyebrows. "It should not surprise you, Mother. You have ever disparaged my personal attractions."

Grand snickered.

Lady Haven colored. "Perhaps, but this is a defamation of your title and lineage, of which there cannot be two opinions."

"Perhaps there are," he said, dryly. "Perhaps there is more than one young lady in the world who does not wish to marry the eminent Viscount Haven. I am not done looking into this, but I would have all of you keep one thing in mind." He scanned those assembled, not excepting his grandmother, whom he dropped a wink at, however. "One: this information should stay in this room. I want no gossip about Miss Dresden should she have decided on an elopement. In fact, I think I would respect the girl *more* if I discovered that she made her own decisions about her future rather than being herded up to Yorkshire to marry a man she has never met. Two: we know nothing for sure at this point, not even that Miss Dresden left the inn willingly. I am assuming nothing. With this new theory in mind I am going to send out a rider to see if any coaches or carriages with a man and woman in them have been seen in the hours following Miss Dresden's disappearance."

The dowager clapped. "Very good, Haven. Spoken like a sensible man. Not like some I could name who would engage in theatrics at the cost of shocking bacon-brained half-wits." She cast Varens a venomous look, letting it slew around to include Lady Mortimer.

"Grand—" Haven said, warning in his voice.

Giving a good imitation of one chastened, she meekly said, "I will apologize for disparaging the intentions or wit of anyone present." Laughter quavered in her voice. "I did not think anyone would take offense at an old woman's maunderings." She rose and started out of the room. "Grandson, when you have a moment for a poor, old, witless woman, I would have a word with you."

Haven shook his head. His grandmother was both a trial and a delight to him. He briefly said good-bye to the others, leaving the dratted pearls in the possession of the baroness, and followed the dowager to her suite. It had been a long day so far and he still had things to do. In the hours since walking and talking with Jenny his mind had become firm on one subject. No matter what his grandmother felt, he was going to ask Jenny to marry him. He felt faintly guilty about doing it while Miss Dresden was still missing, but his own life must go on. His postulation on her disappearance had become almost certainty in his own mind; she had a lover and they had eloped. It would explain much, though he supposed it would leave almost as much unexplained.

"Bartlett, bring tea for myself and the viscount. And some of Cook's excellent biscuits, I think." The elderly woman tapped into her suite as the butler opened the door for her and then disappeared toward the kitchen. In a building as large as the priory, it would take a while.

Haven followed his grandmother, still conning over in his mind the possibilities. He paced to the window and stared out at the high fell, over which Jenny beckoned to his heart. Such a short time ago he had been looking forward to an arranged marriage to a young lady of good birth and lineage. He had not made his mind up about it completely, but was succumbing to the pressure he felt, at the age of thirty-one, to provide an heir for his title and a mistress for Haven Court.

But now he had tumbled headlong into love. What an odd event for someone as unromantical and stolid as he! But the mere presence of Jenny, the smell of her hair, the touch of her skin, the sound of her voice, inspired him. His whole physical being thrummed to life in her presence, but the connection ran deeper than passion to a mating of their souls, a marriage of their minds. Besides Pammy and Grand there was not another female in the world to whom he could speak his mind, and yet as new as the acquaintance was, he knew he could do so with Jenny.

There were hurdles to overcome. Would she marry him

once she knew who he was? He felt capable of talking her into it. It would not be easy for her, but if necessary he would banish his mother to the dower house rather than see her bully the woman he loved. He felt a momentary pang of worry. He had ever valued a peaceful household and it would not be peaceful for some time. Perhaps he had allowed his mother too free a reign. But she was his mother and he loved her. That she disparaged him constantly and in public was a source of pain to him, but he had learned to ignore it most of the time. Perhaps, in hindsight, that had been a mistake. It was possible that he should have silenced her in some way, though his father had never found the key to that difficult riddle.

He turned from the window to see Grand watching him, love and knowledge in her watery old eyes. He crossed the floor and caressed her cheek before sitting down opposite her at her favorite table, the French gilt Cressent, presented to her by her husband as a special gift on the birth of her son, Haven's father, many, *many* decades before. "So what do you think, Grand?" he asked. "Do you think Miss Dresden may have a lover?"

"Oh, yes, I think that she likely does," the old lady said, a twinkle in her eye that Haven did not quite understand.

"It would explain much, including what no one else has seemed to grasp from the hidden reticule and jewel sack, that she must have taken the pearls and money down the stairs with her. I do not want to ignore any avenues, though. I must be sure she has eloped before I call off the search. For if she has truly been kidnapped, I would not have the young lady left on her own."

"What is your reasoning, then, grandson?"

He thanked whatever deity was responsible that his grandmother had the kind of calm, rational mind that made conversation possible without hysteria or posturing. "My theory is this: Miss Dresden, harassed and prodded into this trip north to meet me," he said with a grimace, thinking he understood only too well how a person could finally give in to pressure even against better judgment, "begins the trip with her aunt. She has left behind a beau, an ardent suitor, perhaps, but one whose lineage or position in life is not suitable in the eyes of those around her." He stopped, thinking that he and Miss Dresden might have much more in common than he would have ever thought possible.

"Go on," Grand said, laughter in her voice for some unfathomable reason.

Haven cast her an uneasy look. Why did he so often feel that his grandmother was watching the rest of them live their lives and laughing at them all? "Suppose Miss Dresden's mother has asked her to do this and the young lady acquiesced, only to realize somewhere on the journey that love—" He paused and stared at the fireplace, not even seeing the familiar magnificent carvings and mirrored panels. "Love is not to be abandoned," he continued, his voice quiet. "It has stolen into her heart and will not allow any conclusion but one—marriage to the one she loves. After all, it is the only logical, decent, moral choice, to marry where your heart is engaged." He cleared his throat and sat up straighter as the butler returned, ushering into the room a footman who carried a tray laden with tea, cups, and a plate of buttery biscuits, so hot the steam still rose from them.

"Ah, wonderful," the old lady said, eyeing the plate with appreciation. The serving staff departed and she poured tea and began on the biscuits, layering butter and currant preserves on one. She offered one to Haven but he turned it down for perhaps the first time since he was ailing as a very small child.

"We know, now," he said, frowning down at his booted feet, "that she received a letter at the inn stating that her mother, the moment Miss Dresden had gone from Bath, it seemed, has remarried. I would think if the young lady only submitted to this trip north for her mother's sake, she might well be hurt by her mother's rushed marriage." He stood and paced to the window again, hands clenched behind his back while he talked out his theory.

"That is only a surmise on my part, and may or may not be true, but it seems to be supported by Lady Mortimer's behavior. She clearly was surprised and dismayed by her sister's actions, and they did not directly affect her. How much more upset would Miss Dresden be? Regardless, what I think might have happened is this—a gentleman followed her and convinced her to elope with him. I have found no evidence of such a man—though I have not explored all of the possibilities there, that she received a note, or met someone outside of the inn—but it would explain her disappearance, for one thing, and its timing. Not to mention the missing money and pearls. I can find absolutely no indication that a young lady was molested, kidnapped, or interfered with in any way, even counting in the pearls! The only alternative is that she left voluntarily, but dropped those in her haste to escape the inn.

"I would like Lady Mortimer to go through Miss Dresden's trunk to see if there was any other clothing missing. We have not yet had her do that, since we believed, at first, the kidnap story. But she could have changed her clothes and then abandoned the carriage dress outside the inn, which would explain the serving girl's finding it bundled into a hedge." He paused and pondered for a moment. "It would explain, too, the too-legible note. If she wanted to mislead her aunt as to her whereabouts to give her time to effect her elopement, she—or her beau, perhaps—could have written the note and left it in the stable."

He turned from the window to find his grandmother contentedly munching on the biscuit. "Do you think it possible, Grand? Does it sound likely to you?"

She chuckled around her mouthful and swallowed. "Anything is possible, Haven. Why, it could be possible that the girl is hiding right under our own noses."

He frowned. It was not the answer he had been hoping for. There was something odd about her demeanor. He had never ascribed to the notion his mother had, that Grand's wits were finally wandering, but she did not seem overly concerned with poor Miss Dresden's actions or lack thereof.

"Do you really think that is possible? That she and her beau are hiding somewhere in the neighborhood?"

His grandmother shrugged, visibly straining to contain her mirth. She coughed and swallowed, then took a long sip of tea.

Doggedly he pursued his line of reasoning, trying to ignore the niggling worry that was gnawing at his brain, that his grandmother was beginning to mentally decline. "It would explain, too, why the reticule and jewel sack were in her room, under the mattress. She perhaps did not want to take them with her in such recognizable form. As I said, she could have dropped the pearls, I suppose."

Grand frowned and nodded, her movement arrested in the act of taking another biscuit. "I do believe you are right about that, Gerry. I wonder what she was thinking? I find Lady Mortimer a thoroughly unpleasant woman, but to leave her so worried—were the reticule and sack left as an indication that the kidnapping was *false?* Was it a double bluff intended to reassure, just as the note was intended to confuse? Perhaps the girl is even more clever than I take her for. Why a note at all? Did she only want enough time to get away?"

"Exactly!" Haven said, glad to see his grandmother back to her sharp-witted self. "I must go and continue the search. I will have some of my men search the countryside for information. With this new theory the questions they will ask must, perforce, be considerably different. They will want to see if any man was seen outside the inn, or if someone delivered a note to the young lady. Or perhaps if a strange carriage was seen anywhere. A closed carriage, most likely."

"Stop! Haven, sit for one minute and drink your tea. Everything will surely wait until you can take some sustenance."

He sighed, but submitted. Grand was right, he supposed. His stomach was growling, for he had not taken luncheon, his guilt over his long morning walk with Jenny making him leap into action and spend the time between then and now riding the countryside and asking questions.

He accepted a biscuit from his grandmother and nodded his thanks as she poured him tea.

"You have been to see that girl again."

It was not a question, it was a statement, and Haven steeled himself to answer. "I have."

"And? Tell me more about her, Haven. What is she like? Her voice, her person, her manners."

He was reluctant to discuss her with anyone, even his beloved grandmother. "She is . . . beautiful."

"You've said that," the dowager said, sharply. "Tell me more."

How could he? He shrugged. "Her voice is lovely, nice tone, like a coloratura's speaking voice, I think. Mmm, she . . . she is very pretty, lovely dark hair, curling around her face, gray eyes, beautiful, soft skin. And intelligent." He frowned. "Don't know where she learned half the things she knows. Not good at farming chores, though," he said, with a chuckle, remembering her faltering attempt to milk Esther.

The dowager leaned forward and looked her grandson in the eyes. "You sound to me very much like a young man in love. Why don't you marry her, Haven?"

Thirteen

Evening shadows were long outside the cottage door, but inside was bathed in mellow golden light cast from the fire. Jenny watched Mary wearily rock Molly's cradle and felt a tenderness for the kind woman and her tiny baby. Mary surely must wonder who she was and what she was running from, but though she had asked a couple of times, she had not pressed too hard. The woman had shared everything she owned—her food, her bed, her home—and it just was not right to be taking her time and energy the way she was, for even though Jenny tried to help Mary, there was so little she really knew. As Miss Jane Dresden, she had never needed to know how butter was made, or how long to knead bread, or how hard to scrub clothes to get them clean but not wear holes into them. In all her daydreams of a tidy little cottage with rose gardens by the door and ivy creeping up the chimney, she had never gotten beyond the idyllic life of sitting by the hearth as the fire crackled, or walking in the fragrant woods collecting berries, or picking daisies in a sun-dappled meadow, or drinking tea on the doorstep while neat villagers strolled by and engaged her in conversation. Never had she imagined how much work there was in living when one had no servants.

Every morning the fire must be stirred to life and breakfast made. The cow must be milked, chickens fed, and eggs gathered, wood for the fire chopped, cooking, laundering, gardening, baking, sewing. . . . the list went on and on. Mary's daily routine was staggering in the amount of labor involved, and yet she still found time to tend to her baby and spin wool to make some extra money. And she did it all with a smile and a song. Jenny so far had mastered the simple tasks of feeding the chickens and gathering eggs, but milking Esther remained beyond her abilities. Butter churning had been a failure, for her arm strength had been inadequate for the job; the result had been a watery mess. And her attempt at bread-making was dismal, the loaf as heavy and dense as pudding. It would take years to learn it all, she was sure.

Staring into the fire, watching the flames dance and tangle, she knew that she should be leaving and there was no more delaying it, no more waiting until she had some perfect plan. It was time, and she could no longer mislead herself that there was any reason to stay. Already it was going to make things awkward for Mary when she must tell Gerry that her cousin had just left, without a word. But it was how it must be. Gerry was attracted to her and she to him, but what future did they have?

Just the day before she and Gerry had walked the hills—for only the second time; she could not fathom that she had known him such a short time!—and yet the way he had left her had made her think he was coming back with a question for her. And over the course of the rest of the long day and evening she had tried to tell herself she could make everything come out right in the end, that if Gerry's intention was marriage she would say yes and find a way to make it work. But it was hopeless; even in her rosiest imaginings she had known that Viscount Haven would not look favorably on one in his employ marrying his betrothed bride. It would be the height of awkwardness and she would not—*could* not—put Gerry in that position, imperiling his livelihood like that. The reality had come to her late in the night as she lay awake, sleepless, listening to Mary's even breathing beside her and the baby's soft gurgles. She would never be able to marry Gerry even if he asked her. It had to stop before they were entangled any more than they already were. She had never wanted to hurt anyone, but a man with as tender a heart as Gerry . . . She had to leave, and the time was now.

"I have enjoyed this time, Mary. You will never know how much this has meant to me."

Mary, sitting on the settle by her baby's cradle, looked up with a sad smile. "That almost sounds like good-bye, lass. You know yer welcome to bide here for as long as you need. I'll not ask questions."

"Why not?" Jenny asked. She moved to sit on the brick hearth and gazed up into Mary's honest eyes. "Don't mistake me, I have appreciated your forbearance. I have . . . I have secrets that, while not shameful, are not something I really want to talk about at this time. But why have you been so good to me, and without knowing a thing about me?"

Mary stared down at Molly in her painted cradle, the baby gurgling happily and waving her tiny fists. "I go on me guts, Jenny. I learned long ago that if there be one thing I can do, it be to judge folk. I have ne'er been wrong, an' I think you have yer reasons. It be none o' my business what they are. I was that worrit that you might mislead Gerry, but I see you fixin' to leave now, and I think it might well be that yer doin' so, so as not to hurt 'im." She looked up, her eyes sad. "I trust you," she finished, simply. "And I'll miss you."

There was a light tap at the door just then and Mary frowned. "Who could that be this late?" It was early evening, but already the weak April sun was descending, casting long shadows over the moors. She stood and plodded across the floor, kicking a small mat back into place. She opened the door, and said, "Ah, Gerry, we were just talkin' about you."

Jenny felt her heart thump. She had hoped to leave before seeing him again because it only got harder when he was near. They had only known each other a couple of days, but when he was close to her she could imagine a life where she was accepted for who she was inside, not based on who society said she was. She could imagine a lifetime of sharing and love with a gentle, quiet man like Gerry. It was illusion, a sweet madness that overtook her in his company. But alone with her thoughts she knew that there were too many reasons why it would never work and she was only going to hurt them both. All day long she had tried to lie to herself, tried to deny the knowledge that had stolen into her heart in the night, but honesty was inescapable. She must be circumspect. She must stay away from him as much as possible in this next hour or so. And she must leave. She would have to work out a plan that very night and leave on the morrow.

Mary ushered her friend in and he took a seat on the hearth, setting aside the unlit lantern he had brought to light his way home. Jenny moved to sit up on the settle, away from the disturbing heat he radiated. He gazed up at both women as Mary sat down beside her. "What lovely ladies," he said. "You can certainly see the family resemblance between you. What branch of the family are you from, Miss Jenny?"

Jenny glanced guiltily sideways at Mary, who was coloring, just as *she* was. Now she was placing Mary in the position that she must lie further to her friend; it was unconscionable! Gerry must wonder why such an innocuous question should raise such blushes. She had to escape. Coward that she was, she could not listen to her new friend forced to lie for her. "I . . . Mary, I just realized that we are not going to have enough water for morning. I will go draw some more and then we can put on some tea." It was one of the few skills she had mastered, drawing water from the well.

"I'll come with you and help, Miss Jenny. I'll carry the pail," Gerry said, jumping up.

"No," Jenny said, firmly, putting her hand on his shoulder and pushing him back down. Alone, with him, out in the dark? It was not a good idea at all, not when her lips still had the tender remembrance of his kisses lingering on them from the day before. "You have not had much time lately to visit with Mary. Please, just sit and I will return in a few moments. Please," she added, seeing the hesitation on his face. "Let me do what little I can to help my . . . my c—cousin."

Gerry let it go this once, though his chivalric response was to accompany her. He watched her pick up the pail and head out the door, closing it softly behind her. It was tempting to follow because stealing a kiss in the moonlight would delight his soul at that moment. He was agitated and he wasn't quite sure why. His grandmother's words rang in his ears. "Ask her to marry you." He had stared at her in amazement, because he had been just about to tell her that was what he was going to do and she stole his thunder. He was going to tell her that he would brook no interference in his life any longer, that he was going to marry where his heart was engaged. And then she said it so simply. "Marry Jenny." She had even gone so far as to say she thought he would get no interference from his family once they met Jenny. Puzzling, especially when one considered that his Grand had not even met the girl herself. How did she know? She had only his word for it that Jenny's manners would never raise a blush of shame in or out of the family circle.

And yet there was a ways to go, confessions to make, before he could ask her. Perhaps that was what was bothering him, the knowledge that he had yet to unburden himself to Jenny.

He turned his attention back to Mary. She looked worried. He reached up and took her hand. "Mary, what is wrong?"

She hesitated, but then said, "Gerry, I am that worrit about yer . . . about yer preference for Jenny."

"That is not your concern, Mary, but I know that her being family, it's natural that you should worry. Be comforted. My intentions toward your cousin are honorable. I—" He took a deep breath, squeezed his friend's hand, and then said, "Mary, I want to ask her to marry me."

He heard the swift intake of breath and he stared into her eyes. "What is it?"

"Ya can't, oh, Gerry, ya can't, really, you must not . . ."

"Why are you so upset? I know there will be some difficulty. I have yet to tell her who I really am, after all, and I know that will be a shock to her. But I have Grand's approval, and . . ."

"It's not that, Gerry . . . oh, I swore I wouldn't tell ye, but now I feel I must. Oh, Lord, what shall I do?"

"What is it Mary, is she . . . ?" A dreadful thought crossed his mind. "She is not married already, is she?"

"No . . . no, I don't think so, but I don't know, really. Gerry—"

Haven glanced at the door and said swiftly, "One minute, Mary. I . . . there is a slight complication and I need to tell you about it before Jenny comes back in. It's about Miss Dresden. With the girl still missing . . . I don't know what Pamela told you about her, but I think now that she has eloped, but still, until I find her I feel uneasy about asking Jenny to marry me, so I was hoping . . ."

"What are you blathering on about, Gerry?" Mary's round face was a mask of bewilderment. She shook her head and frowned, saying, "Who is this Miss Dresden? And eloped? What are ye talkin' about? *Who* are ye talkin' about?"

"Miss Dresden, the girl I am supposedly betrothed to."

Mary stared at him as if he had lost his wits and Gerry felt a swell of impatience. He needed to talk to Mary before Jenny came back in. "The girl who is missing, the one Pammy asked you about."

"Pamela didna ask about any girl. Leastways, not in my hearin'. What are ye talkin' about?"

"Idiot," he muttered, about his sister. He briefly reminded her about the family pressure on him to marry suitably—Mary knew much of that already—and told her about his mother's scheme to marry him to Miss Jane Dresden, of Bath, and the young lady's journey north to Yorkshire.

"But when she got to the inn," he continued, "she received a rather shocking letter from her mother and either that, or—well, I think she might have a lover with whom she eloped—caused her to leave the inn suddenly, making it look like a kidnapping. I worry that I am wrong about this and that she really *was* kidnapped. I have spent the last several days trying to find out where she has gone." He frowned into the fire and picked up a poker, jabbing at a log. "And yet if she was abducted, I would think the kidnappers would have come forward with a demand for money." He threw down the fire iron and passed one hand over his hair, muttering to himself, "And the note was not right. It was too well written. I worry though that she is somewhere out there—she disappeared that very afternoon, the last time I came to see you before your cousin arrived."

Mary, stunned into silence, was staring at the fireplace mantel. "Oh, my dear sweet Lord, Gerry!" she muttered. "Oh, my dear sweet Lord! Oh!"

"Mary, what's wrong? What is it?"

"Oh, Gerry, I have somethin' to tell ye. Somethin' . . . oh, my Lord!"

Jenny carried the heavy bucket up to the door and paused, putting it down to flex her poor hand. Much more of this work and her hands would be hardened and callused like Mary's were. Not that that was necessarily a bad thing, but she had always prided herself on her pretty hands. She was unfashionable in almost every other sense, with an undistinguished face, ordinary hair, and a too-plump figure, but her hands were perfect. Not anymore though. There was a blister on the right one. She picked at it and drew in a quick breath of air at the slice of pain. It stung!

She stared at the door before her, taking a deep breath. It was nerve-wracking and difficult being in the room with Gerry, knowing she was going to have to leave without ever telling him the truth. It just wasn't fair to him, she had decided, to put him in the position of being in opposition to his lordship. No matter what Miss Pamela said about Haven being a lamb! He was her brother and was likely to be indulgent with *her*. With a subordinate he would be a much different man, no doubt. As it was she was going to have to write Lord Haven a long letter telling him the whole truth and absolving Gerry and Mary of any wrongdoing.

She pulled the door open just a crack and bent over to pick up her pail. She heard her name, and, ashamed of herself but still overwhelmed by curiosity, she put her ear to the door.

Mary, still stunned by Gerry's statement, stuttered, "G-Gerry, it is *Jenny!* She is the girl. Or the girl is she. It has to be so! Jenny is this Miss Jane Dresden!"

"What are you talking about?" Perplexed by her babbled explanation, Gerry gazed at her warily as if she were mad.

Mary's mind raced. She remembered the night she had gone out to the barn, the girl had struck her immediately as gentry, even though she wore a serving girl's torn dress. Her modest clothing could not hide soft hands and perfect skin and did not change her well-modulated, cultured accents and graceful movements. But Gerry's information clarified everything. Jenny was no longer some poor girl running from an unwanted marriage or a lecherous uncle, but she was Gerry's supposed betrothed! Had she known all along who he was? Had she been playing them *all* for fools? But no, surely there was not a woman bold enough in the world to play the part of a serving wench with the man who was supposed to be her husband. What did it mean?

"Mary," Gerry said impatiently grasping her hands, "what are you talking about?"

His raised voice awoke Molly and Mary took a few minutes to soothe the baby and gather her thoughts. Finally she took a deep breath and looked into Gerry's honest blue eyes, blazing out in the dim light from the fire. "Gerry," she said, calmly, "listen to me carefully. I think Jenny is this Miss Jane Dresden."

"What are you—"

The door creaked and Mary, with a muttered imprecation for the wind, stood and bustled over to it, pulling it closed. "Hear me out, Gerry!" she said. "Four nights ago or so, that same evening after you had bin here for dinner, I heard a noise out in the barn. I went to look, 'cause the door latch has not been working right an' tight. I found . . . I found a girl . . . a young woman with a torn dress, huddled in the corner of the barn, wet an' cold an' scared. I took her in. She slept through the whole next day. When she woke up, I asked her who she was and she told me her name was Jenny. She said . . . she said she was a lady's maid, an' that she got lost."

"Why did you tell me she was your cousin?" Gerry said, pain in his deep voice.

"She was frightened and I didna want to have to explain her presence. She wasn't tellin' the truth, I knew that much. I didna know then what she was running from, but she was so frightened, and I thought it simpler . . ."

"Good God, Mary. Simpler? Why didn't you trust me?"

"I don't know!" Mary said, near tears. "I bin that worrit, Gerry, knowin' I lied to you. After the first day I wanted to tell you, but I didna know how! And I promised her!"

"This means . . ." Gerry had risen and was pacing. "This means that your supposed cousin, Jenny, is the girl who is supposed to be the next Viscountess Haven!"

Both of them paused, not saying another word for a long few minutes. It was a lot to take in, but suddenly Haven started laughing, his laughter a rich, low chuckle, ascending into a bellow of laughter that startled Molly again, raising from her a wail of fear. "I'm sorry, Mary." He gasped, trying to catch his breath while his friend tended to her baby. "But it is just too funny! I came here tonight to propose to her, not knowing that our marriage has already been set up and if we had just let . . . if either one of us had just told the truth . . . oh, this is *too* rich. I do believe that Grand knew all along, the plaguey old besom! That is why she urged me to propose!"

Mary shook her head, a rueful expression on her pretty face. "I'm *that* sorry, Gerry. I should have told you she was not my cousin, but I wanted the girl to tell you herself. She was so frightened, and I didna feel right breakin' faith with her. What do you think made her run, then?"

Gerry sobered and sat back down on the hearth. "God, I think it was probably me, or rather Viscount Haven, she was running from. Knowing her now, knowing how she feels about society and all the stiff-rumped jackasses that people it—and some of the things she said about Viscount Haven . . ." He passed a hand over his face and scrubbed his eyes. "Mary, I have to tell her, reassure her . . . if she doesn't want to marry me . . ."

"But things are different now," Mary said, laying Molly back down in the cradle. "If I am not mistaken," she said, casting her old friend a sly look, "you have both found a spot of romance between ye. I think she'll forgive you yer masquerade, Gerry, when she finds out the dreaded Viscount Haven is her very own country swain. You've both bin wanderin' around smellin' of April and May ever since the moment you first saw her a'sittin' on my hearth."

"You're right there. I have never seen such a lovely young lady and I felt like I knew the instant we met that I could love her. But she is lovely inside, too, Mary, is that not true? Did you not find her so?" He looked to her anxiously, trusting Mary's instincts.

Mary smiled kindly. "Yes, she is truly a sweet young lady and without an ounce of pretension in her bones. I still canna get my mind around her bein' this Miss Dresden! I knew she was special from the very first moment I saw her, but I didna know why." She thought a moment, staring into the fire as it crackled and glowed, an ember popping and causing a twig to tumble and flame up on the hearth floor. "Mayhap it be wrong—an' the *lies* both of you have told . . ." She shook her head in dismay. "And myself, too. I'm not one to cast the first stone. But I'm *glad* for this charade, for it gave the two of you time to fall in love without yer ma and yer sister interferin'. This might never have happened otherwise, both of you being stiff and formal and on yer best company manners. When you just thought she was me cousin, Jenny, you were yerself, not the fearsome Lord Haven some in the village talk about."

Gerry looked chagrined. "I find it hard to be myself when I know people are looking to me to be 'Viscount Haven.' I have never fit the role."

"Ah, Gerry, you mayn't know it, but you fit it to perfection. If you would only let yerself be, and know yer good enough, just as you are."

Gerry, flushing from her compliment, looked to the door. "God, where is she? I want to tell her, I want to ask her . . ." Alarm replaced impatience. He stood and paced to the door. "She should be back by now." He threw open the door and tipped over a full pail of water. One full pail of water.

The next Viscountess Haven!

The night air was cold—dusk had swiftly replaced twilight and the gloom was gathering apace—and she was unprepared. Protected only by her woolen shawl, *Mary's* woolen shawl, she stumbled over a tree root and fell, but got up and sped over the high moor. This time should have been easier, for she had been over the fells and moors a few times with Gerry and knew her way to the Lesley, which ran eventually through the town of Lesleydale. And yet everything looked different by moonlight.

Gerry. Now he knew who she was—she would never forget the pain in his voice as he berated Mary for telling her that Jenny was her cousin—and now he would hate her for her dissembling. She was Miss Jane Dresden, granddaughter to an earl, niece to a baroness, as had been drummed into her head from birth.

And the next Viscountess Haven. By Gerry's own words condemned to a life of stiff and formal living among the aristocracy, wife of a peer of the realm, Mother to the next heir, her main purpose in life bearing that one necessary son.

As she wandered, shivering in the chill of an April evening, she thought back to the trip north and the gradual dawning of her knowledge that once at Haven Court she would be bullied and harassed, if not by the magnificent Lord Haven himself, then by her aunt and his mother. She had never been good at standing up for herself; it was why she had ended up immured in Bath, which she despised, living with her mother in the suffocating atmosphere of invalidism that surrounded the woman at all times, rather than pursuing her dream of life in a little village or the country, where the air was clean and the people friendly.

And then to find, in a letter that must have followed them all the way north, that her mother had married that charlatan Mr. Jessup, with his fake smile and his cloying ways. It was a betrayal of everything her mother had told her to convince her to go north, and it made her own promises meaningless. In that moment she had felt the urgent desire—no, *need*—to get away, to escape, to leave behind everything that was constricting her life into the unnatural shape it took. Who would it be hurting? No one. Who would even care, really? Again, no one.

And so she had concocted a scheme, a mad, unplanned, wild flight from responsibility. She had scribbled a note— she did not even remember now what she wrote, but she had tried to make it sound as unschooled as she could—and had, while supposedly asking for something for her aunt, noted where the laundry was kept and her escape route. In her whole cloistered life she had never done anything so impetuous; she had been frightened, but exhilarated, too. It had seemed like an adventure at the time.

She had surreptitiously placed the note in the stable while conferring with Lady Mortimer's driver, a surly old man named Grouse. Then she had manufactured a reason to go downstairs—the baroness was always wanting something that Jane was required to run and do, and so that was the simple part of the plan to effect—and had swiftly raced down the stairs, her pearls and money secure in the bosom of her dress, changed into a servant's dress that was in the laundry area, and raced into the stable yard. That had been her undoing. She could still smell the drunken bar patron's fetid breath and feel him and his companion's grasping, groping hands as they muttered unintelligible demands and took unconscionable liberties. If it had not been for another man's shouted warning and query as to what was going on, she would never have gotten away.

Shocked and horrified by treatment such as that, she had raced away, not realizing until she was well gone that though she still retained her hold on her carriage dress, bundled under one arm, she had lost her pearls and small embroidered purse of money somewhere in the struggle, likely when her dress was torn. Perhaps they were still lying somewhere in that stable yard under a bale of hay or in some filthy corner. She had stumbled out of the stableyard, and although she had intended to take her proper clothes with her to change into once safely out of the inn, she had been frightened and they had weighed her down, so she thrust her bundle of clothing in the first hedgerow she had found. It was all a blur now, the incident in the stable frightening her so badly it had made her hasty and careless.

And now what was she going to do, out on the moors alone again, and at night? It was just like the first night. She had no money, not even her pearls to sell or pawn, and she was dressed in the garb of a serving wench at the inn. She was running from the very people who had been so kind to her because she could not face Gerry's pain and anger. She had hurt him and placed him in an impossible dilemma, and it served her right for her deception if she must suffer a little now.

She wandered down a slope and glanced up at the sky. It was darkening but the moon was still out, allowing just enough light to see the ground. She could not ignore the possibility that God was having a good laugh at her while teaching her a lesson. Her old vicar, whose kind wife had taught the lady-school she had gone to as a very young girl, had always said that each person was put in their position in life, and to scorn that position was a sin. Well, she had struggled against her lot in life as the protected, pampered daughter of privilege. She had never fit in, not in the salons and parlors, nor the ballrooms and assembly rooms. She had no talent for idle chitchat, she could not gossip, she disdained artifice, and without it in London one was a pariah.

Had she made her own life more difficult by placing obstacles in her own path? Perhaps. But she had always had her dream life to sustain her, the illusion that if only she could find her little cottage, her small, friendly village, the workaday world of the common folk, she could find happiness. Now she knew that she did not even fit there. She was wretched at cooking, hopeless at household chores, and useless at farmwork. Her fantasy was a chimera, dissolving in the cool, calm reason of the night.

The sky was darkening and clouds were rolling in over the moon. She was close to tears, but as she began to shiver, she realized that the wetness on her cheeks was not tears rolling down them but rain. It was starting to spit, and then drizzle. She must, absolutely must, find someplace to shelter for the night. She remembered the shepherds' rude huts Gerry had pointed out to her on one of their walks. That would have to do. With a new determination she glanced around her, took her bearings from the landscape, and set out to find one.

Fourteen

Haven flew out the cottage door, tripping over the bucket in his haste. How much had she heard? How long had she been gone? *Why did she run?*

Where was she?

Spring evenings still closed in fairly early and the dark was gathering, creeping up over the moor and stealing into all of the hollows. Moonlight peeped and winked down at him, but with an experienced eye he could see the clouds form in the west, ready to steal across the sky. Any time now the moon would be obscured and perhaps there would even be rain. Mary came to the door behind him. "Where has she gone, Gerry?"

"I don't know," he said tersely, scanning the valley in which Mary's stone cottage nestled. "And I don't know how long she has been gone, nor what she overheard. Is that why she ran? Does she despise me as Viscount Haven that much?" There was an ache of pain in his voice. "I have to look for her." He turned back to his old friend and saw the worry and fear in her eyes.

"Gerry, she doesna know the moors, how cold it gets at night this time of year. Lord help her, it can even snow on the high fells." She pulled the shawl close around her shoulders and shivered. "She's from . . . well, if she is Miss Dresden, as you say, she is from Bath. This is no Bath."

Grimly, Gerry nodded. He stared out into the dark. "I'll

find her. If it is any comfort, Mary, we walked these hills together and I pointed out the way to Lesleydale to her. Maybe she has headed for town."

"I hope so." Molly started to cry, a thin wail that changed to a lusty bawling that signaled her urgent desire for feeding, and Mary looked back into the cottage.

"Go back to your babe, Mary." He clutched her shoulders, gave them a squeeze, and pushed her back into the cottage. "I will look for Jenny."

Tearful, Mary turned and gazed at her old friend. She wrung her hands together in her apron. "Please find her, Gerry."

"I'll do my best."

But his best wasn't good enough. With only weak moonlight streaking through the trees to guide him, he had to crawl at an invalid's pace. She had only a few minutes', at most, lead; where could she have gone so quickly? Was she running? She was fleet of foot when she wanted to be, he knew that from experience. He took advantage of a brief glitter of moonlight and stood atop a moor, gazing around him, turning in a circle and trying to imagine in which direction she would go. Most of the hillsides were barren, but here and there the sightlines were obscured by gorse and brushy hummocks. Would she have headed toward Lesleydale? Surely that was the way she would go!

He strode down the moor, but the clouds were closing in and he lost the moonlit path he had had. He had to slow and go by memory. Damn but he was an idiot not to bring a lantern! But to go back for one now would be to lose valuable time. As he walked, he muttered a prayer. God help him find her. It was cold and windy and . . . and yes, it was beginning to rain.

Damn the night! And damn his own mouth. What had he said? How much had she heard? That constant refrain raced through his brain, torturing his thoughts. He damned the chance that his and Mary's conversation had occurred when Jenny should hear them. If only he could have seen her face-to-face and explained! If only he had told her the truth the day before, when they were alone and walking on the moors and by the Lesley. Would she then have told him who she was? Would she have confessed so they could both have a good laugh? Then he could have gone down on one knee and asked her the question it was now too late for.

Now she would hate him forever for his masquerade. And he could not blame her. What was she to think? She must have thought, when she heard who he was, that he was toying with her, seducing her. With his new knowledge of her true identity he looked back on their conversations and recognized the powerful, deep-grained streak of skepticism toward the nobility that underlay many of her statements. Knowing he had concealed his identity and made such advances to her, thinking her a serving girl, she must have assumed that his intentions were dishonorable.

And how could he blame her? He had been to London, had had his Seasons, and had found the same distasteful level of artifice and pretension, snobbery and condescension as she evidently had. Men pledged their lives to the ladies they took as wives, and took a mistress in secret, or contented themselves with raiding the servants' hall for sexual conquests. He must have seemed just such a cad, just what she would have expected of Lord Haven, who could not even be bothered coming to London to court a wife but had to have one delivered like the daily post. If he could just find her and explain—

He moved on through the night, pulling his shabby jacket up over his ears against the cold wind and pelting rain.. But the moors were vast, and though he hoped she was moving toward Lesleydale, he had only that general direction to go on. There were a thousand ways to get there and that was assuming she was headed in that direction and that she had not gotten lost in the dark! As it got later the gloom closed in until it was almost impenetrable. He searched and called out her name, but there was no answering hail. She was alone in the moors. His Jenny, alone and cold and wet.

He stood at the top of a long sweep of lonely moor. It was so very dark the hills were just vast, sooty humps looming at the edge of vision. He felt her out there, somewhere, alone and fearful. He knew she was afraid. He felt her desperation in his bones, in his very marrow. And she no longer felt she could trust anyone. Perhaps he was being overly dramatic, but he felt as if he had let her down. Even though she, too, had been playing a part, was his role not more despicable for being so unnecessary?

She, at least, was running from something. Him, to his shame and horror; she was running from him. He was just playacting.

As the moon found a break in the clouds for one brief, shimmering moment, casting the valley below him into silvery light and charcoal shadows, he found the path toward Lesleydale. He knew that for him nothing had changed since finding out she was really Miss Jane Dresden, and not Jenny, servant girl. He was in love with her, needed her.

But what did *she* feel? Had she been creeping toward love, and had the knowledge that he was not who he said he was dashed that burgeoning feeling to the ground and into a million pieces?

There would be time to worry about that later. Right now, fear gnawing at the pit of his belly, he knew she was lost. How was he going to find her? It certainly would not be by standing on the top of a moor and contemplating. With renewed determination he set out down the long slope toward the Lesley.

The clouds closed in again and the rain started, this time more than just a spit. The wind blew it sideways until it felt like needles in his face. He fought a growing panic. Where was she? The temperature was plummeting and the wind rising. If she was unsheltered she would quickly be freezing cold. He bent his body into the wind and strode on, calling her name, hoping against hope to find some indication that he was on the right path.

Hours later he still had not found her and he had to admit, weary and heartsick as he was, that he was not going to find her in the dark. He trudged homeward through the steady rain after stopping briefly at Mary's cottage to report his lack of progress. His friend had tried to calm his worries, but he could see on her face the dread. She was as worried as he and knew, as he did, what a night on the moors with no shelter would be like. Even in August it would be cold and lonely, but it was only April, and in Yorkshire April was a cruel month, full of rapid changes and hard, cold winds.

Haven Court finally came into view. At that moment he despised the old priory, hated the ancient stone and square lines. It made him who he was, and who he was was not who Jenny—Jane, Jenny what would he call her now?— wanted. In the morning he would take his horse and ride every acre. He would enlist every one of his men and get more from the village. Wherever she was, he would find her. And when he did he would make sure she knew that he would make it his mission in life to make her happy, whatever that took. Likely his absence, he thought, gloomily.

Wearily, he trudged up the steps and into the Court. The great hall echoed back the slosh and squish of every footstep. He was almost to the staircase—it was late, and though Bartlett had attended him, he had waved off further help— when his grandmother popped out of her suite, still fully dressed. He groaned inwardly. She was like a cuckoo bird that popped out of a clock he had seen once that someone had brought back from a European tour. She never seemed to sleep.

"Haven," she said, imperiously. "Come!" She disappeared back into her suite and so Haven was left with no alternative but to follow.

She was making him a cup of her infamous dark tea. She handed him the cup, balancing precariously on her cane; as he took a sip he coughed at the fiery flavor. She had seen his state and had spiked it with a generous dollop of fine brandy. He eased back into a chair and closed his eyes, taking another long draft.

"Have you made any progress?" she asked. Her maid creaked around in the background, but with a wave of Grand's cane the woman stopped what she was doing and left the room. "I know you have been out all evening; have you anything to report?"

Haven sat up, put his empty cup aside, and clenched his hands together, leaning forward on his knees. "Actually, Grand, there has been a most . . . startling development."

She sat down opposite him, her brilliant blue eyes gleaming with interest. "Go on."

He paused, but his brief concern that the news might be too much for her heart was rapidly calmed. She was made of sterner stuff than that. "Simply put, my Jenny is also Miss Jane Dresden. They are one and the same. Miss Dresden has never been missing but has been, all this time, at Mary's cottage."

If he expected an open mouth or expression of astonishment, he was to be disappointed. "So you have finally figured that out, have you?" There was a tone of exasperated affection in her voice.

Haven took a moment, but finally said, "You *knew?* How could you possibly . . ." He shook his head. He had briefly considered that she might know, but had dismissed it as impossible. Completely and utterly impossible! She never got out anywhere; she could not have met Jenny/Jane, nor even spoken to Mary.

"Never took you for a slowtop, grandson, but how could you not have figured it out for yourself? And I thought *you* were the brilliant one in the family. There is a girl missing. A girl, coincidentally of the same general description, arrives at Mary's cottage at the exact same time. It did not take a mathematician to ponder the long odds on that coincidence. How could you not even consider it?"

"Because Mary *assured* me she was her cousin! Mary does have a cousin named Jenny, and . . . Grand, why would I suspect anything different?"

"I did," she said. "I have suspected it for a couple of days, now. So, you great looby, have you settled things between you? Am I to meet your future wife? Why is she not here?"

He groaned and held his aching head in his hands. His clothes were soaked through, and he felt that beginning of a fever in his cheeks. But what made him feel even worse was knowing that his Jenny was out there in this wretched, *abominable* weather. "Lord, Grand, if you knew, why did you not tell me? It would have saved a lot of trouble."

"It was rather entertaining watching you all go through such circus contortions trying to figure it out. And I could not be sure, you know. I had only the use of my own brain where other people are able to get about and ask questions." The last was said with asperity. "So, where is the girl? Where is my future granddaughter-in-law? I wish to meet her."

"You will have to wait," Haven said, irritated. "You will have to wait until I find her!"

"What do you mean?"

He stood, agitated, and paced the carpet. "Damn it, Grand, she has disappeared again. She overheard Mary and me talking, as we both figured out what the other was concealing, and she disappeared. It seems her repugnance for the Viscount Haven is so great she cannot even stand to be near me."

His grandmother went rigid, her face suddenly gray, and she said, "She has disappeared, and on a night such as this?

Haven . . . if I . . . oh, Lord, if I had only told you it was she. Where did she go? Where *could* she go?"

Mastering his anger, Haven slumped back into a chair, lowered his head, and stared at his feet. "Oh, Grand, do not blame yourself. You could not be sure, after all. It is my doing. If I had not concealed my identity in the first place . . ."

Her brows drawn down and her arthritic hands picking at her shawl, the old woman said, slowly, "Are you sure she overheard you? Are you *certain* that is what happened?"

He explained about the bucket of water in front of the door, and how it was ajar, and his own surmise that she had opened the door a little so she could bring in the bucket and had overheard him and Mary talking.

"I still do not understand," Grand said, "why Mary Cooper saw fit to conceal Miss Dresden's identity!"

"Mary didn't know about Miss Dresden," Haven said, quick to defend his friend. "I . . . I don't talk about my life here at the Court with her much. It is where I go to get away from such things. So she knew nothing about my supposed betrothal and Miss Dresden's disappearance. I . . . I intended to ask her if she had seen a girl, but I was caught up in that idiotic playacting in front of Jenny and I did not want to say anything that would reveal my true identity. And then Pammy said she had asked them if they had seen or heard anything about the missing young woman. I . . . I suppose she asked Jenny . . . uh, Miss Dresden, but—" He shook his head. "Scott was ne'er so right. *'O what a tangled web we weave . . .'* "

Grand was not satisfied. She stubbornly demanded, "But *why* did Mary claim Miss Dresden as her cousin? Did she not tell you?"

Haven shrugged, weary of the subject and sick at heart. If *he* didn't care why Mary had done it, why should his grandmother? But there was nothing for it but to tell the old woman what he could. "Mary said that the girl was in her barn, shivering and cold and clearly upset. She was wet, her dress was torn, she was lost. Mary was shielding her from too much questioning. At first she thought the girl had been attacked, perhaps even . . . even raped."

The dowager nodded. "I see." She pondered for a moment, her wrinkled face set in a frown. "I suppose I can understand that. With what we now know, I think Miss Dresden must have been the girl who was attacked by those idiot drunkards outside of the Tippling Swan; it would have been a truly alarming experience for a gently bred girl. But Mary should have trusted you, Haven. There is no man in the world more fit to comfort a frightened woman than you."

He gave her a confused look.

She smiled. "So little self-knowledge," she murmured. "Haven, you are the gentlest man I have ever known, and one of the strongest. Your sex is not generally known for its finer feelings, but you are a tender soul."

"Tell the folks in the village that!" He snorted, embarrassed by his grandmother's unusual commendation.

"You hide it well, grandson, under a dour exterior, for fear of being hurt, I think."

"Makes me sound like a woman," he complained.

"And what is wrong with that?" she said fiercely, eyes blazing. "The female of every species has more innate strength than the male."

He shook his head, and said, "Grand, you know I meant nothing by it." He sighed deeply. "What am I going to do? How am I going to find her?"

The old woman's lined face took on a thoughtful expression. "I hate to think of the poor girl out on the moors at night. However, she is presumably not a dolt. She will shelter and in the morning you will find her, Haven. I know you will."

Haven stood and stretched. He was weary beyond the limits of his endurance, almost, but he did not think he would sleep. How could he, knowing Jenny was out on the moors somewhere, alone, cold, frightened? First light would see him mounted and away.

Jenny huddled on a straw pallet in the corner of a tiny shack she had been lucky enough to stumble across. She had wandered for far too long, until she did not recognize any landmarks. She was cold and wet, shivering with misery, and could do nothing more until daylight. It had occurred to her at some point that she had been moving downstream along the Lesley, when the village of Lesleydale was upstream. Come morning she would have to figure out what to do, but for now it was enough to pull her shawl around her and huddle against a wall and think.

The night had taken on a nightmare quality, a waking dream of cold and fear and confusion. Time had no meaning anymore. The moon had disappeared into the clouds and the rain had dissuaded her from looking to the sky for guidance. Perhaps she should not have run.

Well of *course* she shouldn't have run! It seemed that from the moment she set foot on the carriage to leave Bath, she had been taking one misstep after another. It was past time she started acting like an adult and not a silly chit with more hair than wit.

But she had been afraid that Gerry, knowing who she was, would feel compelled to take her to Haven Court and she didn't know if she was ready for that yet. Especially now, when it would be known how foolish she had been. For she had been *beyond* foolish, she had been cowardly and weak.

She was a grown woman. No person alive could force her into a marriage she did not want. And just because she found it hard to withstand excessive bullying under the guise of "persuasion" did not mean she could not learn to say no. She sat up straighter. She was intelligent. She was not without courage, though one would not know it by the actions she had taken in the past week. But the first shock of finding out her mother had married that weasel, Mr. Jessup, and realizing she had no home to go back to—that must be the excuse for her ludicrous actions.

And in the end it had led to a new knowledge of herself. She could stand on her own. Oh, perhaps she had not proved it yet, but she began to be certain she could.

She had lost Gerry with her foolish lies, but then she had never really had him. He had cared for Jenny, a servant girl. Miss Jane Dresden would be a different matter. She had to accept that and plan her own life now.

But first she must, in the morning, straighten out the mess she had made. She was still unashamed that she had upset her aunt, for if the woman was truly worried, it would be a salubrious experience. Perhaps she would begin to see that she could not force her own ideas upon others and expect them to fall in joyfully with her plans.

The wall was cold and Jenny felt the frigidity settling into her bones. She longed to curl up and sleep but the pallet of straw was, she felt certain, alive with vermin; she was not so tired that she could stand the thought of what might crawl through her hair in the night. As it was she could hear scuttling in the corners and once had felt something move next to her booted foot.

She was so very weary, but it was more than just tiredness. It had more to do with a deep down exhaustion, the burden of always doing what others expected. It was what she had hated about London, where every move one made was for public perusal. A misstep, and she had made many, could lead to social ostracism. That was not necessarily an unhappy outcome if she was solely guided by her own wants, but she had deeply wanted to make her mother happy and happiness, for Mrs. Dresden, was a matter of public acceptance.

But no more. Miss Jane Dresden, Jenny to her closest

friends and her old Scottish nanny, could live for herself now and would. She had come to the painful understanding that there was no escaping your life, there was only dealing with it. What form "dealing with it" would take she was not sure, but the morning would see her new life begin. At least it would once she found her way to Lesleydale.

Despite her intentions to remain awake through the night, she felt the drifting, hazy numbness of sleep overtake her and she was soon adrift in the arms of a forgiving Morpheus.

Fifteen

The morning dawned with a brilliant display of rosy light from the east and Jenny awoke, confused and stiff, aching in every joint. She awoke to the miserable awareness that she had been excessively foolish the night before and had, through her own actions, made many people unhappy. She lay, staring at the rough timber of the roof above her, feeling the prickling of the straw pallet through her dress. What must Mary be thinking? And Gerry? Especially Gerry. He likely headed out to find her and who knew how long he would have wandered before giving up?

She stretched, rolling her shoulders and moving to sit on the edge of the low, crude wooden structure that held the musty straw pallet. How she had taken for granted all her life the presence of servants for the simplest things! She attempted to comb her ratted hair out with her fingers. It was hopeless and she no doubt looked like a madwoman. The Dresdens had not lived lavishly, indeed her mother had oft lamented their "impoverished" state, but Jenny now understood that she had accepted without a second thought simple comforts like hot food and tea prepared by other hands and served to her on pretty plates.

Tea! How she longed for a cup of tea, she thought, trying to swallow, her mouth dry with the dust of the straw and dirt floor. A beam of morning sun found its way through a chink in the wood walls, and she saw how dirty her once-fine hands were. She would need to wash in the Lesley just to be bearable to herself. And that was *another* thing she had overlooked—a hot bath whenever she wanted one. Clean clothes, warm fires, fragrant mattresses and linens; she had accepted them all, taking them as part of nature like the budding of the trees and the blooming of daffodils. She had thought that a simpler life in a cottage would be endless sweet and summery days of picking flowers and strolling country lanes, drinking tea in the garden, gentle conversation with the cottage cat. Evenings were to be taken up with reading and sewing and chatting about the day.

Instead, as evidenced by Mary's life, living, for the poor, was a constant struggle that they expected and accepted without question or complaint. They were accustomed to long hours, hard labor, inconvenience, cold, and conditions that could only kindly be called simple. Call them rather rough, often inadequate, occasionally brutal and squalid. And yet Mary, Jenny knew, considered herself fortunate, and indeed she was. She had a home. After her husband died, the right of her accommodation died with him. She could well have been cast upon the charity of the parish, but instead she was allowed to stay in her snuggery. And she had animals, chickens, and a cow, she had firewood, thanks to Gerry, who made sure her woodpile was well stocked, and she had her spinning to bring in extra money with which to purchase "luxuries," like tea and flour, sugar, molasses. She traded for other things, like eggs for honey, butter for salt.

Jenny moved her aching legs, cramped by the cold pallet, and tottered out the door to find a place to relieve herself. And that was yet *another* luxury she would never again take for granted—a chamber pot, and a maidservant to empty it.

Oh, for a hot cup of tea, she thought again, groaning at the ache of muscles and smelling the dampness of her skirts. She was distasteful even to herself. There was nothing romantic about poverty, she decided. She had had too little contact with the realities of life before this experience; never would she be so mistaken again.

Her crude morning ablutions completed, she looked about herself.

Ah, but the simple life *did* have the occasional compensation. She took in a deep breath of untainted air and gazed out over a dewy landscape sparkling in the early spring sunshine, beaming happily down on the moor that the night before had been a dark and threatening wilderness. A mist rose from the grass and drifted, whirled into threads and fingers by the breeze that flitted up the moor. She glanced back at her shelter, finding that it was a crude shepherd's hut, little more than a daub and wattle shack on a low-rising hill.

The valley of the Lesley spread out below her, the jewel green trees following it like an emerald necklace. In the hazy distance, the valley fog lying like a comforting blanket among the dwellings, was the village of Lesleydale. She was not so far from it after all! During those long hours of wandering she must have circuitously made her way closer and closer. Granted, distances were likely deceiving, she thought, in this open country, but still, it couldn't be more than five miles.

Filled with a new determination, she vowed that it was time to stop being a coward and start taking control of her life. Perhaps she had limited options—as an unmarried young woman that was indubitably true—but she was also firmly on the shelf. After this debacle no one would consider her marriageable. Perhaps a cottage, after all, in the countryside near Bath, with a respectable companion and a couple of servants. Definitely a couple of servants. Perhaps three or four. For her there was no joy in the labor inherent in a life without them. She turned her mind firmly away from Gerry and the life of love she had envisioned with him. She absolutely *would* not endanger his livelihood; Lord Haven would no doubt be furious at her hoax. He would not look kindly on one in his employ marrying his betrothed, especially since it meant she was rejecting *him* in the process! Even if Gerry had asked her—her heart throbbed at the memory of his kisses and caresses, but she put a halt to her wayward thoughts—even if he had asked her to marry him, she would have had to say no.

New determination in her step and in her heart, she took her bearings and moved off toward Lesleydale.

"Is it true?" Pamela said, jumping down from the bottom step in the great hall in a most unladylike fashion. Her silky skirts bounced and floated around her slim legs.

Haven, wearing his disreputable old clothes again—he did not know how long he would be or where he would have to go to find Jenny—was ready to head out the door toward the stable. "Is what true?"

"Is that jolly girl, Jenny, *really* Miss Dresden?"

"Yes, infant," he said, ruffling her curls with a casual caress. "They are one and the same."

"And are you going to marry her?" She hopped on one foot.

"No . . . yes . . . I don't know!"

"Well, make up your mind," she said, settling down and staring at him quizzically.

"I have to find her first. And then, well, it is not so easy. She has an aversion to . . . to my position that makes it highly doubtful that she will wish to marry me, now that she knows me as Haven." He nodded to a servant, who brought him a canvas sack containing food and water. If she was lost he might be gone for some time trying to find her and he did not want to be without provisions. He was taking one of his best hunters with him and would stop at Mary's first to try to pick up Jenny's scent.

"Ah yes, Grand told me about your little . . . mmm, *'indiscretion,'* I think she called it. How romantic!" She clutched her hands together and struck a giddy pose, eyes rolling upward to peer into the vaulted reaches of the great hall. "The great lord poses as a simple shepherd lad to gain the love of the maiden, who in turn is disguising herself as a simple serving wench, when really she is a great heiress and niece—or is it cousin?—to an earl or a duke, or a marquis, or whatever!"

Haven gave her a quelling look and she giggled. "Well, really, Haven! It is just too deliciously Goldsmithian, if there is such a word! She Stoops to Conquer. He Stoops to Conquer. They *All* Stoop to Conquer." Her expression becoming more serious, Pamela said, "But truly, that is ridiculous! How can she dislike a title? I thought she was a sensible sort, but if she is going to take against a silly title when she likes the man behind it well enough, then I think she must not be so very . . ."

"Stop prattling!" Haven glanced over and saw he had hurt his favorite sister. He tweaked her cheek, shouldered the canvas sack, and said, "Sorry, poppet, but I must go. I do not know why she has taken against the title so, but when we talked—she did not know who I was then, remember—she said much against the titled nobility. I fear it is an old and ingrained prejudice against some of the more frivolous and insensitive of our class."

"But Grand said . . . and you had all that time together. Maybe now that she knows it is you and that you are not some ridiculous, puffed-up man milliner, like some of the titled noddies we met in London, she will reconsider."

Haven smiled. "I can hope, brat, but I do not think it will make a jot of difference. After all, she ran away again, did she not?"

"Coward," Pamela said, with a disparaging sniff.

"Not everyone has your courage, infant. And not everyone has been raised so indulgently. I have always let you say what you will; even when you were younger I let you run wild and did not even spank you when you so often, so *richly* deserved it. But most young ladies feel a certain inability to say what they really want or need. We will be charitable toward Miss Dresden until we know her story." It was a warning as much as a statement.

"I suppose so," the girl said, wistfully, adding, "She seemed so jolly. I should like a sister like that instead of the plaguey one I have."

Haven held his tongue. He did not see a happy resolution to this saga. He would have to be satisfied with helping Miss Dresden—Jenny—as much as possible. It horrified him to think that she was running away because she could not bear the thought of being tied to him for life. When he had agreed to allow her to come up to Yorkshire—though it had never been said, it was done with the knowledge that he would be looking her over, much as one would a mare before purchasing—he had found it repugnant even then when it was only his own feelings he was considering, but he had never stopped to consider what the young lady was thinking and feeling. It was so much what was done, so much a part of life for his class, that he had assumed that she understood the rules of the game and was content to abide by them.

But he feared his own reputation in London circles was not altogether as a bright and shining example of noble manliness. The Seasons he had spent in London—years ago now but still vivid in his memory—had been little better than torture and he knew it had brought out all of his worst qualities, a tendency to sullen surliness and an uncertain temper. He had been brooding and dour, certain that every joke was at his expense and all laughter aimed in his direction. Not an attractive image to attain but there it was, it was too late to do anything about it now. If she had heard of him at all in advance, it would not have been a happy picture to form in her mind. And now, knowing she had likely been bullied into coming . . . it did not bear thinking about. He set off without delay, scorning accompaniment. The other teams of men he sent out across the fells. But his fervent hope was that he found her himself.

* * *

It was not as simple, Jenny found, as following the Lesley. At some point in the day, she had become confused by a branching of the river and had followed the wrong branch. As a result, afternoon was waning by the time she thought she was on the right track. Even exhausted as she was, she dreaded stopping to ask for help, though she would have to if she ran out of daylight or energy.

And she *was* deeply weary, down to her very bones. Her cheeks were burning from their unaccustomed exposure to the sun. Her nose was running, her eyes scratchy and dry, and her body was drooping along with her spirits as she finally found the bridge that crossed over the Lesley into the village of Lesleydale. It was a most picturesque village, she realized now, nestled snugly on the slope of a hill, but as tired as she was, its beauty could not touch her as it might have at another time.

She paused to catch her breath on the humped stone bridge and stared up at the tiny, winding village of stone houses, smoke curling from the chimneys. The inn was near the river, if she remembered right. She could only hope it was not too far now, because she felt that she only had a finite number of footsteps remaining in her strength before she collapsed, utterly spent. She plodded across the bridge, over the sparkling Lesley. Quaint stone and brick houses huddled close together, their white-painted windows covered in fresh curtains and their doors painted cream and azure, apple green and even primrose. The first buds of spring flowers were pushing through the earth in tiny garden plots squeezed in beside stone steps. If she had been in a mood to admire she would have been charmed by the sight. As it was she just hoped that each weary footstep found her closer to a bed.

She passed by an elderly, hunched woman who gave her a startled look and bustled away from her. Jenny wondered what she looked like. She had been tidy enough when she left Mary's cottage the night before, but she had wandered the moors for hours in a stiffening breeze and drizzle, then had sheltered in a hut on a straw pallet and had wandered again all day. She touched her hair and was alarmed at how it felt, like a bird's unsuccessful first nest. Her finger-combing that morning had not done one jot of good. And she was so very weary and hot and hungry. She had slaked her thirst in the sparkling springwater of a gill that fed the Lesley, but food had not been a thought nor a possibility.

The inn could not come into sight too soon. And there it was. She sighed. Her strange odyssey, living the life of a class so different from her own well-tended existence, was over. Wearily, she climbed the steps of the old stone inn and entered the low-ceilinged front room.

"Miss Dresden!" The innkeeper was a rotund man, but quick and agile for all his bulk. "Miss Dresden, we bin that worrit abat ya! Where ha' ya bin? Who was it that took ya away? Miss Dresden? Miss Dresden!"

She almost collapsed. She had not understood how truly bone-deep weary she was until she knew that her journey was at an end. Every last bit of energy drained from her and she sagged against the bar. "Mr. Barker, may I . . . may I have a room?"

Haven handed the reins to his groom and limped back up to Haven Court. His best hunter, Olivia, had been of some help. He had followed her lead and knew that Jenny had stayed the night in a shepherd's cottage high in the fells, but at some point she must have gone into the spring water and the dog just could not pick up her scent on the other side. His only hope now was that Jenny had found her way to Lesleydale. He would have to send a servant to town, because he was sure he could not ride another foot. He had never been much of a rider, preferring "shank's mare," and now was paying with a hip that would not stop aching.

Just as he was going up the steps to the house, a young fellow, a groom from the Tippling Swan, galloped up on a hack. "My lord!" he cried. "They found her! That there ledy o' yourn. She be at the inn, safe an' sound!"

With a surge of relief so sharp it was more like agony, he saddled a fresh horse and recommended the young man to the tender mercy of his cook. Invigorated as he never thought he could be, aching limbs forgotten, Haven galloped off as the evening sun met the horizon and began its night ritual of sinking into the earth. She was safe . . . safe, safe, *safe*. The word thudded through his brain with every beat of his horse's hooves on the beaten earth of the road into Lesleydale.

And he loved her with every fiber of his being, every bit of his body, and every whiff of his spirit. He was "pissing mad," as the Yorkshiremen in the village might say, that he had suffered such agonies of apprehension for her safety through a long night and day, but more full of fear for what she had endured. He needed to see her, to touch her, to be sure that she was whole and healthy.

He was into Lesleydale faster than ever he had, realizing as he arrived that he had not even left word for his family that the Jenny was found. He had to hope that word would make its way up from the servants' quarters once the stable fellow's message was relayed.

As he rode into Lesleydale he came to understand how much he loved Miss Jane Dresden, his own dear, sweet Jenny. His darkest fears had gone unadmitted until that very second. He had been desperately afraid that she had fallen into the Lesley and drowned, or off a cliff somewhere, or . . . or anything. His imagination had conjured the direst consequences.

He handed the reins of his horse to a waiting groom and

raced into the inn, finding Barker and almost shouting, "Where is she?"

"First room on the left at the top o' th'stairs, milord. Can I . . ."

But Haven did not wait to hear what the landlord had to say. He took the ancient, worn stairs two at a time, but stopped, suddenly, at the top. He stared at the door, thinking that his future lay beyond it and what happened in the next few minutes might determine its course. What should he say? How could he calm her fears, answer her questions, win her heart?

If that was even possible at this late date and after everything that had come to pass. He took in a deep breath and opened the door. It would come to him. It would have to.

As quietly as a man of his bulk could enter, he did, tiptoeing into the room, the dim light from the stable yard lanterns and the lamps from the hall outside the room the only illumination now that the sun had slipped beyond the horizon. He could hear the soft, snuffling breath of a sleeper, of Jenny.

He crept toward the bed to find her sleeping soundly under soft, worn covers, her dress over a nearby chair. She looked so peaceful and sweet it turned his heart inside out. What turmoil of mind had she been in to make up that preposterous kidnap note and run from her aunt and the fate of marriage to Viscount Haven?

He knelt by the bed, noting the soft "whoof" of expelled breath out of her pursed lips, and remembered the breathless kisses they had shared on the turf by the Lesley. He had known her but a short time and yet in that brief passage of days she had become everything to him. He should be happy that she was Miss Dresden, acceptable bride, but something in him longed for the battle he was willing to wage to marry his Jenny, the wholly unsuitable bride of his heart.

But he might face a battle yet.

He kissed her forehead and stroked back her tangled

curls, pulling a piece of straw out of them and tossing it aside. She shifted uneasily but did not wake. He kissed her burning cheek, inhaling deeply her essence, brushing his lips across the velvety skin and feeling a surge of mingled love and desire.

Drowsily, she opened her eyes. They were hazy, the clear gray muddied by exhaustion, but she blinked and her vision cleared. "Gerry! What . . . what are you doing here?"

"What do you think?" he said, laughing shakily. "I have come to get you." He smoothed back her curls, running his fingers through and untangling knotted strands like finest embroidery silk, unhappily snarled.

"Get me?" She struggled to sit up, pulling the thin blankets up to modestly cover her body, clad only in a shift. Her mouth twisted in an unhappy frown and her eyes darkened. "You mean you have come to take me back to your master, Lord Haven, now that you know who I am."

It was like a blow to the solar plexus, the sudden knowledge that she did not know the whole truth. She didn't know! His heart thudded. She must have heard only a portion of his conversation with Mary and did not know he was Haven. She still thought of him as Gerry, the farmer. He opened his mouth to clarify, but the words would not come. He heard the bitter unhappiness in her voice, the anguish. Was his position so repugnant to her then? Would he *never* win her as himself?

"Jenny," he said softly and pulled her into his arms, needing the touch of her, the reassuring feel of her in his embrace before he tore them asunder once more with the truth. She resisted at first but then allowed him to draw her close. She burrowed her face into his neck and he held her there, stroking her hair, feeling the dissonant pounding of their two heartbeats. His own leaped and fell into beat with hers.

When she pulled away a little and gazed at him, breathless, wide-eyed, he put his hand behind her head and pulled her to him, kissing first her eyelids, then her nose, then her lips, where he lingered, savoring her, feeling the exquisite blossom of passion burgeon.

She threaded her arms around his waist and he pushed her down onto the bed, relaxing against her, feeling the tantalizing eroticism of her soft, plump body being pushed into the mattress by his own bulk. Soon they were entwined, arms and legs, a happy tangle of sweet passion. He kissed her throat and felt rather than heard her muttered exclamation of breathless desire.

"Jenny, dearest, sweetest girl, heart of my heart, I love you!"

There was silence and he looked up, afraid. Had he said it too soon? Was there no hope? Tears were streaming down her cheeks.

"You . . . you do? Even knowing . . . even knowing I am Jane Dresden, that I m—misled you?" She touched his face, flattening her hand on his cheek. "I am so sorry I lied to you, so very sor—"

"Stop!" He couldn't bear for her to apologize, couldn't stand the hypocrisy of his own lies. And yet he couldn't tell her. Not yet. *Please, God,* he said in his heart, *not until she has told me what I need to hear.* "I love you Jenny, no matter who you are. Can you say the same of me? Can you tell me you love me, no matter who or what I am?" His plea was urgent.

"I can." She sighed. "I love you, Gerry. I love you with every beat of my heart and every particle of my being and soul."

"Then marry me." The words tumbled out in a rush.

"M—marry you?"

"Marry me. 'Come live with me and be my love.' Be my wife. Oh, Jenny, how wonderful that sounds. Does it not? Do you want to be my wife?"

"Mrs. Neville. Oh, I like the sound!" Her voice was giddy with surprised delight. "Gerry, can we?" She sat up and bounced on the bed. "You would marry me, just like that? Knowing . . . knowing who I am?"

"Who you are does not make a jot of difference, my love. I would marry you if you were a scullery maid or the Princess Charlotte. I love you. I want you to be my wife."

She threw herself back into his arms and they tumbled down onto the bed, passionately kissing, so close together there was not even a hair's breadth between them. "Oh, Gerry, I will marry you. Right away. We can go to Scotland, or . . . or anywhere."

He smothered her words with his mouth, lost to everything but her agreement. She was pledged to him and he would never let her go now, never let her back out of her promise.

"Lord Haven, my lad came back wi' yer carriage driver, thinkin' ya might need it fer the young ledy, seein' as how . . ."

Gerry and Jenny both looked toward the door and saw the innkeeper, his round face poked into the room, his eyes wide and filled with shock, his words dying to silence.

"My lord!" the innkeeper cried, shocked beyond further speech at the sight of the dour and fearful Lord Haven tangled in the bedclothes with the young lady.

Knowing he was caught and knowing that Jenny had not missed the landlord's ill-timed repetition of his title, Gerry sat up on the bed and thrust his fingers through his rumpled hair. The landlord, confused and embarrassed by the scene he had witnessed, bowed and said, "I'll just leave ya, milord, or . . . I'll be down th' stairs should ya be needin' anthin'."

Jenny, her eyes round, had sat back up and pulled the covers back up around her.

With a rueful smile, Gerry gazed at her and said, "You did say you loved me no matter who I was, my dear."

"You are Lord Haven."

"I am. To be exact and complete, I am Geraint Walcott Neville, Viscount Haven, Baron Lesley."

Sixteen

In that one moment the brilliant hope of her lifetime burned down to ashes, cold and dirty cinders. "Viscount Haven," she repeated. Her voice was as bleak and barren as she felt. It echoed in the room, bounced back, and taunted her with the desolate sound.

Gerry winced. "I *am* Lord Haven," he admitted, "but I am still just Gerry Neville, local farmer. Or at least . . . I would be if I could, my love. Haven is just my title, not my soul. Can you not love me anyway?"

"But you asked me to marry you, knowing who I was, but not letting me know who *you* were!" Anger replaced the pain of that betrayal. "I don't know you. You say you are the same man, but you aren't!"

"Look, Jenny, we lied to each other! Can you not forgive me as I have forgiven you?"

"Oh, no, it is not the same thing at *all*," she said, scrambling from the bed, dragging some of the bedclothes with her. "It is not the same." She struggled to get her dress on without letting her blanket drop. "I was afraid . . . afraid of being coerced into a marriage I abhorred, afraid of a future of insipid days and unthinkable nights. So I ran. And I lied about who I was. But you!" Her voice trembled. She stood straight and glared accusingly at him in the dim light of the inn room. "You lied to seduce a serving wench! You lied thinking to crawl into my bed. It was only when you found out who I was that you asked me to marry you."

Thunderstruck at how she viewed their relationship thus far, he was speechless. What could he say that she would believe? It must look that way to her or she wouldn't have even thought to say the words. He damned the caution that had made him wait, even though he had known he was going to ask her to marry him before he found out she was Miss Jane Dresden. But she would never believe him now.

He stood and faced her. "Jenny, I . . ."

"Don't call me that!" she said, straightening. "I am not Jenny anymore. I am Miss Jane Dresden, to you, my lord."

The ride back to Haven Court was achieved only after Haven offered to ride his horse back, leaving Miss Dresden—he called her that, knowing she would answer to nothing less—the carriage in solitary safety.

The household was awake and gathered in the great hall. Lady Mortimer let out a cry and made a great show of rushing at her niece; Jane dutifully allowed the embrace but there was no real warmth there.

The introductions were even more uncomfortable.

"Mother," Haven said, daring not even to take her arm as he would want when introducing the woman he would marry to his mother, "this is Miss Jane Dresden."

"I do not understand," Lady Haven said, irritability writ deep in the lines on her face. "Why was Miss Dresden at the inn? I could not make any sense at all of that brainless dolt from the inn stable, and, Haven, why did you not tell us yourself before haring off to the Swan?"

Haven cringed inwardly at the impression Jenny must be getting of his family.

"Something havey-cavey here," Rachel said, her narrow, pretty face twisted into a frown.

"There's nothing havey-cavey, it is a romance," Pamela,

A COUNTRY COURTSHIP 201

adorably disheveled in her nightdress, said, before Haven could stop her. "Miss Dresden was masquerading as a servant girl and Haven fell in love with her thinking she was a maid."

Lady Haven wheeled and faced her youngest daughter. "What nonsense are you spouting, Pamela?"

"She's all about in the head," Rachel jeered, pinching her younger sister's shoulder.

"I am not," Pamela denied hotly, slapping at her sister's hand. "It happened exactly that way, did it not, Haven? I think it is romantic." She turned shyly to Miss Dresden, who was standing, mute and frozen among the din echoing in the great hall. "You remember me, Miss Dresden? I came up and saw you at Mary's . . ."

"What on earth is she on about, Haven?" the viscount's mother shrieked. "You met Miss Dresden? Where? And Pamela, too? How? And why . . ."

"And I want to know why my niece looks like she has been dragged through a thicket backwards," Lady Mortimer demanded. "What is wrong, that she should appear so disheveled, so . . ."

"If everyone will just keep silent for a moment!" The elderly dowager, unnoticed, had entered the hall from her suite. Silence did, indeed, fall. She tapped over to the newest arrival and looked her over. A sly smile stole over her wrinkled visage. "I can see why he mistook you for a serving wench."

Lady Mortimer bridled but the dowager fixed her with a steely stare, and for once the baroness remained silent.

Jane was not sure who this old lady was and why she was saying such a thing, but anyone who could make her aunt shut her mouth was formidable. She met the woman's direct and challenging gaze. If the experiences of the past few days had taught her anything, they had taught her that it was no good to be bullied in her life. It was the only life she was given and to live it any other way than by her own conscience would be a travesty. She straightened and defiantly glared directly into watery blue eyes that snapped with an intelligence that was unnerving, to say the least. But she would never be afraid again, least of all of these mad people. The old woman nodded once.

"I am Haven's grandmother, his father's mother. I am, though I hate the title, the dowager Lady Haven. You understand, it is not the 'Lady Haven' part I despise, it is the 'dowager' appellation that makes me cringe. Makes me sound old." She looked Jane over from the top of her head to the tips of her toes. "What an appalling mess you are. I am quite sure there is an interesting tale behind the straw in your hair. But to get to the point, you have led the entire county quite the dance, my girl. How did it suit you, living as one of the serving class?"

Jane considered her answer. She glanced over at Haven and her heart ached, remembering the carefree delight of falling in love, uninhibited by any class requirements or stuffy ballrooms, proscribed manners, elegant, stifling surroundings. Though she had accused him of lying to seduce her she had, during the carriage ride, reconsidered. That could not have been his motive. After all, what lord of the realm would have made himself less than he was to debauch a maidservant? Would he not have expected his position in life to have helped him, rather than hurt his chances at a liaison? So he would not have lied about his position for that purpose.

And there had been times when he was the one to pull back from the brink of impropriety. Why? If it was seduction on his mind, she had given him no reason to believe that she found his advances repulsive. It made her blush to recall how readily she had welcomed him into her arms.

"I learned much, my lady," she said, turning her gaze back to the old woman. The collected group had remained silent, the force of the old lady's personality holding them captive.

"I would wager you did, young miss, and I will want to hear some of what you have learned. But at what price knowledge, I wonder?" She turned to the rest of them. "This child is clearly exhausted and distraught by her experiences. She will become ill without proper care. I would recommend sending her to her bed and she can explain herself and her actions tomorrow."

"I concur," Haven said.

Lady Haven, arms across her bosom, said, "But I want to know . . ."

"Mother, no!" Haven glared at the woman, who bridled but remained silent for once. "We will take this up in the morning." He turned to the butler, waiting at a discreet distance. "Bartlett, have a maid show Miss Dresden to her chamber."

Jane was grateful and turned to go. But not before the elderly woman grasped her elbow with one crabbed hand. Her grip was steely. Voice low, she said, "I will see you in the morning, young miss. I want first crack at the explanation."

It was like returning to someone else's life, Jane thought. She had awoken wrapped in luxurious Irish linen sheets, clothed in her best muslin night rail. A young maid had peeked in just then and, seeing her awake, had entered and opened her curtains for her. It was another brilliant spring day but a world apart from the past week, sharing a bed with Mary Cooper and sleeping in her shift. Now, after dining on tea and toast in bed, she was gowned in one of her best gowns, an indigo silk with forget-me-not blue silk ribbon roses edging the low bosom and tiny cap sleeves. Feathery lace adorned her clothes, and the pink-cheeked maid assigned to her had combed out her ratted hair and pinned it up. Jane peeped out her bedroom door, not ready to meet with any of the household just yet.

She had been surprised after the events of the evening that she had slept so soundly, but she supposed she had been physically exhausted and that had taken over. But now all of the confusion of the previous day and night came back to trouble her mind. What was she going to do now?

A maidservant bustled by with a pile of linens in her arms.

"Excuse me," Jane said, softly. "But could you tell me where the elderly lady—his lordship's grandmother, I mean—where her room is?"

The girl curtsied. "Her ladyship has a suite down off th'great hall, miss."

"Would she be awake at this hour? She asked me to see her first thing in the morning, but I do not want to disturb her if she is still abed."

"Oh, no, miss. Her ladyship rarely sleeps. Dodd—that be her maid, miss—she says as how her ladyship hardly closes her eyes at night. I believe she has already breakfasted."

"Thank you. Just off the great hall?"

"Yes, miss."

Jane descended the winding staircase. She had almost reached the door to the suite off the great hall when she heard a noise from above. Her heart thudded. She did not want to meet anyone else yet. As acerbic as the old lady seemed the previous night, there was still some empathy in her old eyes. The viscount's mother, on the other hand—

Jane flattened close to the wall and waited, but what she saw next astonished her. It was Pamela, and she was creeping down the stairs dressed in that same disreputable pair of breeches and old cambric shirt. She had a riding crop in her hand and moved stealthily.

She smiled at the girl's subterfuge. "So, Miss Pamela, this is how you manage to evade notice?"

The girl jumped and Jane could not keep from chuckling.

"You won't give me up, will you?" the girl pleaded, coming into the great hall as Jane moved toward her into the huge, echoing area.

"Of course not," Jane said. "but why do you feel compelled to creep out like this?"

Pamela rolled her eyes. "I would get an endless jaw-me-dead if my mother knew I still rode astride. It is not ladylike, don't you know," she said, with a wicked imitation of her mother's querulous voice.

"I know how you feel," Jane said, and the girl eyed her curiously. "I have often been accused of the same . . . of not being ladylike enough."

"You? But you're . . ." Pamela paused and cocked her head to one side, looking Jane over with sharp eyes. "I always knew there was something odd about you as a servant, you know. And when I said as much to Grand, she got that calculating look in her eyes, the one that makes m'mother shiver."

"Grand?"

Pamela indicated, with a movement of her head, the suite Jane had been about to go to. "M'grandmother. We call her Grand."

"You . . . you spoke of me?"

"Oh, Lord, yes. Grand was no end interested. Made me describe you, you know, when we thought you were Mary's cousin. Made *Haven* describe you." A noise in the hall above made her jump and her gray-green eyes grew huge in her tiny heart-shaped face. "I have to go," she whispered and trotted off toward the back of the house. She paused, though, and glanced back over her shoulder. "Go see Grand. She's what the old folk 'round here call a 'right knowin' old 'un.' Talk to her. But I want to know everything when I come back. Good-bye, Jenny!"

The noise from above was just a footman. Jane moved toward the door of the dowager's suite and scratched on it, and was admitted by a hard-faced maid. The elderly Lady Haven was by the window, and she turned as Jane entered.

"Ah, good. I see you took me at my word. I appreciate that. Shows good breeding, despite what I feared."

Stung, Jane said, "What did you fear, my lady?"

"That you were in some way unworthy of my grandson."

Her first instinct was to resent the dowager's words, but curiously, she didn't. They had the merit of being honest at least, as blunt as they were. "Why did that worry you?" The watery blue eyes were shrewdly assessing her, Jane knew, with every word and every movement. Would she be found lacking after all? Did she care?

"It worried me because I love my grandson. And he had fallen in love with a girl who was flighty enough to run away and silly enough to apparently play the part of a maid instead of take her rightful position as daughter of an old and well-placed family."

"Fall in love with?" Did the woman know what she was talking about? Jane moved slowly toward the viscount's grandmother, and so the window. The view was of the high fells and Jane recognized one rise as the moor over which Mary Cooper's cottage lay. She looked back at the elderly Lady Haven and examined her seamed face. "Does that mean that you had gleaned the truth, my lady? That Mary Cooper's visiting cousin was really Miss Jane Dresden?"

"Well, really," the old woman said, acidly. She moved slowly over to a table and sat in a straight-backed gilt chair. "It was just too great a coincidence, a young lady of your description arriving at Mary's just as Miss Dresden disappeared?"

"But no one else caught on?"

"No. They, meaning Haven and Pamela, chose to believe that Mary was telling the truth. No one could imagine why she would lie. I can think of a hundred reasons why she would lie."

Jane frowned. She joined the woman at the enameled table, sitting opposite her and watching the expression, the sharp intelligence, flicker through watery blue eyes, eyes so like Haven's, only rheumy with age. "Such as?"

"You could have told her the truth and offered to pay her. There is never enough money when one has a fatherless child to feed and clothe. Or perhaps she did not know about the missing Miss Dresden, and she thought she was hiding you from some sort of persecution. Or possibly—"

Jane sat back. "All right, I think I understand. For your interest, I think the last is the most true. She did not know about the missing Miss Dresden and I made sure Lord Haven—Gerry the farm manager, as I thought of him then—did not have a chance to tell her."

"Ah. I did so want to know the *exact* reason. Curiosity is my failing, especially when it accompanies infirmity." The old woman eyed her with a sharp look and raised her white eyebrows. "That must have made for an uncomfortable week. Lying to your hostess. Lying to your lover."

"He is not my lover," Jane shot back, stung into a hasty reply.

"No? Is he not? Then you are a fool," she said, disdain in her quavery voice. "More than I even thought you to be." The dowager squinted. "He does love you, you know. Do you love him?"

"Really, Lady Haven, you can hardly expect . . ."

"But I *do* expect you to answer me," she said, with a rap of her cane on the floor. "It is why I asked you here. In a few hours, when the household is awake, Haven's mother and your aunt will decide what to do about you. You have made yourself notorious and they will, between them, decide on your fate. Should you marry Lord Haven? Have you made yourself unfit for him with this wild kidnap story and your disappearance? What scandal will ensue?"

Jane covered her face with her hands. It was true, every word of it. Lady Mortimer and Lady Haven, between them, would hold a council of war to determine her fate. But what should she do about it?

As if in answer to her thoughts, the old lady said, "Do not let them do it!"

Jane uncovered her face and gazed steadily at the old woman who faced her across the table, arthritis-knotted hands flat on the tabletop. "How do I stop them? They are two very determined women."

"Are you a woman or a child?" The dowager's tone was impatient, bracing. "Make up your mind what you want, and take it!" She put out her hand and closed it into a fist. "It is *your* life. Take what you want and be damned to the world. If you want Haven, take him."

"Why are you saying this to me, my lady?"

There was silence for a moment, but then: "I think my grandson is in love with you. Again I ask; do you love him?"

"How can I know? He is not the same Gerry that I . . . that I f—fell in love with."

"Idiot girl. Are you not the same young woman, though now you are Miss Jane Dresden and then you were plain Jenny, maidservant?"

Jane thought about it. Gerry had taken the chance of asking her to marry him after finding out that she was not who she said she was. But it was not the same! Was it? She shook her head, feeling like she had cobwebs forming, clouding her thoughts, bundling them up in a gauzy wrapping until she couldn't sort out the truth.

"I don't know. *I don't know!*"

The dowager made an exclamation of disgust. "Then figure it out, or you will be coerced and bullied again into a life you are not sure of. Make your own decisions, young miss, or your life will *never* be your own."

That advice stayed with Jane as she sat in the morning parlor awaiting, as she had been commanded, Lady Haven and Lady Mortimer's presence. She was staring out the window when she heard the door open and then close. She turned her head to see, staring at her, a young woman of surprising beauty and elegance. Her loveliness was spoiled only by a haughty look in her eyes and a proud tilt to her head.

"You are Miss Dresden," the young woman said.

"I am. We met last night, but I do not believe I caught your name," Jane said. "And you are . . . ?"

"Miss Rachel Neville, Haven's sister."

Ah yes, Jane thought, *the unpleasant sister.* "Pleased to make your acquaintance, Miss Neville," Jane said, standing and offering her hand.

The young lady took it but only briefly clutched it before dropping it again. "Are you going to marry my brother?"

Stunned, Jane did not know quite how to answer such an impertinent question—the family seemed expert in that area—and was saved when the butler opened the door, bowed, and said, "Sir Colin Varens, to see the ladies." He bowed again and exited, as a young man came in, his homely face lighting to a glow when he found himself in the presence of Miss Neville.

"Miss Neville, what a pleasant surprise. I had not hoped . . . that is, I had not dared to hope . . ."

"What is it, Colin?"

His eyes wandered finally to Jane and he bowed before her, but his gaze was curious and just a shade bold. "Sir Colin Varens, at your service . . . Miss Dresden? Am I correct?"

"You are, sir," Jane said, rising and dropping a brief curtsy.

Just then Lady Mortimer and Lady Haven swept into the room after Sir Colin. "We wish to speak with you alone, Jane," Lady Mortimer said to her niece. "Come."

"May I speak with you ladies first?" Sir Colin asked, casting a sidelong glance at Jane.

"What is it, Sir Colin?" Lady Haven replied, impatiently.

He moved toward them and whispered something to her and Jane's aunt. There was a hiss of displeasure and both women talked in low, furious voices at once. He shrugged and whispered again, and all three stopped and looked at Jane.

She moved uneasily under their unfriendly scrutiny. Jane could not like the calculation in her aunt's eyes, but that moment Lady Mortimer moved away from the two others. Standing apart from them but facing her niece she declaimed, in a loud and ringing tone, "I did not know this before and it changes everything. Jane, you did not tell me that you had been compromised by his lordship, that he forced himself on you and that it was witnessed. I must demand, now, that the viscount make speedy plans to marry you and save your poor reputation!"

Seventeen

"No!"

The chatter in the room silenced with that one word from Jane.

"What do you mean, 'no'?" Lady Mortimer said, glancing around uneasily at the others, then looking back at her niece. "You have no choice in the matter. Your reputation has been sullied and there is no alternative but that the man who ruined it *marry you.*"

Jane felt a surge of strength as if that one word had unleashed her power. "No." Yes, it was working—she felt a new boldness and fresh energy. "I will not marry Lord Haven simply out of social need. I will not marry him because you all want me to. I will not marry him because I should, or because I have nowhere else to go, or because I am getting old. *I will not!*"

"Very good," the dowager, who had come into the room unnoticed, said.

Lady Haven whirled and confronted her mother-in-law. "What do you mean, 'good'? Don't you want Haven to marry?"

The old lady shrugged. "If he wants to. *When* he wants to. But I don't want some girl marrying him just because they were caught in a compromising clinch." She glanced over at Jane. "Although that does raise one or two interesting questions, my girl."

Jane felt a blush rise.

"That 'compromising clinch,' as Grand so eloquently puts it, occurred when Miss Dresden had already agreed to be my bride." Haven's voice, hard and unyielding, made the gathered assembly look toward the door. The viscount stood, legs apart, arms over his chest.

Jane felt a throb of emotion and it frightened her. It was desire, pure and raw, and she almost could not breathe, suffocated by an overwhelming excitement just at the sight of him. The night before, their heady lovemaking at the inn had revealed a new world to her, a new dimension to relations between man and woman. She knew that the dowager was watching her, but her throat had constricted and she could not look away from Haven; he looked not at all like her gentle country swain. He was dressed in buff pantaloons and a charcoal coat of exquisite fit, with a perfectly tied cravat in a waterfall knot, a pearl stickpin in the folds. Somehow his shoulders seemed broader, his legs more muscular, and his height more imposing. He was as intimidating as every Corinthian who had ever sneered at her in a London ballroom.

And yet for all that he was still Gerry, the man she had fallen in love with the moment he had sat down by her side, beside the hearth in Mary's cottage. Or was he? His expression was stormy at that moment, his brilliant blue eyes blazing with fury.

"If any one of you has a single thing to say about our behavior, then you will address me, not Miss Dresden!" he said. "She is perfectly innocent of any wrongdoing."

A babble of voices, both Lady Mortimer and Lady Haven, along with Sir Colin and Rachel, erupted.

"They are already engaged," Lady Mortimer said. "Lord Haven said so himself!"

"But that is not possible, or he would have . . ."

"I do not see what all the fuss—"

"But that is not what those in the vill—"

"Stop!" Haven's voice carried over all and as silence fell the only sound was the dowager chuckling.

Jane, watching the viscount's face, thought she could detect weariness in his expression along with something else. He glanced over at her, but then looked away again, fixing his gaze on the wall.

"We . . . we are not yet *formally* betrothed, though I may have thought so at the time of the embrace everyone is so concerned with."

"Not an embrace, old man. Heard you and Miss Dresden was rolling around on the bed like a couple of—"

Haven's blue eyes blazed with azure fire. "Shut your mouth this instant, Colin, or I shall be forced to shut it for you." The words were hard and the tone was flinty.

The baronet paled, but the threat had the desired affect and he was silenced.

Haven glanced around the room. "Listen to me, all of you. Miss Dresden did not know who I was when she agreed to marry me and I am heartily sorry to have tricked her in such an underhanded way." He looked directly at Jane. "Miss Dresden, will you walk with me? I think you will agree we have much to discuss."

She took a deep breath and nodded. He gave one hard look back at those in the room and said, "This discussion is private, as is the decision of whether we shall marry or not."

He guided her outside to a rose garden sheltered by a stone wall and strolled with her down a pathway paved in crushed limestone. Just as she feared, the clothes seemed to make him a different person and she was torn in a thousand directions as to her feelings. On the one hand he had defended her right to make her own decisions . . . or had he? It had certainly sounded like it, but would he now present to her the very arguments the ones left back in the parlor would make, about propriety and decency? Or would he hold by his words that their decision was between them?

She found herself attracted to and yet at the same time repelled by his commanding aura, and thought she understood now what the girl who had known him in London meant by his dour air. He was uneasy and aloof. As she sat down on a bench he stood by the wall and gazed out, a brooding expression dimming his magnificent eyes. This was everything she had feared, the circumscribed life within the garden walls, the awkwardness of no conversation, the frosty distance between them. Already the memory of the sweet freedom of life in the cottage was beginning to fade, the hours of roaming the fells and by the Lesley. How had she ever mistaken him for a farmer, she thought, examining him as he stood, staring off into the distance over the fells. He was every inch the nobleman.

He turned and caught her gaze. "I meant what I said, Je . . . uh, Miss Dresden. I will not have you badgered into this marriage. But I am yours if you so desire."

She bridled. "What, to save my sullied reputation? I think not."

"Not only for that," he said, his voice gentler. "I thought we had established a . . . a relationship, a *rapprochement.*"

She looked at him sadly. "But that was when I was a servant girl and you were a farmer."

"Are we so different now?"

Was that a note of appeal in his voice? She must be mistaken.

"Are we not who we were when we were just Jenny and Gerry?" he continued.

"No." She spread her arms wide and indicated all around them—the old priory, magnificent in its age, the walled gardens, the stately landscaping. Trees tortured into boxy shapes, herbs in perfect round balls, an Elizabethan knot garden, impeccable in its straight lines. "This—all of this— makes us different, makes *you* different. I can see it in your manner, I can hear it in your voice." She stood and walked quickly to the wall and indicated the wide world beyond.

"And even in the village . . . you are his lordship, Viscount Haven, master of many. That is not the man I fell in lo . . ." She stopped abruptly, and her voice hushed. She stared out at the distant hills, closing her eyes to the spring breeze that swooped down from the fells. "Not the man I learned to care for."

He was silent for a moment, but then said, "I . . . I feel I must apologize for asking you to marry me without telling you the truth. It was wrong."

"Yes, it was. I . . . I trusted you."

"Why did you run from the inn? In the first place, I mean? Leaving the kidnap note and changing your clothes. What were you going to do? Where were you going to go?"

She leaned against the wall and gazed out over the landscape. Clouds rolled up over the fells and darkened the tops with their shadows. Taking in a long, deep breath, she expelled it slowly. "Did you ever wish you could just leave behind all of your worries? All of your cares? Did you ever long to just live, to just exist without anxiety?"

He leaned on the wall beside her and chuckled, a dry, unhappy sound. "Oh, yes. I have often wished to do that. It is what I do when the world becomes too much. I go to see Mary and for a while I am just Gerry, just her childhood friend."

"Then you will understand that I have long felt that, but being a woman and a lady of a certain class, there is no retreat as there is for you. I am circumscribed by society to perform a certain role. I may marry, but only within my class. I may not work. I may not walk alone. I may not travel alone. I may not mingle and enjoy the company of those 'beneath' me." She beat her fist on the rock top of the wall. "I may do nothing outside of the rigid expectations of a lady of my station! I may marry and bear my husband an heir, and that is all. Then, for the rest of my days I may do pretty stitchery, attend balls and routs, pay morning calls. I may entertain the vicar, take the water at Bath, sit in this prim and trim garden, and then descend into my dotage never having known one moment of freedom, of unfettered movement, of real conversation!" She closed her eyes. "And I *long* for freedom! I breathed the sweetness of it for such a very short time."

Silence. She turned to look at him and his expression was thoughtful, but closed. She could not read his eyes. Couldn't he say something? Had she shocked him so badly with her unladylike outburst?

"My trip up to Yorkshire was only to appease my mother," she continued, looking away from him again. "She promised that if I at least came up here and gave it a try— that is, met you, and gave it an honest chance—that I could come home and she would never plague me to marry again. She promised . . . or at least . . ." She paused and sighed again. "No, I suppose she did not promise, but I understood that then we would be able to get a little cottage together somewhere in the country and live a simpler life."

"But there was a letter awaiting you at the Tippling Swan."

She flashed him a look. So he knew about that. "Yes. I expect my Aunt Mortimer has told you about that, for I know she received a letter from Mother, too, and it likely held the same hideous news. My mother married a horrible little toady of a man the moment my aunt and I were out of Bath. She never, *ever* intended that I should come back. She advised me to marry you, as that was my best opportunity at a 'settlement.' It was offered to me as my only option."

"I'm sorry, Jenny."

"Don't be sorry," she said, looking up at him through a mist of tears. "That was not your doing, after all. I decided that I could not go through with it. I determined that I would go north to my old nanny's cousin's home in Scotland. Morag and I are friends and I know she would take me in. I had some money and my pearls. But I did not want to face my aunt—I am a bit of a coward—and so I crept to the laundry and s—stole a dress and wrote that ludicrous note. But then, in the stable yard . . . oh, those awful men! Is that what it is like for young women of that class?" she asked, looking back up at the viscount.

He grimaced and shrugged. "Barmaids and servant girls learn early to either fend off threats to their modesty or to allow the familiarity and make some extra money from it."

"Oh. I did not know what to do. A man shouted and the one let go of me, but the other had hold of my dress and it tore. I . . . I lost my little purse full of money and my pearls, I think, just then. I r—ran, and I got lost. I had intended to go up the road a ways and stop the next stage, going north to Scotland. But I was afraid those dreadful men were following me and I thought to evade them, and then it started to get dark. I got lost. I must have wandered for hours, and it started to rain. When I found shelter, I crept in. I did not even realize there was a cottage nearby, or I would likely have gone to the door."

"Jenny," Haven said, pushing her back down onto the stone bench and sitting down beside her, "I wish we had been honest with each other right from the beginning, but I cannot take back the past. And now . . . well, I will not have you badgered into this marriage, but your aunt is right in some respects. Your reputation is in tatters and I am responsible. But I wish to make it right, and . . ."

"Lord, but you do not understand at *all!*" Jane rose and stalked away from the bench. She looked back at him and the bewildered expression on his face. "Forget any responsibility you feel toward me, my lord. I have no desire to live in society. So ease your conscience and I will go away and you need never hear of me again!" With that she turned and ran away.

What on earth had he said to make her bolt? He started after her but the dowager was in the doorway and she put her cane across it.

"Grand, I have to go after her! I must make her see . . ." He started to push the cane aside but she jerked on it, making him halt.

"Dolt. I did not think you such a slowtop, Haven. I heard you. You have intolerably insulted the girl and she will likely never listen to you again, now."

"How have I insulted . . . Grand, what are you saying?"

"That you are a great looby in a family of great loobies. Come with me and we will talk. I think I shall have to explain to you a few things about women, Haven. Among them, how impossible it is for a woman in love to marry a man to whom she will be a burden, or whom she does not think loves her."

There was one last thing to do before she left, Jane thought later that afternoon, glancing around before slipping out of Haven Court alone. The next morning she was going to go to town, get on the stage, and return to Bath. She would go home, seize control of her finances in any way possible, and make her own life.

But right now she had a task to accomplish. She took her bearings and started up the long grassy rise, hoping she could find her way on her own. A half-hour later, out of breath but triumphant, she was tapping on the door of Mary's cottage.

"Come in."

Mary's voice was musical but Jane entered hesitantly, poking her head in. She was at her spinning wheel, keeping up the even movement of the treadle as she spun her fine and even wool.

"Come in, come in," Mary called, smiling at her. She finished off the bobbin she was spinning and left the wheel. Molly was sitting on a blanket on the floor, pushing some square wooden blocks around with chubby, clumsy fingers.

Jane took a deep breath and entered the cottage, thinking

it had only been two days but she felt so separated already from the person she had been while living in Mary's home.

"I'm so glad you came back," Mary said, reaching out and enclosing Jane's fingers in her warm, callused hands. "I've bin that worrit about you, tho' Gerry sed you was all right, but I prefer the proof of my own eyes."

"I . . . I'm so sorry Mary, for . . . for everything."

Mary's face split into a grin. "An' what part would you be sorriest for, Jenny—ah, I keep thinkin' of you as Jenny!"

"That's all right, Mary. Jenny is the name my Scottish nurse called me. It is a diminutive of Jane for many."

"Jenny it is, then. So, what part would you be sorry for? That poor attempt at milkin' you made? I think Esther has still not recovered! Or that brick of bread you baked that even the birds scorned?"

Jenny giggled, happy once again in the confines of the cozy cottage. "You know what I mean. I am so sorry for lying to you, for misleading you. It was wrong and I apologize." She picked up Molly and put her on her hip, as she had seen Mary do. "I did learn how to do one thing, though. Shall I make us some tea?"

"You know," Mary said, once they had their tea and were settled by the hearth. The day had turned gloomy after a promising start and the wind beat at the door of the cottage, but inside the fire made it warm and welcoming. "Gerry has bin here, an' he told me much."

Jane felt the rush of blood to her cheeks.

"So much heartache," Mary murmured.

"I just don't know what to do," Jane admitted.

"Do you love Gerry?"

"I . . . oh, how can I know? I thought I loved him, but that was when I knew him as Gerry, the local farmer. Lord Haven, the viscount, is quite a different man! He is . . . intimidating. Powerful. He . . . he just is not Gerry."

"Oh, but he is!" Mary sighed and took a sip of her tea out of the pewter mug she cradled in her hands. She glanced up at Jenny as she cradled little Molly in her arms. "When I was thinkin' of my Jem's proposal, I was not certain. He was a man o' few words, was my Jem, and I have always liked conversation. But with me he could talk. Oh, he ne'er was a big talker, but when it were just us, alone, he would open his heart and say things he could ne'er say otherwise. Jenny, men spend their lives bein' strong an' silent; they must command and direct and it leaves precious little time for the other side o' them. But with th'right woman, if you give 'em a safe place to feel and just be, they open their hearts and show you what's inside. That's what Gerry found with you, Jenny, a safe haven for his heart to rest. He's the same man. Viscount Haven and Gerry are just two parts o' who he be. Just as you have a private side and a side you show in the parlor."

Jane pondered that for a few minutes. Mary took a sleepy Molly from her arms and put her in her cradle, and then came back to the fireside.

"He has a good heart, Jenny. I know this of him. I have known him all my life, and he has a good heart, and nobbut more gentle than Gerry. And he loves you. I ha' never seen him in love before, but he is in love with you."

"I have been afraid to believe it," Jenny said, slowly.

"Well, believe it."

"I . . . I thought it was just because he thought me a servant girl. I don't know. It has all become so jumbled and confused, I don't know what to think."

"Ah, but, lass, it is really quite simple," Mary said, with a sad smile. "Love is a rare and precious thing. You might ha' bin foolin' each other as to your identities, but you canna disguise the heart. Don't say nay to him just 'cause yer hurt right now. Look inta his heart, lass, an' yer gonna see what is true."

There was a tap at the door and Mary opened it; it was Gerry, looking weary and discouraged. He looked up and saw Jane and his expression flickered between hope and sadness.

Mary made an exclamation of disgust. "You two poor fools! Go, both of you, and don't come back to me cottage until you have a date set and plan to have the banns read next Sunday!"

Still afraid, still uncertain, Jane was nonetheless willing. When he held out his hand she took it and stepped out in the breezy afternoon, tying her bonnet more securely against the tugging of the breeze. They walked for a while, wordless, and she felt all the tension ease out of her. Could she pretend just for a while that they really were just Jenny and Gerry? He was wearing his disreputable "farmer" garb again, with the beaten and battered hat. But she looked down at her own gown. It was a well-tailored traveling dress of gold wool. Expensive and tasteful. And she wore a poke bonnet of modern structure.

When she realized where he was leading her she hesitated, but he gave her a pleading expression and she allowed him to direct her to the top of the long rise. They looked down. They were overlooking Haven Court. Clouds scudded across the leaden sky and the stiff breeze lifted the skirts of her dress, tugging at them. She pulled off her bonnet, wanting to feel the breeze in her hair again.

He turned her to face him, held her smaller hands in his large warm ones, and said, "I have been doing a lot of thinking since our last conversation. First, I should say what I neglected to say earlier. I don't want you to marry me because you have been compromised. Nor do I want you to marry me because you are, at twenty-seven, at your last gasp!" He moved his big, strong hands up her arms and clutched her shoulders in his hands. She gazed up into his face. "I want to marry you because . . . because I love you!"

She was speechless.

"We have both been beyond foolish, acting as if who we are is not good enough, somehow! But it is, Jenny! I fell in love with *you,* not with who I thought you were! I don't care if you are a dairymaid or a duchess, I would still want to marry you!"

"Truly?"

"Truly! And we are masters of our own fate, my love. No one can make us dress up in court dress and retire to London. No one can make us kowtow to the rest of the aristocrats, or leap and caper at Almack's, or grimace and grunt at the annual farce that is the London Season!"

She giggled giddily at his exemplary choice of words. "You mean no diamond tiaras or fancy court gowns?"

"Not unless you want them. Jenny, oh, Jenny, please say you will marry me. I love you with all my heart! Will you marry me knowing you will be Lady Haven to the rest of the world, but my own dear Jenny, my heart, my life, to me?"

She looked deep into the brilliant blue of his eyes and saw only honesty and love there. He was Gerry, her own dear love, deep in his heart straight down to his soul. And he loved her. She moved closer and he surrounded her with his powerful arms. She could hear his heart pound as she laid her head against the solid wall of his chest. It reminded her of her recurrent dream, of the man who held her close and loved her. It was Gerry. "I . . . I will," she whispered. "I will marry you and I will love you forever."

"Jenny!" He tipped her face up to look directly into her eyes.

She closed them as he lowered his face and the first reverential touch of his lips confirmed for her the love she had been afraid to admit into her heart. He pulled her even closer and the steady throb of his heart promised her that she was doing the right thing in marrying where her heart truly led her.

She pulled away a little, after a moment. "Will you"— she was breathless, but stammered—"will you p—promise me one thing?"

"Anything, my heart."

"Will you build me a snug little cottage in the woods, with a hearth and . . . and a little cradle, f—for our first baby?"

He laughed out loud and the joy in his voice boomed through the valley, down to the old priory, even where a figure supported on a cane stood in one of the windows. He picked her up and spun her around until all she could see, all that was still, was the love and exultation in his eyes.

"I will go one better, my love. I will build one for our honeymoon, so that I can take you away from Haven Court for our first weeks as man and wife. I love my family, but for a fortnight at least, I only want to see you by my hearth every evening, in my bed every night, and at the fire every morning."

He kissed her soundly on the lips. "And then," he continued, "forever after, when the strain of being Lord and Lady Haven becomes too much, it will be our retreat, the one place in the world where we can be just Jenny and Gerry."

"Jenny and Gerry," she echoed, locking her arms around his neck and knowing, for the first time, that she really was doing the right thing. "I think I shall like that. But I think that we will always be just Jenny and Gerry, even . . . even in our bedchamber in Haven Court."

She saw the flame of desire alight in his blazing blue eyes and it took her breath away.

"Oh, Jenny," he whispered, "don't make me wait too long."

Happiness welled and gurgled like a spring, flooding her heart with hope. "Gerry, my own true love, my handsome farmer husband-to-be, we can be married the moment you build me that cottage."

"I'll start at dawn," he murmured, and bent toward her, taking her lips in a kiss that became more demanding. Breathing heavily, he added, "Or sooner."

About the Author

Donna Simpson lives with her family in Canada. She is currently working on her next Zebra Regency romance, *A Matchmaker's Christmas,* to be published in October 2002. Donna loves to hear from readers and you may write to her c/o Zebra Books. Please include a self-addressed stamped envelope if you wish a reply.